# NIGHT BRINGS NIGHT

ALSO BY KRIS LORENZEN

*The Cold, Cold Voice*

# KRIS LORENZEN

WOODSHED BOOKS
- Indianapolis -

Published by Woodshed Books
www.woodshedbooks.com



First Edition 2022

Designed by the author

Printed in the United States of America

1 3 5 7 9 10 8 6 4 2

"My mother was dead but we still had duties which we ought to perform; we must continue our course with the rest and learn to think ourselves fortunate whilst one remains whom the spoiler has not seized."

-Mary Shelly,
*Frankenstein*

# NIGHT BRINGS NIGHT

OR

# WHOM THE SPOILER HAS NOT SEIZED

# ONE

# A LONG, LOW WAY DOWN

Detective Lieutenant Powell Dixon sits rigidly upright with elbows squared off, and his nose resting on laced fingers. He stares at the paper bag slumped in the middle of his desk. The clock tower two blocks east finishes its twelfth chime.

He lifts his head up and to the right, straining through his office door out into the bullpen, looking for the remnants of cake or pizza or anything from Morgan's retirement lunch last week. No luck.

His gaze falls onto DPEA Agent Singh's desk, his occasional officemate. He's usually got something in there, but the fucker hasn't been in all week.

It's now or never.

Sighing, he slowly lifts a bottom corner of bag with a thumb and forefinger and its measly contents slide out onto the blotter like dying fish from a net.

A turkey—fucking turkey, again?—sandwich, maybe six or seven pretzels, and one of those small seedless orange things. Jesus, he'd rather have dying fish.

He thinks that maybe his service revolver would taste better.

A knock on his open door mostly snaps him out of it.

"Special Agent Singh?"

Dixon looks up and says, "Clementine."

The woman in the doorframe glances around confused.

"No, I'm Rebecca," she says. "Rebecca Perlin?"

Now Dixon looks confused.

"What, no, not you, the…" he says and points at the clementine on his desk, looks back at her, gives up. "Is there something I can help you with?"

"Yes, Agent Singh, I've left—"

He puts a hand up and stops her.

"I'm not Singh," he gestures towards the empty desk, "that is, sometimes anyway. I think he's in Indy or something. I'm Lieutenant Dixon."

She's heartbroken.

"I've been trying to reach him for weeks," she stammers.

"Well, as the DPEA liaison for Northern Indiana, he's got lots of small and midsize towns…" Dixon trails off, deflating. "Why am I covering for him? I don't know what the hell he does with his days."

She smiles slightly, still exasperated, but appreciating his honesty.

"Thanks," she says, shaking her head, "I'll try for him again tomorrow."

He nods and returns his focus to lunch. Immediately he regrets it.

He pushes himself away from his desk, stands up and puts on his jacket. He tucks the clementine into his pocket and eats the pretzels as he walks out the door. He doesn't shut or lock his office.

"Where you headed, Lieu?" Ruthie calls from across the bullpen.

"Hospital," he says. "I've got my phone."

"Say hi to Carol for us," Ruthie says.

He nods his consent as he pushes through the doors.

St. Joe's looks quiet and he parks on the curb because, why not? Nobody tows police cars.

Inside, it's quiet too. If this was one of the newer hospitals up north or west of the city, it'd be bustling but it's not. It's rundown and old and where they push-off the drug addicts and diabetics and cancer patients—everything the medical community isn't interested in anymore and hasn't been for six years now.

He takes the elevator to the fourth floor.

Carol's in bed with the TV muted, staring out the window.

He knocks on the doorframe and enters.

"Hey," she says and smiles. She's so skinny and bald and her color's grayish. But he still sees his little sister in there somewhere.

"How you doing?" Dixon asks.

She bobs her head and swallows.

"Oh, you know me. Picture of health," Carol says, and spasms into a mild coughing fit. She adds a soft, "Sorry."

"Sure," he says. "And it's not your fault chemo hasn't made you funnier."

"Ha ha," she says. "I do feel bad, all this money—"

He lays a hand softly on her arm and tries not to notice how frail she feels.

"Stop," he says. "It's just money. There's nothing else it's good for."

She continues bobbing her head slightly.

"I don't think I'm going to last much longer, Powell," she says. There's no sadness or fear in her voice, just exhaustion.

He squeezes her arm slightly and keeps a lid on his platitudes. Neither of them would believe him.

"Do you want me to talk to your doctor?" he asks. "See if there's anything else to try?"

"I don't even think he's in town," she says. "There's nothing else to try. Everything, all the resources, go towards…"

She trails off but gestures vaguely at the TV. As if he doesn't know what she's referring to. He picks up the remote and turns the thing off without looking at it. Like that's what the world needs. More news coverage, more statistics, more think-pieces.

"It's not good for you either, Carol," he says. "It's only bad news now."

"It was only ever bad news," she says.

He puts the remote on her tray, so she can reach it when he leaves.

"You want some lunch?" he asks her. "Think you could eat? I can go down and get us something."

She laughs at him. It's dry and short, but it's a laugh.

"What was it today?" she asks. "Turkey sandwich?"

"Fucking turkey sandwich," he agrees.

He gets up and heads to the door.

"I don't want anything, but you go ahead," she says.

"C'mon, nothing?"

"Chemo makes everything taste weird," she says.

He shrugs.

"I'm going to get you a couple different things," he says, "and if you don't eat all of it or any of it, I won't be offended."

She bobs her head OK and then laughs again.

"I'd love a fucking turkey sandwich," she says.

The next day, Dixon sits rigidly upright with elbows squared off and his nose resting on laced fingers. He stares at the paper bag slumped in the middle of his desk. The clock tower two blocks east finishes its twelfth chime.

"I think I've done this before," he says out loud to himself.

He pokes the bag with an index finger. Sure feels like a sandwich.

Somebody knocks on his open door.

"Clementine, you're back," he says.

The woman looks confused again.

He stops her.

"It's Rebecca," he says. "I remember."

She smiles and nods towards the other empty desk.

"Still no Agent Singh?" she asks.

"Nope. But if you're here for DPEA matters, I can maybe help you out," he says. "Most of it falls under local jurisdiction. That's why I have to share my office with, well, an empty desk."

She smiles, then reconsiders once she's given it a second of thought.

"Are you the entirety of the staff for…these concerns within the department?" she asks.

"That's me," Dixon says, spreading his arms out to encompass the whole room.

"Jesus," she says. "I knew you were understaffed, but…"

"Hey," he says, "maybe I'm Superman. You don't know."

She blinks.

Dixon pops up from his chair.

"Do you like Chinese food?" he asks.

"Huh?" she manages between more blinks.

He struggles into his jacket.

"Mr. Wong's? On 7th? I hate bringing my lunch," he explains. "It's the most depressing thing I can imagine. Except maybe the toy section they used to have at Goodwill."

She looks impossibly sad at this last remark, and of course she does. Idiot. There's a reason she's here looking for this exact department.

With one swipe of his arm, his lunch is trash.

"Come on, now we have to go," he says, looking in the garbage can and regretting he hadn't spared the probable pretzels from his dramatic gesture. He could've snacked on them later.

He's already past her and out the door.

"You can talk in the car," he says over his shoulder.

"Do you need to lock up or something?" she asks once they've cleared the front steps and stand by his cruiser as he fishes for his keys.

"What, why?" he asks. "The cops never close."

"I didn't see anyone else in there," she says. "I walked straight past reception and roamed around until I saw you."

"Really," Dixon says, without a hint of question in his tone, then shrugs it off. "Eh, someone's around somewhere. Ruthie sneaks a cigarette after her salad most days."

He holds his keys up triumphantly. "Ah. Success."

They drive off, hook off Broadway, then up Van Buren. They pass a boarded-up mosque, large neon green stickers adhered to doors and windows. A block on, a church with the same.

She looks behind them frantically.

"Was that a Catholic church?" she asks.

"That? No," he says. "First Assembly or something. The Catholics haven't gone cultist. They compromised to save themselves, of course. Recovering Catholic myself. You religious?"

She laughs, "Hardly. You just never know what to trust, you know? The news I mean. One site says they've been declared cultists, another says something else."

"The truth is usually somewhere in the middle, I suppose," he says.

A block in silence as she struggles with something.

"I'm worried about my sister," she says, finally.

"OK, what's going on?" he asks. "Sister" tweaks him, especially after the church talk.

"She's been avoiding me for weeks. Over a month now, I guess," she says. "She'll answer her phone or return my calls, but I haven't seen her in so long. She keeps making excuses. At first, I thought she was mad at me. The last time I saw her I mentioned she was putting on a few pounds—I meant it positively, she was always too skinny—but I haven't seen her since."

Weight gain, shit. He wills himself not to accelerate.

"Look, a few years ago," she continues, "at their house I found a weird Bible. It was her husband's."

Shit. Shit, shit, shit.

He says nothing, using the uncomfortable silence to coax the rest of it out.

She sighs.

"I got something in the mail for her," she says. "She stayed with me a year ago or so when they were having problems, and some of her stuff still comes to me. I never open it, normally, but—"

Dixon cuts her off.

"Where did this letter come from and what did it say exactly?" he asks.

"I have it with me," she says, digging through her purse. "Here."

Dixon glances, sees the Humanity Legacy Association letterhead, and doesn't need to see the rest. He wishes he hasn't seen it before. He wishes he had stayed at his desk and eaten his bagged lunch.

"Food is going to have to wait," he says.

He flips the lights on and pushes the accelerator to the floor.

"No," she says looking at him with wide, terrified eyes. "No, please."

"I'm sorry," Dixon says, straightening up in his seat. "I'm afraid your sister might be pregnant."

They tear through town. Rebecca stares out the windshield, absently giving him directions as needed. Dixon white-knuckles the steering wheel.

They're well into the outskirts of town now. Of course they are. Religious whackos who tie their wives up in the attic don't usually want neighbors. Even though they're right, by God. Even though God himself told them to do this, told them that they're special. Somehow, they're always just sane enough to hide their actions from the larger world.

"Does your brother-in-law have any guns in the house?" Dixon asks.

"I'm not sure," she says. "I, yes. I think he has a rifle or a shotgun."

"Is it a rifle or a shotgun?" he asks. When she glances at him blankly, he explains. "Look, can he get me coming out of the car, or does he wait until I'm at the door?"

Still nothing.

He pops open the center console, pulls the shotgun out

most of the way.

"Is it more like this, or more different?" he asks.

She falters, visibly at war with herself.

"All right," he says and lets it slide back into place, tries another approach. "Does he keep it above the mantle, or under the bed?"

"The bed," she says immediately, face lighting up. "I was helping Emily clean up once—"

"That's good, that's good," he says cutting her off as gently as he can. "It's a big help. At this red light, I'm going to pop the trunk and I need to you to step out and grab two bulletproof vests. They should be on the right."

"Two? Am I coming inside?" she asks.

"God, I hope not," he says. "No. But you're going to wear one in the car, OK? I just want you to be as safe as possible. Sounds like he probably has a shotgun, and those can be a bit indiscriminate, understand?"

"Yes," she says and is out of the car immediately, and back long before the light changes over. She even remembers to shut the trunk. She's calming down. Or going into shock.

"I need the layout of the place," he says, because it's true, but also to keep her talking and give her something to do. "Start with where you think he would keep her. An attic? Any outbuildings?"

She nods, unclenching her hands.

"There's a garage, but it's full of junk," she says. "They park in front of it. He wouldn't put her out there. He wants the baby. He'll try and keep her comfortable until…" she trails off.

They both know what will happen.

"The attic is the same," she says. "There's just an access in the closet. Not even a pull-down ladder or anything. The basement…it's full of junk the last time I saw it. But it's finished and heated and everything. There's furniture down there."

"Is it a walkout or anything?" he asks.

"No," she says. "Just the stairs in the kitchen. Maybe one or two of those half window things along the right side of the house."

Dixon swears under his breath. Of course that's where he's keeping her.

"OK," he says. "When's the last time you saw her?"

"Six weeks," she says after a moment.

"How much weight had she put on?" he asks.

"I don't know," she says. "She was wearing baggy clothes. Maybe twenty pounds?"

"How long before that had you seen her?" he asks.

"Another month or so?" she guesses.

"Could it have been another six weeks?" he asks, trying to keep his voice level. "Two months? Four months or more between that time and now?"

"God. Maybe. I can't be sure," she says.

"I don't want to ask you this," he says, then stops. There was no way around it. "Would he cut the baby out of her?"

"Jesus. What?" she asks.

"If she's seven months or more along," he says, "and from everything you've said she could be, and he sees a fucking cop car, is he going to cut the goddamn baby out of her?"

"I…I don't know," she says.

"I need you to guess, Rebecca. If she goes to term and has the baby naturally, well, we know what that means. But is he also the kind of man who could handcuff her to the bedposts and slice her open?"

"I just don't think so," she says. "He always seemed to

love her so much. Maybe he's one of those conspiracy nuts. Thinks the last six years has all been media bullshit or something."

They arrive at the drive to the house and Dixon kills the engine.

Bright NO TRESPASSING and NO SOLICITING signs leap from the dull, rusted metal of the fence. Cold fingers squeeze his guts.

"I guess theorizing that he's slowly gone insane over the last half-a-dozen years wasn't as comforting as I intended," she says.

Dixon shrugs. He's thinking the same thing.

Dixon moves slowly up the drive. He leaves Rebecca in the car, low in the seat, and with the doors locked. He tries the radio again, gives up and shows her how to use it instead.

"Try every five minutes until Ruthie or one of the fellas comes through. You might have better luck than me," he says.

He isn't out of sight of the car when he goes back and gives her the keys.

"Leave in half an hour if I'm not back or I don't radio in," he says. "Do not get out of the car, just climb over the console."

He glances at his watch. Shit. He's eaten ten minutes coming up the walk, sticking his head in the garage, and checking out the two vehicles parked in front of it. Oh well. If she leaves him here, he'll commandeer one of those. He's always wanted to commandeer something.

Half-windows on the right side of the house, she said. He should have made her clarify. North or South or, at the very least, stage left or stage right.

Not her house, he reasons, so she pictures it from the

outside, facing the front. So right means stage left.

Bingo.

Overgrown grass and some seen-better-days bushes cover most of the windows, but he's pretty sure there's a light on in the basement.

He circles the house. The shades are up, curtains pulled back. No lights on, even though it's mostly cloudy. No movement.

He winds his way back to the south-facing elevation, edges closer to one of those basement windows—

And crunch.

He falls backwards, tucks his knees in and rolls left. He flattens to the ground and pushes himself against the concrete foundation of the house.

He checks his shoe—thin, white glass shards. He cranes his neck out enough to see. Sunlight glints off something in the grass in front of both windows. Crushed light bulbs—a makeshift proximity alarm.

A shadow passes in front of the window closest to him. Dixon hears the unmistakable sound of a round chambering into a pump-action shotgun.

He lays on the grass and listens to his own breathing. That cha-chunk echoes through his brain. There's no other sound in the world.

He scoots back towards the garage, keeping his left shoulder against the house. When he's in the front lawn, he stands back up. Still no movement on the first floor. Of course—why would he give up that prime basement spot? Dixon needs to give him a reason to stay by those windows.

He gets down on his haunches and checks the slope of the ground with all the seriousness of a professional golfer. It might work.

Dixon walks to the garage, taking a long, low way around and ducking or crawling when necessary.

He checks the doors on the sedan. No dice, but the rear driver's side door is unlocked on the SUV. There's a fucking baby seat back there. He spies a peeling strip of masking tape on it that reads $1. He instinctively checks his sidearm.

He opens the driver's side door, shifts the car into neutral and cranks the steering wheel as far left as it'll go. This forces the front end of the car right. He checks the angle, gets behind the car and pushes as hard as he can. The car inches forward. He checks the angle again, pushes harder—he's parallel to the ground. He's committing everything he has. The car inches forward. When it's lined up with the edge of the house, he pulls the emergency brake and walks over to the front door. He's too exhausted to crawl or stay hidden. He sees his watch as he jimmies the front door. Rebecca's long gone by now. Where is that backup?

The front door pops. He just barely opens it—the knob turns and the lock springs—and heads back to the car. He checks the angle a last time. Releasing the parking brake, he gives the car a final sturdy push past the south side of the house and bolts for the front door.

He hears the shotgun go off as he clears the threshold. The sound's in this weird kind of stereo—half resonating from outside, half from inside. He imagines he hears the shell hitting the basement floor, but that's impossible.

He wishes he heard two shots. With a pump shotgun, the fucker might have four more shots before he needs to reload.

Dixon risks not sweeping the first floor. He's got to get down there before the husband realizes it was a feint.

He opens the basement door. With the lights on down there and the cloud coverage up here, he doesn't think there will be a discernable difference in light quality.

Something makes him duck at the last second and a kitchen knife takes his sheriff's hat off and sticks it into the door jam. The husband struggles to unstick the knife for a second then gives up and lunges at Dixon.

He wonders how the husband got behind him.

He should wonder where the shotgun is.

They grapple to the kitchen floor. Dixon's foot slams the basement door shut, snapping the butcher's knife in half and sending pieces into the basement. Other shards skitter under the stove.

Dixon's on his stomach, pinning his own arms under himself. He can't reach anything. The husband's straddling him and launching blow after blow but they're wild, untrained shots and they glance right off. He barely feels any of them. He jerks his head back and feels it connect with the husband's chin, who makes an "urk" sound as he falls off him. Dixon twists, pulls his TASER and fires as the husband lunges for him a second time.

The probes hit him in the torso—one in the sternum and one in the belly. He drops to one knee but doesn't collapse. Why isn't he falling?

Dixon fires the TASER again. One probe gets his shoulder, but the other goes wide. He hits him with the juice again on the first pair. The fucker still won't fall. He's inching closer.

Dixon had to volunteer to get zapped with the damn thing before they'd let him carry it. He's fond of telling people that it is the most painful five seconds of his life, but what he really remembers is how he couldn't move. How is this fucker still moving towards him?

Then he thinks of a guy he used to partner with, Tim.

Totally normal cop, until you put a whole day of drinking into him. Then he became a superhero. The last thing to go out on Tim were his legs. He could be puking, blind drunk, speech gone, passed out, snoring and he'd still be standing, stumbling around. Some guys are just built that way.

"Fall down, goddammit!" somebody shouts close by and with Dixon's own voice. "I said fucking fall down!"

His thirty-eight's in his right hand, the TASER shucked to the ground. He's never un-holstered his pistol on duty in twenty years. He's certainly never fired it.

The husband gathers the thin copper wires protruding from his body in his large right hand and yanks them out. They clink on tile somewhere far away. He reaches out for Dixon.

Dixon fires twice. The husband grunts, wobbles and pitches forward. Impossibly, he catches himself on his elbows and knees, and dies like that—hunched over on all fours, forehead resting gently on the cool tile, eyes open and mouth barely parted. Still he doesn't fall.

Dixon stands up, reflexively checks the man's pulse, then kicks him over onto his side into his own blood.

"I told you to fall down," he pants.

Dixon takes a glass from the drying rack, fills it from the tap and drinks it down. He rinses it out and places it back. He opens the basement door and descends the stairs. A shotgun blast takes his legs out from under him and he climbs down most of the stairs with his face.

Maybe he passes out or maybe he stops focusing on his surroundings. He kind of just lies there, hearing his own breathing and feeling his heart beat his blood out through his shredded legs.

The wife hovers into view, shotgun in hand, pointing it at him.

"I'm sorry," she says.

"Not as much as I am," he says. Or tries to, anyway.

"I'm chosen," she says.

He laughs, then coughs and spits.

"You're really not," he says. "You're going to die. The baby is going to kill you, like every baby has killed their mother for the past six years. You can't survive it."

She shakes her head, her eyes sad for him, like he's the idiot here.

"I'm special," she says. "God's chosen me. I'm going to not only survive this—I'm going to thrive. I'm going to start a new and better world."

Her eyes are glassy, her expression is far away. She isn't really seeing him—she's looking at some perfect world inside her own head.

Dixon laughs again.

"This is where you start your new and better world?" he asks. "In this shitty fucking basement? Can I ask you a question, Chosen One?"

She snarls at him, but doesn't pull the trigger again.

"Why haven't you asked about your husband?" he asks. "If you're so special, so important, why don't you care about anyone else?"

Her mouth tightens. The shotgun barrel doesn't so much as dip, but her eyes focus on his. He hopes it's enough.

"You killed him," she says. "It's what you came here to do. You came here to murder all of us. You came here to murder the truth."

He shakes his head, being extra careful to maintain eye contact. He's willing her not to glance down and see his hand inching towards his belt and his fingers, niggling with the holster.

"I came here to save you, Emily," he says. "Your murderer has been growing inside you for months."

He thumbs the hammer back. The sound deafens in the basement. Her eyes dart down to the thirty-eight pressing into the side of her belly. His finger's firmly on the trigger.

"I'm trying to save your life," he says.

She smiles. She actually smiles.

"You can't do this," she whispers.

"I don't want to," he says. "I told you that. I don't want any of this. I want to be at my office having a boring day. You did this. You could have applied for a birth, legally."

"Right," she says, "and be tied up in bureaucratic hell for years just so they could tell me no. My life's not more important than my child's life."

"You don't have any children, Emily," he says. "No living woman does anymore. You know this as well as I do. And it's fucking terrible. I know. We all know. But throwing your life away is not going to fix it."

She tosses the shotgun into a pile of blankets on the floor. She shakes her head, her face relaxes.

"No," she says, calmly taking two steps back from him. "When I said you can't, I meant you're too late."

She reaches down slowly with both hands and pulls at the end of her long cotton nightshirt. She's short enough that it almost touches the ground. Dixon's mind screams at him. Don't let her show you. It's a trick. It's a last gambit to get her way. But he lets her show him.

She pulls the shirt up, and even in the gloom of the basement, he sees the wetness glistening on her thighs and he can't pull the trigger now. Not now that the baby is the only one of them that has any chance of surviving.

He lowers the gun into his lap.

"You're too late," she says again, at the exact moment he's thinking those same words in his head. It gives him a weird feeling, like déjà vu or like his stomach dropping in a dream. A feeling like dread.

She climbs up the stairs and leaves him in the dark, not looking back once.


Backup finally arrives ten minutes later. One car picks Emily up halfway down the road as she shuffles along in her bare feet and nightshirt, doubling over every so often from the intense pain in her abdomen.

The other car, the one with Rebecca now in the backseat, gets to the house and finds the husband cold and dead and stiff on the kitchen floor. They find Dixon sweaty and alive on the basement floor, white-knuckling his revolver like it's a steering wheel. He sees familiar faces in uniform, thinks they look more terrified than he feels and finally gives himself permission to pass out after they positively answer his one question: "Did you find her?"

He wakes in the hospital the next day and realizes, to his utter fascination, that he can wiggle his toes on both feet. He lies there doing that until he's convinced it isn't a hallucination.

He finds the device and signals for a nurse. Three of them come in moments later, check his machines, prod him and ask him basic questions about his name and birthday.

When there's a gap in the questions, he scratches out one of his own.

"Did she have the baby?" he asks.

All three of them busy themselves with other things, avoiding looking at him, eyes darting this way and that.

"Ah, c'mon, goddammit. Did she have the baby yet or

not?" he asks again.

They leave as abruptly as they entered, but the taller of the three, with the plain brown hair, looks directly at him before she's through the door. She nods yes, and her eyes are suddenly much older, her pleasant face more grave.

He lies back into the pillow and shuts his eyes and thinks of nothing and hears nothing but the machines beeping and blipping and whirring around him.

The shotgun was loaded with single-aught birdshot so most of the pellets barely made it through his pants, let alone broke the skin. The doctors said the fall down the stairs had done more damage.

His wife comes to see him. He has this irrational fear she'll bring him food so he won't have to eat the delicious hospital stuff, but it never happens. A couple boys from the precinct stop by. The chief is in and out in five minutes, but Dixon really wants to be alone anyway.

Rebecca comes by later that same day.

"I thought maybe you'd bring the baby," he says in place of hello.

"Did you want me to?" she asks.

"I don't know. Kinda, yeah. How is anybody supposed to feel about this?" he asks.

She has no answer, so says nothing.

"Boy or girl?" he asks after a moment.

"Girl," she says, her face in complete sorrow.

He nods. She'll have to go through this again, in twenty years or so, possibly, with what's now basically her daughter.

"She's mine, now, I guess," she says. "Our parents are dead. It falls to me."

"My wife and I couldn't have children," he says, before

he can stop himself. "I mean, even before all this. Fifteen years ago. We…"

"What?" she asks.

"Nothing. Never mind. Stupid," he holds up his hand with the tubes protruding from it. "Whew. What's in this fucking thing?"

They sit silently for a while, smiling at each other every so often, neither knowing what to say or how to excuse themselves from the situation.

"How long?" he asks after a time, knowing she'll know what he means.

"She was in labor for about fourteen hours," Rebecca says. "Refused any drugs. She swore, she swore up and down, right until she lost consciousness, that she was going to make it, that she was going to undo all the pain and death of the last six years. That she was going to live through it. God. She really, really believed it."

"I wish I could tell you I hadn't seen it before. If I thought that would help," he says.

She wipes her eyes, but they're mostly dry anyway. It's just a new habit picked up over the past few days.

"She passed out as the baby was crowning," Rebecca says. "She lasted four minutes, I think, after the umbilical was cut. That's not even close. Doesn't even rate. Not record breaking. Not even in the top million. Fuck. That woman in Ohio lasted over ten hours?"

Dixon nods.

"Yeah, last year," he says. "Or maybe two years ago. I heard of a woman in Canada lasting most of a week, but who knows what to believe."

"Officer Dixon," she says, "the baby's perfectly healthy. There's nothing wrong with her, she's just a baby."

"They all are," he says.

"But who do I blame?" she asks. "Who do I get mad at? Who took my sister from me?"

"I don't know," he says. "The world, I guess. You can blame me, if that helps."

She laughs, and they move on to small talk, the weather and other useless things. She leaves after a bit and he lies there, staring at the TV but not seeing it.

His wife picks him up the next day and they stop by the nursery on the way out of the hospital. There are only two babies behind the soundproof glass—the rest of it's empty and unused.

Before he gets in the car, he asks his wife to take him to another hospital—St. Joe's downtown.

"Now?" she says. "You don't want to go home for a bit?"

"Nah, I need to see how Carol's doing," he says.

It wasn't the first time he tried to talk a pregnant woman off the ledge and failed. He looks at the lined face of his wife in profile as she drives and feels nothing but love for her.

He knows it isn't the last time either.

# TWO

# NO PURPOSE BUT ENDLESS POTENTIAL

Valerie watches Charlotte carefully push the refried beans away from the shell of her lettuce and cheese taco while she complains the rice is "weird" because it has tomatoes or something in it. Yeah, it has tomatoes in it. It's Spanish rice.

Val tells herself—for the thousandth time—to never eat with her again.

She dislikes picky eaters and Charlotte is the pickiest eater ever.

"I don't think I'm that picky," she said once because of course she did. Part of the reason it bugs Val so much is that picky people can't just admit what they are. They make it a problem with the world, not something wrong with them.

"I can find something to eat anywhere," she said once while eating a hot dog bun with nothing in it but mustard and onions. "Most anywhere."

"Without making a subtraction or substitution?" Val said. This was years ago, when she still engaged Charlotte's inane behavior. "Is your hot dog-less hot dog on the menu? I'd say it doesn't count."

"Hot dogs are disgusting," she said.

She calls all food she doesn't like—or, most likely, never tried—either disgusting or nasty. This from someone who has Mountain Dew and chocolate for breakfast regularly. Sure, the world's full of disgusting food. That makes more sense.

She had let it drop because she'd have to argue in favor of hot dogs and that's hard to justify even though Val finds them delicious.

Charlotte finishes her lettuce and cheese taco and eats around the tomatoes in her rice. A grown-ass adult acting like stubborn child.

When Val was a kid, tough shit if she didn't like what her parents made for dinner. This is what we're eating tonight. No, you're not allowed to go to bed hungry. We made this— you are eating it.

She knows, from gentle prodding over the years, that Charlotte's parents let her eat whatever parts of whatever meal, or completely refuse it and eat a stack of Kraft singles or whatever the fuck she did and continues to do. Nobody stopped her and now it's too late.

Val sighs and looks out the window. She can't watch her pick at her food any longer. She can't think about her eating habits anymore. At least Val always eats less when she's with Charlotte—the woman's disgust for food morphs into a disgust for the woman herself. This then turns, like everything, into rage, depression, and into herself. As much as she hates her habits, they've been friends for twenty years and she hates herself more. Shit always loops back on her.

Charlotte waves the waiter off when asked if she wants a box. She never eats leftovers, of course. What kind of disgusting monster does that?

Val asks for one.

They sit there while Val finishes her margarita and Charlotte gets refill after of refill of Mountain Dew. She doesn't drink either, and not out of some moral code. It's the same reason she doesn't eat meat—not because she's a vegetarian or because she believes in anything—but because she doesn't like the taste. Valerie used to be able to get her to try things; little sips of hard cider or Champagne or an amaretto sour. The most basic, girly drinks imaginable all met with that pinched face of revulsion that's her default expression.

Even Champagne—the sweet kind. Hopeless.

Val gave up making her try shit mostly because she tired of the effort, not that Charlotte has gotten any worse. What's the phrase about trying the same things and expecting different results that proves your craziness?

That's the frustration—Charlotte isn't worse. She isn't pickier. The years pass, and she stays the exact same. It seems weirder precisely because she doesn't change. Val's mom had a close friend who died when they were in high school, right before prom, and her mom keeps an old photograph of them in her house. She talks to it, just mentions things to it occasionally, like when Val turned sixteen, something like "I have a daughter, Debbie, and now she's the same age as you." Or, "Christ, I think I've doubled in weight since high school, Deb, but you get to stay the same size forever." Little, normal things like she's frozen in that moment of time and not just dead and gone. Part of Val's mom is stuck there with her, watching in horror as everything else moves past them.

Val thought it was sweet that her mom kept her friend updated on her evolving life but that's when she was a kid and still believed the dead could hear you, before she connected the fabled Debra McMahan with her own real friend Charlotte Hartz and how annoying it is to have a friend that never changes.

Val swears she'll never share a meal with Charlotte again, but they always wind up eating. Besides what her brother Randy says in his wisdom, "You gotta eat" which sounds too clever to have originated from her borderline-moron brother, it's not like food is the only thing Charlotte is weird about.

Charlotte also, as a woman of thirty-two, still lives at home in her childhood room, sleeps on a twin bed and routinely doesn't wake up until noon. She was a school administrator, but now just substitute teaches so she works two or three days a week, sometimes. She has no partner. In fact, she's never had a boyfriend or girlfriend, never gone on a date and never had sex—not even once so she could make a repulsed face and swear off it for the rest of time.

Val's ex, Warren, theorizes that she was molested or something, but Val's known her since grade school and it's just part of her weird stubborn thing—her strange romantic idea of what the world used to be or should be.

So, what are they supposed to do besides get a late lunch once every other month or so? Talk? What in the actual fuck do they have to talk about? Jane Austen novels? Christ.

"Do you want to go to the mall?" Charlotte asks.

Val realizes they've sat here staring at the table—two people alone together.

"Sure," Val says. Why not?

Charlotte spends two hundred dollars at Lush like it's nothing. Like she has a reason to treat herself, or has someone waiting for her at home. She works and has no house or car payment, so she spends her money freely when an activity or item doesn't conflict with her upside-down revulsions.

Val spends forty bucks and immediately feels terrible, her buyer's remorse complete and total. She mentally looks for gaps in her calendar this week when she can get back here to return all this shit she doesn't need, hoodwinked by the bright colors and powerful smells. She knows in the secret, deep part of her where she knows true things about herself that she'll leave the bath bombs and moisturizer in the bag for a week until she admits to herself that the hassle of returning isn't worth the money that's already gone. She deserves nice things too, and she might as well use the shit before it spoils.

They stop into Sephora and repeat the experience. Val intentionally steps away so she doesn't hear Charlotte's total and envy-jumpstart a shame spiral.

"She's nothing to be envious about," Warren told her. "She has nothing going on in her life but money. She has no one to spend it on. Do you think it'd be worth it to have a few thousand in the bank and live at home with your parents?"

He's right. Well, they both are. It's not like she didn't know that before Warren told her—she hadn't put it into words but she felt it. He's all words and articulated thoughts. She's emotion and feelings. That doesn't make him smarter, it makes him colder. He's a block of text, she's a song.

Charlotte holds up her shiny, foil-embossed bag.

And Charlotte is, what? A caution sign? A list of psychosomatic allergies? Val doesn't miss Warren much, not really, but he'd be able to finish the analogy.

They go to a furniture store and Valerie feels bad for Charlotte for the first time in years, embarrassed for her and her stubborn refusal of everything, her unshakeable belief that the world's insane, and not her.

Charlotte needs a new bed because she's had the same bed since she was ten. Of course you fucking have and whose fault is that? When they find a salesperson, the lady's happy to help and takes them to the queen-sized section but Charlotte says they're too big and the fulls are too and where are the twin beds and the sales lady apologizes at assuming Charlotte's buying a bed for herself and before she can say, yes, I am, the lady zips them over to the modest children's section and Charlotte explains that no, she is purchasing a bed for herself, a twin bed for an adult and she says this with no embarrassment or self-awareness, not registering the look on the sales lady's face, the pity and shut-down nature of her expression, her utter dismissal of Charlotte as something even human and Val's own facial expressions must echo the lady's and she thinks of all the times she's felt this way towards her friend and feels bad for her and depressed that she's so close to being normal but isn't and that she can't recognize how goddamned weird she is.

Val hates pity.

She hates being pitied and she hates feeling pity for others.

She suddenly knows what Charlotte is.

Warren's a block of text, Val's a song.

Charlotte's an adult twin bed.

Charlotte has more shopping to do, but Val makes an excuse and gets the fuck out of there.

She said she needed to check on her brother, which isn't true. He'd burned his arm—and most of Mom's kitchen in the process—trying to make french fries a couple weeks ago, so she might as well check on him anyway. Warren would call this "retroactive truth" or some such thing, like it travels back in time and makes the lie true even though her intent is to get away from her friend.

She wishes she could tell Warren about the twin bed thing, knowing he'd find it fascinating. He always finds Charlotte stories fascinating, like a slug or spider is fascinating, but also a little gross. Not that they don't still talk or text or even see each other every other week or so. They've had sex only once since they broke up but everything else is pretty similar—she just doesn't live over there anymore. She probably would have more sex with him, but he acts like he doesn't want to, even though he used to pester her constantly.

She can tell Randy about the twin bed thing, but he won't get it. He'll ask the wrong questions because that's what he does. Maybe because he's still in high school. It's like he's another species.

She checks her dash-clock and is pretty sure her mom won't be home. Who needs that stress? She heads to the house she grew up in. Charlotte will also head to the house she grew up in as well except, impossibly, she still lives there.

She pulls into the driveway and doesn't see her mom's car. That'll make this easier to deal with. She sees what's supposed to be Randy's car parked on the side of the street. It had been Matt's car, their older brother. He let Randy have it, but it hasn't moved in three years; the insurance and plates long ago expired after Randy failed his driving test twice. Wait. Or was it three times?

She sees the tiny basketball court their dad and uncles poured for the kids back in the day off in the corner of the lot near the streetlamp, so they could play well into the night. Basketball eventually morphed into sitting on the court with friends smoking and drinking.

Matt and his friends used to tie fishing line around small

stuffed animals and drag them across the road under that streetlamp when cars passed by, hiding in the brush, their laughter giving them away when someone from the car yelled "What the fuck was that thing?" They let Val and her friends tag along sometimes when everybody got older and suddenly your kid sister's kinda cool or kinda has boobs. But Randy's the baby in the family, in every way, and was never allowed to hang out with Matt and his friends or Val and hers.

The garage door is cracked open about six inches. Either it's broken or her mom's taking in stray cats again and housing them in the garage. She draws the line at letting the raggedy things inside the house.

Val steps over a few small turds on the driveway when she exits her car. Cats, for sure. She wonders if mom still names them the way she did when they were kids, calling them by vague descriptions. "Hey, look, Half-ear is back," or "Broken-tail is hogging all the food."

Val's favorite was Orange-face, the name entirely apt—Orange-face was entirely black/brown over its body except for its bright, orange face. Plus, she was sweet, coming up to Val without coaxing and instantly purring when she rubbed her. Some of the cats wandered in and out for years; Orange-face had only been around a month or two, but she's the one Val remembers.

It's weird that the front door's locked, that Randy and mom keep it that way now. It was barely even shut when all the kids were here with a flurry of activity, people and pets streaming through the house at all times. Mom says the neighborhood isn't as safe anymore, but Val remembers where the weed dealer lived, where the crack house was and where the handsy adults were when she was a kid and figures it was never that safe. Somebody blows a shed up in a meth explosion and you can't look the other way anymore.

"Why don't you move?" Val asked her, so she'd stop complaining rather than expecting an actual answer.

"Move where?" her mom said. Val couldn't find fault in that reasoning.

She finds the key in the bottom of her purse and enters.

It's hot and stuffy in here for March. Light glows soft and warm from the drawn curtains. The house is a split tri-level, so you enter on the ground level in a foyer no bigger than the welcome mat. The eat-in kitchen is off to the left with the garage—possibly bursting at the seams with cats—beyond that. Straight ahead is the living room and the sliding glass door to the patio and yard. To the immediate right is a split staircase, ascending and descending half a floor. Up the half-flight are three bedrooms and a bathroom, down the other half-flight is the basement, which is only half underground. The basement has its own living room, bigger than the one upstairs, a tiled area that could be a kitchenette, but instead is nothing, another bathroom and a large storage room converted into a bedroom, first for Matt, then for Josh and now for Randy, leaving all but Mom's room upstairs unoccupied. Val never lived in the basement. She's the second oldest, so she certainly could have claimed it after Matt moved out into the world's shittiest apartment, but she never saw the appeal. Must be a boy thing.

She intentionally avoids the kitchen—doesn't want to see the damage Randy caused in his stupidity—and descends the stairs, hearing faint TV sounds from down there somewhere.

No lights are on and the curtains are shut over the basement half-windows. It's stuffier down here, somehow, and there are extra bandages, ointments, painkiller bottles and half a dozen empty glasses and jugs of Gatorade. Randy sleeps on the couch, his right arm plastered-up in a cast, and a video game controller dangling from the protruding fingers of that hand. He snores lightly.

She turns the overhead fan on and begins pulling the curtains open, flooding the basement with afternoon light. He moans and squirms in protest.

"Ugh," she says, defaulting into big sister mode. "Get up, you piece of shit."

"I'm sick," he says, muffled from the throw blanket he rolls over into.

"You're not sick, you're an idiot," she says. "You burnt your damn arm up trying to make fries and you almost burnt the whole house to the ground."

"I saved the house!" he says, perking up to defend himself, about the only thing you can count on him for. "I carried the pot out through the garage and threw it into the street. That's how I burnt my arm."

He holds his arm up and shows her the cast as proof.

"Congratulations," she says. "You only burnt down half the kitchen and a bit of the yard. How're you doing, dummy?"

He smacks at the cast, mimes scratching it with his good hand.

"I just wanna touch the skin," he says in a pseudo-Buffalo Bill voice as if *Silence of the Lambs* had been a creepy Saturday morning cartoon.

"You don't have any skin," Val says. "You burnt it all off."

He sits all the way up on the couch, tossing the controller away.

"You're not very nice today," he says. "Why'd you open all the things?"

"Curtains?" she hazards. "Drapes?"

"Be nice. I'm on mucho painkillers," he says.

She shakes her head at him.

"Another child drug addict," she says. "Mom's right. This neighborhood."

"Uh, I'm pretty sure I'm nineteen," he says, slurring his voice more and more for effect, playing along. "I'm an adult drug addict."

She points at his face where he has a small bandage. A couple drops of burning grease leapt from the pan as he carried it out through the house. A neighbor told mom that she heard him screaming.

"You changing that thing when you're supposed to?" she asks.

"Mom helps remind me," he says.

He pokes at the cast as if petting it.

"I juuust wanna touch the ssskin," he repeats, exaggerating further.

"What the fuck is wrong with you?" she asks, laughing this time.

He shrugs.

"I'm the youngest, so I'm pretty much guaranteed to be a fuck-up," he says.

She stands up.

"You want a fresh Gatorade or something? Any food?" she asks.

He shakes his head and makes a nauseated face.

"Just drink," he says. "One of the blue ones, if there's any left."

She bounds back up to the mid-level and into the kitchen. It's half destroyed, like that one Batman villain with the half fucked-up face. Warren would know the one.

The right side of the kitchen is black and yellow with fire

and smoke damage. The cabinets above and next to the stove are ruined beyond repair. The stove top itself is rippled and blackened, melted looking. The kitchen table to the left is fine and the curtains are all right. The window's cloudy from smoke or condensation and the fridge and rest of the counter and cabinets look normal.

The stuffy smell of the house, she realizes, is emanating from the burnt kitchen. She should open windows, not just curtains. They must be breathing in some nasty shit. She checks her phone. It's only sixty degrees out, too cold for opening windows this late in the day.

She opens the fridge—a Diet Coke for her, a Gatorade for Randy.

"Sorry, no blue," she says when she's back downstairs and hands it to him.

"Red it is," he says and pops the nozzle thing open and takes a few pulls.

She cracks open her Diet Coke can and gestures with it towards him.

"Does it feel weird drinking from that nipple thing they put on those bottles while you sit on the couch all day playing videogames and watching Netflix?" she asks.

"You're being super judgey today," he says, taking more drinks. "I'm not being lazy, my arm's all fucked-up and I have to take pain meds, and then because the pain meds turn my shits into clumps of jagged glass, I have stool softeners and laxatives, so I'm either stopped up or raining huge liquid dumps from my sore asshole, all without much use from my right arm. And I am right-armed. Or right-handed or whatever it's called."

"Gross," she says, and relents slightly. "But you're right. I had a half-day and was hanging out with Charlotte earlier.

That whacko puts me in a mood."

Randy nods, picks the game controller up and starts scrolling around.

"I think Charlotte's hot," he says.

"Gah! Oh my God, what?" Val screams. "Your watery shit talk didn't get me to barf, but this might do it."

He shrugs.

"She is," he says. "Got a nice bod."

"Are you fucking serious?" she asks. "Because she's skinny, that's why she's hot? Dude, she is skinny because she is very, very unhealthy."

He shrugs again.

"If it works," he says.

"God, how are we related?" she asks. "You know, she's probably never had sex or even masturbated? Her pussy is probably sealed over from disuse."

He drops the controller and bends over onto the couch, making gagging sounds that turn into fits of laughter. Val laughs too.

"How can there be three brothers in this family, and the sister is the grossest one of all?" he asks, genuinely marveling at this thought.

"Grossness is equal opportunity."

She finishes her Diet Coke, rinses it out in the bathroom sink and crushes it slightly. She sets it on the stairs, so she can toss it in the bin in the garage on her way out, maybe see a kitten or two.

"I'm gonna head out before mom gets here and guilts me into moving back in here with you crazy people," she says. "You need anything?"

"Nah," he says. "Thanks for checking on me."

When she gets to the stairs he calls her back.

"Shit, I almost forgot," he says. "I was gonna call you anyway. Can you take me to an appointment on Wednesday? Mom has something at work she can't miss."

"Wednesday is tomorrow, you realize. What time is it?" she asks.

"Uh…"

"Jesus, Randy," she says. "Before or after lunch.?"

He starts nodding his head vigorously.

"Oh, after lunch, for sure," he says. "One hundred percent."

"Uh huh," she says. "Whatever. I can work from home on Wednesday, so just text me and remind me. With the time."

She leaves. The outside of the house is dingier than she remembers or noticed when she arrived. The basketball hoop she glanced at fondly is starting to lean slightly to the side and the court has huge weeds—some three or four feet high—sprouting up from the cracks. A kitten darts between them. A stack of business cards for landscapers are scattered around on the front porch next to a pile of newspapers. It makes her feel weird, like her mom hasn't been coming home or Val's in some psychological thriller where the big reveal will be that her mom has been dead the whole time. *Oooh*. But Val remembers this behavior from her youth. Her mom works too much, enters and exits through the garage and doesn't check the front door. Probably not the mail either.

She scoops up the fanciest looking card that also has a Spanish name—a thick one-sided card in matte green with a nice foil embossing with no rates listed and a number to call or text, plus a website to set up appointments with a guy named Manny—and makes a mental note to check the mail tomorrow when she picks Randy up.

She glances at her watch. She really must go.

She drives to the clinic and signs in, hitting that sweet spot of low traffic minutes before rush hour which puts her next in line for walk-ins since the after-work crowd has yet to hurry over or wander in after a quick dinner.

She always uses this brand of clinic. They're owned, staffed and run by women. How could a man really understand what this is like for her? But let's be honest—she's been neglectful. She hasn't been in…probably a year? Jesus, maybe two? Warren got snipped before she knew him, and she was careful with anybody on the side. And only around the beginning of their relationship had she done that.

The lady before her is called back and Val uses the free Wi-Fi to book an appointment for Manny to tidy up her mom's house tomorrow morning. Maybe he'll still be there when Val comes by and she can tip him in cash.

The receptionist comes up to Val and touches her arm lightly, saying her name with gentle quietness, and leads her back into one of the rooms. Like the green of that business card was chosen carefully to make an association with a healthy lawn, the clinic is equally well thought-out and designed. The soothing colors of the room, natural light and the gentle, personal nature of the well-trained staff. She has friends who never go to the same clinic twice, never quite satisfied in their quest for the perfect place. Exhausting. Val's too lazy for that. She's tried others, of course, but this one and its consideration of all facets of its presentation impressed her. The fact that it's women owned and operated clinched it.

She sits in the room for ten minutes before the nurse practitioner enters. They chat briefly, small talk stuff. Val's pretty sure she's never met this woman before, but her friendliness lands without being patronizing or condescending. The woman segues seamlessly into Val's reason for her visit.

"My, ah, boyfriend and I broke up," Val says.

"I'm sorry to hear that, Valerie," the woman says with genuine concern on her face. "That's always hard."

"Yeah," Val says. "We were together awhile, so I let my stuff go. Kinda got away from me."

She nods sympathetically and glances at the iPad in front of her for the first time since entering the room. She scrolls a few seconds and then turns her attention back to Val.

"I see you had an IUD," she says. "Is that still the way you'd like to go?"

"Yes, I think so," she says.

The woman nods.

"Since you've been here last, a few new laws and ordinances have been passed and are in vigorous enforcement," she says. Then, seeing the worry on Val's face, broadens her smile and touches her forearm lightly. "Don't worry, it's still your choice and an IUD is perfectly safe and reliable and still very popular, but legally I am obligated to go over any new pregnancy protections with you and to recommend tubal ligation. It's entirely safe, painless, and the procedure takes about an hour. Even though it is permanent, it is also completely reversible, if the fortunes of the world should reverse."

Val becomes annoyed for the first time. The way everybody talks about it without talking about it. She knows this woman is merely doing her job and is only explaining the procedures to her as she's legally obligated to, but it grates on her. She's most likely also legally obligated to mention motherhood bringing certain death and the decreasing hope for changing that, but the way she said it, not in clinical terms, even, but like government doublespeak. Like corporate bullshit, and nothing grates on her more—attempting to add subtext when whatever's said is easier plainspoken. After more than seven years, you'd think people could at least talk about this openly.

She pushes this away and tries listening to the woman as she explains a few new birth control methods that have become available in the last two or so years. She's heard or read about them, she's pretty sure, so she nods along and daydreams until the woman's posture tells her that she finishes talking. Val says "Yes, thank you," but she likes and responds to the IUD well, so let's stick with that. The woman smiles and nods and makes a few clicks on her tablet, not at all put out by the fact that she spent twenty minutes on other techniques and Val barely pretended to listen. She's a goddamn professional.

"Since it's been so long since we've seen you, we'll have to do a pap smear and a pregnancy test and a few other things," the woman says.

"Of course," Val replies, and they start. The woman takes a tiny amount of blood, seals it, they both sign it and then send it through a pneumatic tube in the wall. Val climbs into the exam chair and stretches into the stirrups, closes her eyes, and thinks about other things. It's over quickly. The woman glances at her tablet which just lit up and excuses herself, ducking out for a minute.

She sticks her head back in and asks Val a question which she can't really understand but she answers it and the woman leaves and returns with another woman—a doctor?—and they tell Val that she's pregnant and they'll need to remove it before they can implant the IUD and she nods in agreement and says "Of course, of course" and "I understand." She signs forms on the iPad and initials here and signs there and places her thumbprint on that and they lead her down the hall into another room and another woman helps her onto the table, which is like a couch without a back to it, and they give her something to drink and a pill and something else to drink and tell her to "Lie back" and "Breathe easy" and "Try to relax" and the lights have dimmed imperceptibly during her time in the room and a soft music plays and was it playing when she came in here? And she lies there and knows she'll never sleep again, or even shut her eyes.

The first woman comes back in later. Her warmth the same, her smile a little restrained now, and she says everything has gone fine and they can prep her for the IUD now and Val stops her, puts a firm hand on the woman's forearm when the woman's has always been tentative on hers.

"No," Val says. "I want my tubes tied."

They won't let her drive herself, so she leaves her keys and takes a Lyft home.

She eats something from the fridge, some leftover something, not even bothering to warm it up or use a fork or anything, just eats it out of the carton with her fingers, pushing past the nausea, and finishing it. She puts the empty carton back into the refrigerator without realizing it.

She calls Warren before she knows what she's doing.

He answers after a ring or two and she's glad—who else could she go to? Not her mom, not the ever-virginal Charlotte and not her other friends who she realizes now are acquaintances or work associates at best.

"What's up?" he says like it's completely normal for her to call him this late during the week for no reason.

"Warren," she says, and hears something very wrong in her own voice.

"Are you OK?" he asks, his cheeriness falling aside. "What's wrong?"

"Can I see you?" she asks.

"Of course, Val," he says. "Stop by."

"I don't have my car," she says. "Can you come here?"

"Yeah," he says. "Where's your car? Did you get in a wreck?"

"Please," is all she says.

"OK," he says, and hears him rustling around. "I'm leaving. Are you hurt?"

She doesn't know how to answer.


He's there in ten.

She tells him about it while they sit in her kitchen and he makes her tea. She suggests the couch, but he says here is fine. Her brain waves mesh with his—the couch symbolizes other things, like what got her in this damn mess.

He listens patiently and holds her hand when appropriate, and rubs her back and even gives her a peck or two on the top of her head.

"I'm sorry, Valley," he says, bringing out the big guns of his special nickname for her that she hates. She realizes she misses it.

"You should get yourself checked," she tells him. "That procedure you had loses effectiveness after so many years."

He nods.

"Clearly," he says. "I've been meaning to go in for a tune-up."

If you had already, this shit wouldn't have happened, she thinks, but can't be bitter at him, not for that, not when she's done the exact same thing.

She looks at him, and he smiles at her, and she has trouble

remembering why they are no longer together.

"I'm sorry you can't have a baby, Valley," he says, ruining it.

"What?" she gasps.

He shifts in his seat, his body trying to tell his stupid brain that "Oh no, this is not what you want to say right now" via uncomfortable soreness in his ass and legs, but it is, after all, a stupid brain and he continues.

"I'm sorry that you had to go through with that," he says. "And alone, too."

"Better," is all she says.

"I'm sorry it probably rehashed the fact that you'll never have kids," he says while squirming, his body knowing what his mind does not.

"Ah," she says, "you lost the thread again."

She pushes her tea away with her fingertips, making the barest of contact with the mug as if it's turned to ice suddenly and she can't stand touching it or to even to have it near her, radiating the cold.

"I never wanted kids," she says. "I've told you that."

"I know, but—"

"No," she says. "Never. Not now, not ever. Not because it would cost me my life. I never wanted kids. My house was fucking chaos. Loud insanity all the time. I don't have it in me. I don't like to be needed."

"You used to like when I needed you," he says.

"No, I didn't," she says. "I liked when we were partners, when we were friends, when we were on the same page."

"Right," is all he says, not looking at her, but over her, as if picturing her saying similar words weeks ago when she told him she was moving out.

"I'm not going to try and keep you here if you don't want

to be here," he had said. Something about that had made her want to remain friends with him, which she doesn't regret, even now.

"You're right. You did say that," he says, echoing that understanding between them. Their understanding, their commonality, it meets and meshes together somewhere between them as if they have auras, as if there are parts of themselves that are bigger than their bodies and where these parts touch, the lines blur and there's something that is both of them. A union.

Val smiles. She thinks of a t-shirt she bought for him years ago. It had a Venn-diagram on it, on the left, red circle it said "Music I Like," on the right, blue circle it said "Music You Like," and in the overlapping purple middle, "Music I Used to Like." This sums them up and their understanding of each other. They are mostly themselves but a tiny sliver of each of them is also the other.

"What are you smiling about?" he asks, smiling himself because she is and maybe the storm has passed without a fight.

"Do you still have that t-shirt?" she asks, drawing a vague outline on her own shirt. But they're in the understanding place now and he nods, knowing what she means immediately.

"Yeah, I'm a little chunky for it right now," he says, "but I live in hope that I'll be able to wear it again someday."

He sips her discarded tea.

"Oh, I get it. We're the shirt, right?" he says. "Our bubbles merging?"

"Yeah," she says and gets up from her chair and goes to him. He doesn't stand, but they're tall counter chairs so he's approximately his natural height. She leans into him and he puts an arm around her and holds her. He kisses the top of her head and she tries to relax the tension in her body and be held.

"Thank you for coming over," she says.

"Of course," he says and gives her a little squeeze before letting her go. "I'm still here for you."

She nods.

"Until one of finds somebody else, probably," she says.

"Yeah probably," he admits.

They share the rest of her tea until it's gone.

"Do you want me to stay tonight?" he asks.

She shakes her head.

"No, no," she says. "Well, kinda, but no. I've got a conference call first thing and I'm sure you have to work."

He nods and gets up, gives her one more hug and tells her he'll check on her this weekend and leaves.

She sits in the chair he sat in. The warmth from him fades as she sits there, or she becomes used to it or replaces it with her own body heat, or it melds into her. She doesn't know which is true and maybe it's all of them. She sits there and holds the empty mug they shared and thinks about how a mug's only purpose is to be a vessel for something else, how it has no use besides its empty part, and before it's a mug it's clay and it has no purpose but endless potential. It could've been anything, and instead is defined by the void at its core.

She thinks of this in vague terms, in the abstract.

Maybe it's more of a feeling than a thought.

She sleeps fitfully. She's exhausted, but jerks herself awake as she begins to drift off. She does this several dozen times throughout the night. She hits the snooze on her phone until the absolute last minute, until she must turn it off and go right into her work app, joining the conference call while still in bed.

She's the last one to call in, but only at three past eight and she doubts anybody notices. She mutes her phone and shuffles out of bed, hits the coffee maker button, opens her laptop and moves onto the toilet. She hopes nobody asks her a numbers-specific question in the next however long it will take her to pee, get caffeine, and remember her passwords.

She sits at the counter and sips her coffee, farting and blinking at her computer screen, unmuting her phone from time to time to answer a question or agree with something. She forgets the questions before she finishes answering them, but nobody notices. The meeting drags on and on and round and round like meetings do, but she's pretty detached from it, so it strobes by—static shots that flip abruptly into the next shot with barely perceptible forward motion. The meeting as a clattering old film projector.

Finally, it's over and the call ends, and she makes a few half note-type things in her laptop before she forgets them, hoping she can make some kind of sense out of them later.

She puts an "Away for Fifteen" message up in the work chat system and moves herself and her coffee to the damn couch. As soon as she sits down she wishes she'd posted the "Away for an Hour" message.

She curls up with pillows and blankets and sips her coffee and her phone buzzes at her with a text.

She has four texts from Randy.

reminder you're taking me to docs.

hey it's before lunch. 10.

hope that don't fuck things up.

you alive right?

Shit dammit butt-fuck. She jumps up and gets to her bedroom before she remembers that she doesn't even have her car with her.

She checks the time: 9:19. Nope. Not a chance she makes it to the clinic and then to the house and then to the hospital.

Fuck. Fuck fuck fuck. She could swing by in a Lyft and pick Randy up. She checks the app. She'll have to leave in two minutes, out the door and with minimal traffic...

She looks at herself in the hallway mirror. Nope. Not a fucking chance. Not this morning, not today.

She texts Charlotte, grasping at straws.

U awake?

A second later:

Strangely, yes. What's up?

Can U take Randy to a dr.'s appointment? On my way, had car trouble.

Sure, no problem.

Life saver!!! OWE YOU BIG TIME!!!!!!

Leaving. Let me know if you need picked up from the garage or anything.

Val sends her a couple dozen heart and trophy emojis and texts her brother that yes she's alive but her car isn't and Charlotte's going to pick him up and be nice to her and be ready when she gets there and try to give her money for gas even though there's no way she'll take it.

She sits back down at the counter, too keyed up to snuggle on the couch, and pounds through her emails and chat messages.

Satisfied for the moment that work stuff is at bay, she showers quickly and applies a minimal ammount of make-up and pulls her hair back, what she'd use for going to the gym if she did that anymore, or running out to the grocery for a few things.

She has zero new emails or chats, bizarrely, and even though it's just after ten, she readies a lunch icon. When her phone tells her the Lyft is one minute away, she posts and hops downstairs.

She picks her car up from the clinic and grabs a sub on her way home since she's supposedly on lunch and her stomach is doing something weird. Either she's hungry already, or whatever the hell she scarfed down last night isn't agreeing with her. Ugh. How long had whatever that was been in the fridge?

She sits at the counter and eats her sandwich with sparkling water and answers emails and other stupid questions while her stomach settles.

It's well past noon and she hasn't heard from Charlotte or her brother, so she texts Randy to make sure everything went fine.

He responds fifteen minutes later with

yeah, sorry forgot to tell you I'm home and it's all looking good

She asks if he wants her to come over and he says no, they gave him new pain stuff and he's going to try and sleep.

She says good luck and sends him the Zs emoji.

She doesn't hear anything from Charlotte, but Randy has probably driven her crazy and she's remaining silent in the hopes that Val will forget her offer to come pick her up as well.

Hmm. She probably should Google some easily fixable car problem she can pretend her car had but she won't. Just shrug and act completely ignorant of automobiles, which won't be acting.

She finishes working, and the rest of her sandwich, over the next few hours and then sits around on the couch and watches TV without really absorbing any of it, but that's what it's for. She tries coming up with a believable scenario in which she can work from home tomorrow and Friday but talks herself out of it. She doesn't like being there, it is work after all, but she does like knowing what's going on. She gets more work done at home in some respects, but is certainly more out of touch with exactly what work needs doing.

She doesn't hear anything from Warren all day, but that's for the best. She wants to be alone and he knows that. She knows it's hard for him to not pester her about how she's doing, which is his default handling of all situations.

She doesn't hear from him until mid-afternoon on Friday and she acquiesces to get drinks with him that night.

As she's waiting for Warren to pick her up, she realizes she still hasn't heard anything from Charlotte. She's begins texting with her right as Warren pulls up in his old Jeep. The smell and feel of the Jeep is more comforting than she believes possible.

"Setting up your next date?" he asks.

"This is not a date," she says, moving her free hand in a circle motion to encompass the whole interior of the vehicle. "This is drinks."

"Right," he says, faking an injury to his heart. "But, ouch."

She holds up her phone towards him.

"And this is just Charlotte," she says as her phone blips again.

"Ah," he says, perking up, "and how is that most fascinating of weirdos?"

She makes a half-hearted disgusted noise.

"She's not that fascinating," she says. "She's just weird and the older we get, the weirder she gets. Or her weirdness seems more insurmountable."

"You guys having a spat?" he asks.

Val sighs.

"No, not at all," she says. "We're fine. She really helped me out this week, actually. She's just, her whole thing is exhausting."

"So, you told her about the…" he trails off not knowing how to say it, letting it hang there instead.

"What? No, God no," she says shaking her head vigorously. "I tried to talk to her about going to the gynecologist once, and she changed the subject so fast…ugh, God."

"What?" Warren asks, attempting to drive and look at her phone at the same time.

"She's watching her second Jane Austen movie of the evening and complaining that her mom keeps trying to buy her low-cut shirts, so she can catch a man. See? Exhausting."

They sit in silence for a moment, driving closer to downtown.

"She thinks the world should be a certain way," Val says. "But does nothing about it. Just stubbornly sits in her parent's house waiting for shit to change. She's positive she's right. That's what drives me nuts. She's one hundred percent sure that she's right and the rest of the world is crazy."

Warren nods in agreement. They've had this discussion so many times, Val thinks. Maybe she's the insane one. Nope, because of that right there. She has doubts, she has questions, she searches for answers. The insane don't do that.

"What'd she help you out with?" Warren asks.

"Oh, I had to leave my car at the clinic, remember? Anyway, I was supposed to take Randy to the doctor's the next morning and I had totally spaced it, so at the last-minute Charlotte bailed me out."

Warren chuckles, but without malice, as if she'd related a

sitcom plot.

"Oh yeah," he says, "how's Randy's arm?"

"Better than my mom's kitchen," she says, sounding more bitter than she intended. "I don't know how she's going to get that fixed. Oh! You want to know the grossest part? Randy thinks Charlotte is 'hot'!"

"What the fuck?" Warren asks, full-on laughing now.

"Right?" Val says. "It's just because she's skinny."

"Skinny?" he says. "She's not skinny, she has no nutrients. She's probably fucking dying."

"That's exactly what I said!"

They laugh and turn onto Broadway. When Val realizes where they're going, she vetoes it. They argue for a bit, but she refuses to get out of the car if they go to The Brass Rail, that dump. He accuses her of not wanting any of their friends to see them together. She insists that, no, she just hates it. It's a fucking hole in the wall. It's a dive bar, he argues, but she won't be swayed. How is that different anyway? They were having so much fun. He relents, and they agree on Henry's. They drive the few blocks and park, mostly in silence.

Once inside, it's warm and familiar like his Jeep or his holding of her the other night and they soon fall into easy conversation and Red Stripes.

They sit in a booth on the bar side. It's crowded but they know people and some stop and say "What's up?" and some give them "Are you guys together again?" looks but nobody says anything—except for when Warren bumps into this guy and he looks like he's going to kill them—so they can easily pretend everything's normal, Val pretends her secret fantasy—that they never got together and they just stayed friends and that's all they've ever been.

To Warren's credit, he acts like a friend. He doesn't try to sit too close or touch her or anything weird. She knows it's hard and appreciates the effort. She'll have to leave soon before they get drunk and confused. The table dips slightly. Well, more drunk, anyway.

"You know something Charlotte told me the other day at lunch?" she asks.

He gives a mildly interested look. She shouldn't tell him anyway.

She shakes her head and waves it off.

"Never mind," she says. "I shouldn't talk about it."

He perks up at the deflection. She finds it so easy to bitch about Charlotte—this must be something special. God. She really shouldn't say anything. She tries searching her memory for some weird detail about Charlotte that's strange enough that he doesn't know but comes up blank. Val can only see that thing she told her in confidence. Told her specifically not to tell anyone.

Warren's giving her this c'mon face. She's painted herself into a corner.

"OK," she says, lowering her voice way down in the noisy bar. "But this absolutely cannot leave the table,"

"Scout's honor," he says and holds three fingers up. She half-expects him to cross his heart or make the sign of the cross. She ignores the mockery.

"All right." She looks around one last time. It's thinned out a bit, in that time between the after-dinner crowd and the late-night creeps still trying to find their keys or whatever the hell it is that takes them so long to get anywhere.

The guy Warren bumped into is still in the booth behind them, but his back is to them as he talks intensely into a cell phone, oblivious to the world.

"Charlotte has a hundred grand saved," she tells him.

He shakes his head. All right, all right, like it's a perfectly reasonable thing for a thirty-two-year-old to have, but he does whistle, subtly impressed.

"From substitute teaching?" he asks.

"Remember she was an administrator at that East Allen school for a couple years?" Val reminds him. "She banked almost all of that."

"Must be nice," he says.

"She's saving up to buy a house," Val tells him.

"She knows you don't have to pay for a house outright, doesn't she?" Warren asks. Then, thinking about it for a moment, "Hell, with that kind of money, in this town? She could buy two."

"Right? That's what I told her, but you know how picky she is about absolutely everything," Val says. "She'd rather sleep on a twin bed in her childhood room than, God forbid, live in an apartment or a house that wasn't absolutely perfect. It's sad. She's losing by being so stubborn, look at her life and compare it to things that are supposed to make up a life. She's a fucking loser."

"Yeah," Warren says, "a loser with one hundred thousand dollars."

Val nods and lifts her beer to her lips, savoring the next part. Even Warren can't act cool after hearing the grand finale.

"A hundred thousand dollars," she says, taking a sip. "In cash."

It'd be a spit-take if she'd timed it better. Instead he chokes on his swallow of beer and has a minor coughing fit.

"No way. Cash?" he hisses. "Is she insane?"

"Well, yeah," Val says. "I've been saying that for years. She's weird about everything—you didn't think she'd be weird about banks?"

He rests his elbows on the tabletop and rubs his eyes, trying to massage the madness of it into his brain.

Val changes the subject suddenly, not wanting to talk about Charlotte anymore, knowing it'll just go in circles. They'll just nod and agree, and nothing will be solved, like her silly old-fashioned vision of how the world should be.

The place thins out, their side of the bar emptying completely.

Then, almost immediately, it begins filling again with clubbers and other late-night assholes, so they bounce. She punches in a Lyft to get home, he half-heartedly protests, but they hug, and he leaves. She won't miss his mass in the bed tonight, stretched-out and taking up as much of the bed as she can, like it's all perfectly normal.

She wakes up sort of hung-over, but pushes through it. Saturday and Sunday fly by like good weekends do and she heads back to work feeling kind of refreshed for the first time in a while. She stops in to see her brother and he seems different too, somehow. He's wearing grown-up clothes and his hair is combed. His arm is still in a cast and he still isn't in school, but the house seems in better shape. Even the kitchen is getting some of the melted and burnt crap out. Dad and some of his brothers come by and start redoing it. Val's sure her mom won't let them do it for free, but it's deeply discounted. Her parents are even civil towards each other. Val stays for dinner one night, popping around the corner and picking up Lee's Famous Recipe Chicken when her mom gets home. She looks so fucking exhausted in her scrubs.

A couple weeks pass like this—just normal shit. She hasn't seen Warren or Charlotte again yet, but they text here and there. Normal for her and Warren, a little strange that

Charlotte seems so busy. Busy with what?

Val also keeps doing strange, absent-minded things. Like getting home and realizing she forgot to lock her front door or leaving her laptop on all day and finding it dead in the evening. Finishing food and forgetting to write it on her grocery list in her phone. Small things—no big deal.

Entering her apartment now, she's debating whether she should ask Charlotte if she has a boyfriend or something as Charlotte just texted her that no, she can't get lunch tomorrow but maybe next week, when her key sticks weird in the front door lock and the lock turns strangely, jaggedly like there's sand or something in there, but she only half-notices, relieved that she remembered to lock the thing this time. She closes the door, locks it and feels that jaggedness again and puts the chain on and goes into the kitchen.

There's a man in the kitchen and he has something hard and shiny in his hand. He points it at her.

"Put your hands flat on the counter," he says in a gravelly voice.

She does.

It's a gun. There's a gun in his hand. Why is there a gun in his hand?

He edges her phone away from her with his free hand. He glances down at it long enough to turn it off and put it in his pocket.

"Let's go sit on the couch, Valerie," he says.

She moves from the kitchen in slow, deliberate steps. He follows behind her. She feels him behind her. She tries to brace herself for whatever is coming.

He motions for her to sit in the corner of the couch, next to the lamp which is already on and bent to a weird angle, so it shines in her face. She sits. The ottoman has been moved and is positioned across from her carefully chosen spot. He sits on it and rests the gun on his knee, but he still holds it firmly and it still points squarely at her.

She opens her mouth to speak but, like everything in the last few moments, this too is in slow motion and he stops her.

"If you scream or yell," he says calmly, "I will shatter your jaw."

He then nods at her to continue and, somehow, she does.

"You've been in my apartment before," she says. "A few things have been…off. I thought I was losing it."

That same curt nod.

"I needed to use your computer, Valerie," he says, as if that makes sense.

He shifts on the ottoman, trying to sink back in the shadows. There's something almost familiar about him.

"Everybody seems to call you Val," he says, "but I'm going to stick with Valerie. I'm not everybody else."

"Why did you need to use my computer?" she asks.

"Your friend, Charlotte," he says, "she's weird about everything, even banks, but she's just normal enough to have a Facebook, isn't she?"

"What?" is all she can manage.

"You know," he says, conversationally, "I almost just barged up here that first night and beat the information out of you, but I stopped myself. Thought I'd play this one smart."

He sticks his hand out farther, she shrinks back from the gun in it. She'd scooted to the edge of her seat, despite herself.

"I'm proud of myself for that," he says, glancing at the gun. "I usually have poor impulse control."

"You're from the bar," she says. "A couple weeks ago. Warren bumped into you."

He smiles.

"Congratulations," he says.

"I thought, I thought you'd left," she says.

"I was eavesdropping on you two most of the night," he says. "I heard about the hundred grand, then I waited for you outside, followed you home. It was no big deal to get into here while you were at work, root around on Facebook, discover you only have one friend named Charlotte and then learn all about her. Like, where she lives."

"You're going to steal her money?" Val asks, feeling slow but not caring.

"It's just money," he says. "It's not hers, it doesn't belong to anyone. It just floats around, lands on some people, and then moves on."

He sounds so much like a lapsed monk or a first-year philosophy major that she almost laughs in his face. She stops herself, but he notices.

"Do you believe in God, Valerie?" he asks her, then waves her answer away before she gives it. "Your Facebook has you listed as an atheist. If you don't believe in benevolence, you can't rightly believe in malevolence."

He shrugs and raises his eyebrows at her.

"Things just are," he says.

She sits there stunned by the ridiculous justification of his actions.

"Then why take the money at all?" she asks before she can stop herself.

That shrug again, only more cartoonish, like he doesn't even believe the bullshit he's spouting.

"Well," he says, "all this Zen won't feed my children, now will it?"

He stands up swiftly and places the gun right up against her temple. The cold of the metal sends a jolt through her body. She goes cold to match the gun barrel, her vision clouds and her stomach bottoms out. He puts his free hand around her throat and squeezes just enough. His hand feels like fire. He whispers harshly in her ear, all the humanity gone from his voice, dropping away and revealing that it's an act he performs, a mask he wears. He's really a monster.

"Or think of it like this," the monster rasps in her ear, "something my father used to say, after he'd hit me, randomly, no matter if I was good or bad. 'You can't plan for crazy' he would say."

They're parked in her car across the street and down from Charlotte's house. When she drove them here, he sat in the passenger seat speaking only to give her directions, even though she's been here thousands of times.

Before they left, he told her if it didn't go well, if she tried anything, he'd make a stop and visit her mom's house. He gave her the address casually.

"Give me the keys," he says.

She hands them to him.

"Put your hands back on the wheel," he says. "No, lower. There."

With one quick movement, he zip-ties her hands together and to the steering wheel.

He reaches up and turns the overhead light off. He opens the door.

"I'll be right back, just cutting their house phone," he says. Then, as he's halfway out of the car, "What year is it? Can you believe they still have a landline?" He shakes his head and is gone.

It's the first moment Val's been alone since she saw him standing in her kitchen. She lets out a long, slow breath.

She must do something—she must. But what?

She wants to slam her body into the horn and start waking people up, but how fast can anyone get to her? Faster than he can shoot her in the face and then kill her family and Charlotte's too?

Jesus, he's probably going to kill Charlotte and her parents anyway—

But Charlotte's car isn't there.

Val blinks and shakes her head. No, she's right. Charlotte's car isn't there. It's well after midnight. Where the hell is she?

If she can get a call to her, or a note or something. Val can't think of any way to warn her or her doomed parents inside.

And there he is, on his way back already.

She's out of time. Did he notice Charlotte's car isn't here, or does he not know what it is? Of course he knows what her car looks like—he's thorough about everything. Did he figure out some way to keep Charlotte away?

Jesus—has he already hurt her?

Val's pretty sure her phone's still in his jacket pocket. She must get it away from him.

He opens her driver's side door and reaches in with his left hand. Metal gleams briefly and the ties binding her to the wheel fall away. His right hand remains in his right jacket pocket.

"Out," he says, and pulls her out of the car by her arm in a smooth, forceful motion. She doesn't think her legs will hold, but they do.

"Go up the steps to the porch, approach the door but don't knock or ring the bell," he says, angling her towards the house. "I'll be right behind you."

She walks. He follows right behind her.

When she was a kid, maybe six or seven, Val was riding her bike down the street and she looked away from the road for a moment, focusing on somebody's dog or a car or something—she couldn't even remember what it was now—but when she glanced back up, she was barreling straight at some mailboxes. She saw them loom up at her and, even though she was propelling herself forward under her own power, she couldn't stop. The mailboxes bearing down on her was so shocking, so impending, that she couldn't remember how to break or stop pedaling. She crashed into those mailboxes, watching herself do it in slow motion and knowing it was going to hurt. Knowing there was some way to avoid it, but her brain refusing to tell her how. She plowed into them, her front wheel caught in the tangle of poles and metal boxes, and jammed to the right, twisting her arms over each other like a spastic dance pose. At the same time her inertia pushed her ass-over-elbows and her head hit one of the boxes square on the side of her face. Her body continued somersaulting over her own head like it was a pivot point and she landed hard on her back on the ground. Gravity restored time to its proper speed. She lied there in the gravel along the shoulder of the street, the breath knocked out of her, and stared at the sky still trying to remember how to stop her bike. Her breath came back and so did the answer.

You pedal in the wrong direction. You must move your feet backwards.

She sees Charlotte's house approaching her in the same way those mailboxes did years ago, and she knows she cannot let him get inside the house. If he gets in, it will be pain and horror and breathlessness. If she can keep him outside, it might be OK.

"Keep moving," he says and pushes at her with her free hand. "Think of your family, a few blocks away."

He rattles off the address again and a description of her mother's house.

They reach the front steps. There's no porch light, and no security light pops on. Is there usually one? Had he cut the power too? She can't remember. How many hundreds of times has she been here, and she can't remember?

"Your friend's not even here," he says. "Her car's gone. Were you going to tell me, or what?"

Val stammers out that she hasn't noticed. He jabs her in the back with the gun. He must've slipped it out of his pocket once they moved out of the streetlight's glow.

"Is there a spare key to get in?" he asks her. She uses every ounce of mental strength she has to keep her eyes from flicking over to the potted plant to the right of the door under the window.

She stares at him and her mouth refuses to invent even a simple lie.

"You really don't want me to wake her parents up, do you?" he asks, the cold menace in his voice stabbing through her like the knife he used to cut her free from the steering wheel.

"I think," she says after a moment, after she's able to speak again once those cold knife-like words have sliced through her, "I think there's a spare key around the back, under the grill on the patio."

He nods and looks from side to side, assessing the best way to get back there. There's a fence—maybe they'll make enough noise getting back there that someone will wake up and see them skulking around.

His gaze settles back on her and his right hand—the one

with gun in it—shoots out and hits her on the side of the face, connecting with her left cheekbone. The night explodes with light and color. He catches her with his other arm and lowers her soundlessly to the ground.

She lies on the cold floorboards of the porch and feels the side of her face. It feels wet and wrong, and the fingers she uses to feel it don't feel like her own somehow. The lights and colors in her vision wink out one by one and the darkness returns. Air catches cold in her throat.

He stands over her, clenching the dripping gun in one hand. He says something like "I told you not to try anything" and then he turns his back on her and heads towards the flowerpot because he already knows where the key is because he already knows everything and—

Wait, no. That isn't the important part.

He's turned his back on her.

He hasn't restrained her in any way. He just turned his back on her to retrieve the key. Her head pounds. She knows this is important, but can't complete the thought.

He leans into the pot, but it makes a loud scraping noise. He swears and puts his gun in his pocket again. He needs both hands to tilt it up far enough to pull off the duct tape on the underside and get the key.

He's not looking at you, and both his hands are busy.

The world's time slows down again but this time Val moves at top speed inside of it like she's faster than anyone.

She props herself up on her left arm and leg and rolls herself over and keeps rolling over and tries to be careful with the side of her head and not smack it on the porch. She has a last glimpse of him turning towards her, impossibly slow, as she rolls off the edge of the porch on the other side with this hilarious *What the fuck?* look on his face. His eyes and mouth are perfect round circles.

She lands in the grass and flowers and edges under the lip of the decking, so he can't get a clear shot at her. She has an insane head start on him—he's still standing back there with the flowerpot half lifted, completely dumbfounded.

She yells at the top of her lungs as soon as she's made it off the porch and, now that she's running around the side of the house, she bangs on the windows and kicks the siding as she runs, making as much noise as she can. She knows where a gap in the fence is, down by the edge of the house where the back decking starts. She doesn't think he can fit through it, even if he knows it's there. She pulls herself through roughly, scraping her sides and back in the process. It stings like hell, but she also nips herself on the side of the head where he pistol-whipped her and that's much worse. The flashes subside as quickly as they start. She has no time for them anyway.

On the back patio, she kicks over the grill and the sound is insane. Lights pop on in the house and a few neighbor's houses as well.

She hears him at the fence trying to figure the thing out, but she isn't planning on staying back here. She clamors over the low part of the fence to the next-door neighbor's and ducks down low. She moves carefully and slowly towards the front. He's in the backyard looking for her now, but she's in the other yard and he might not figure it out if she stays quiet enough.

More lights come on in the neighborhood, and she hears front screen doors and voices. Nothing too close, but he'll cut his losses soon and head to the car.

But she's in the front and he's in the back. He doesn't want to be seen and she does. He has the car keys—but not the only one.

She explodes into a full sprint from the neighbor's front yard and makes it to her car in seconds. She pulls the small magnetic box from the driver's side back wheel-well and jumps into the car, and has it on in another few seconds.

She hears a bellow of rage from the direction of Charlotte's house and hits the headlights—the brights.

The lights blind him, and he stumbles and fires the gun into the asphalt. The sound echoes back and forth off the houses.

She wrenches the wheel to the left, turns the car completely around. The U-turn destroys a large chunk of somebody's front grass.

She shifts, and is a moment from flooring the gas pedal when her back windshield explodes. She hears the shot after she feels the shards of glass rain through the inside of the car, which seems wrong, but she still feels like the world is in slow motion so maybe it makes sense.

She glances in the rearview mirror and sees him loping towards her, and he looks ridiculous. Out of breath and out of shape, he stumbles more than runs at her. Even the gun, the still very dangerous gun, swings from his hand haphazardly, more like a sack-lunch than a weapon.

She's no longer afraid of this pathetic creature.

She's not sure she says "Fuck it" out loud, but thinks later that's what was on her mind.

She shifts back into reverse and stomps the pedal.

She turns from the mirror just in time to see the trunk of her car smack into him and the gun leap from his grasp. The force of the car carries him backward for a few feet and then he slips beneath the car. She feels and hears him crunch apart under the vehicle.

She stops when he's fully exposed under the glare of her headlights—all red and twisted.

She drives over him again on her way out of there.

She wakes up still in her car in her mother's front yard.

She sees Charlotte's car parked on the side of the street behind Randy's car that never moves. But that can't be right.

She hears the front door. All the lights in her mother's house have come on when she wasn't looking, and her mom and Randy and Charlotte are standing by her car saying things to her.

She passes out again.

Val awakes when the EMT arrive. She sits on the curb while Charlotte and her brother sit on either side of her, trying to figure out what happened. Mom paces and barks things into her cell phone.

She tries to refuse medical attention or a trip to the hospital, but can't form the words and is soon on her way. Mom rides along with her, punching into her phone and checking her over.

Everything speeds up as they poke, prod, swab and ask questions. They hook her up to things and give her things to drink and stick things in her veins. Two cops come by, but a nurse shoos them away. They place a card by her bed as they leave. Mom ducks out for a minute and Val's alone for the first time and she needs to get the fuck out of here.

She pulls everything out of her. She leaves the bandages on her head, slips out and finds an unguarded courtesy phone. She calls Warren because it's the only number she knows by heart anymore.

He meets her out front in a Lyft for some reason, takes

one look at her and waves the driver on.

He walks her back inside and finds someone to help them to her room. Mom sees them in the hall and thanks him for bringing her back, and Val feels intensely betrayed and tells him to leave and won't look at him. He stays in the room with her mom and she hears them chatting. One of them will pop out for a few minutes for coffee, or whatever, but neither leaves at the same time.

She passes in and out of sleep and it's suddenly the next day or maybe even the day after that and she's feeling much better, or she at least isn't trying to escape the hospital.

The police appear again and ask questions, and she answers and they seem satisfied, genuine concern on their faces, but cops are good at pretending to be your friend when they aren't. When they leave, she doesn't have to go with them, though. And they don't leave her handcuffed to the bed.

"Is he dead?" she asks the detectives as they're leaving her room.

"Oh yeah," one of them says. "Before we arrived. You nailed him good."

She wakes hours later to hushed talking, punctuated with giggling every so often. She knows what it is before she opens her eyes and sees them, even though she's been telling herself for days that, no, that's impossible—it must have been a hallucination. It must have been something her mind invented out of thin air, created whole-cloth from nothingness, the lights and colors swirling in her head from the crack on her noggin, congealing into inane fantasy.

Nope.

There they are, snuggled up in a chair in her hospital room making gooey eyes at one another. Charlotte and Randy.

Charlotte and her brother. Her youngest brother.

"What the fuck, guys?" she says hoarsely. "C'mon."

They spring up from the chair. Charlotte stops to compose herself. Randy makes his way straight over, grabs her drink and holds it so she can sip.

She sucks on the straw and notices that his cast and bandages are gone. The hair on his arm is growing back except in those smooth pink strips and spots where it never will.

"This," Val says, gesturing at Charlotte with her head, "is more fallout from you trying to burn mom's house down, isn't it?"

He ignores her dig and smiles warmly.

"Yeah," he says, and looks over at Charlotte. "When you asked her to take me to that appointment, well, I don't know if it was the pain medicine or what, but I told her how hot she was."

Charlotte laughs and puts an arm around him. She honest to God no bullshit blushes like a fucking teenager over Val's loser brother. Jesus Christ.

They prattle on and on about that night, stepping all over each other's words to try and convey all the information at once. Then they both stop, waiting for the other to speak, and erupt in a duel of giggles.

"Jesus Christ, stop," Val says and pushes at them, pushing them away from her hospital bed. "You guys are going to make me fucking barf."

They attempt to control themselves, which of course leads to more uncontrollable laughter. Finally, Charlotte gets a hold of herself long enough to send Randy out for sodas, so Val and she are alone together.

"Do you want to talk about it?" Charlotte asks.

"Not really," she says. "Not now."

"Do you want to talk about how you kept a guy from robbing me and possibly killing my parents?" Charlotte asks, her eyebrows up in an almost holy amount of awe.

Val releases a long, stale breath. What's there to say?

He's dead, but he's still with her. He's in the room right now, off to the side and just out of focus. He's in the corner of her eye. In the shadows and in the dark areas. Behind her. If he was in jail instead of dead, or if he'd escaped capture, she knows it'd be worse. She knows it'd be impossible to sleep. She'd have cops in her hospital room, at her apartment and watching Warren and her mom, hiding in ridiculously disguised police vans circling between her mom's house and Charlotte's. She knows it'd be worse. She knows it'd be constant fear.

Yet she's still afraid.

Everyone else has moved on, she can tell. They're relieved that she killed him, and so is most of her, but there's a part that's linked to him forever. He's a ghost and she's the house that he haunts. What can she do? How can she get rid of him? She killed him and still he's with her.

Her grandfather had been absent-minded. He always forgot this or that—things little and big. He'd leave to go retrieve something and, either forget what he'd come into a room for, or get distracted by something else along the way. Often both. He'd constantly called Val by her mother's name, usually not ever correcting himself. He said it's because he knew so much that it appeared he knew so little. Every time his brain learned something new, it pushed out some older thing it'd once known. As if his brain had hit capacity before Val was born.

He'd always said it with a smile and a wink and Val knew he was kidding but now she isn't so sure. What parts of her has she lost to make room for the inclusion of the man with the gun?

"No," she says. "I want to talk about that even less."

Charlotte cocks her head and raises an eyebrow in her direction.

"Fine. Jesus," Val relents. "Tell me what the fuck it is you think you're doing with my brother."

Charlotte nods and does her best to keep her smile restrained. No more uncontrollable giggles, please. She breaks eye contact and that seems to help.

"It just happened, I don't know. Isn't that what people say?" she asks.

"He's a fucking teenager, Charlotte," Val says. Let's get the difficult shit out of the way.

"He's nineteen. He's an adult," she says.

"You're thirty-two, c'mon," Val says, trying to explain it without having to explain it. Like using a shrug to say So what?

"I know," she says. "I was thirteen when he was born. We were friends then already. I remember when he was born."

Val tries—and fails—to keep a disgusted look off her face.

Well, she doesn't try too terribly hard.

"That's not, like, weird to you?" she asks.

Charlotte shrugs. So what?

"What about me isn't weird, Val?" she asks in return.

Val sighs again.

"Is that what's bothering you about this?" she asks, a slight edge to her voice. "That your brother is with such a weirdo?"

"No," Val says. Then, "Maybe a little, I don't know. You're both really fucking bizarre, so whatever, I guess."

Charlotte relaxes noticeably with this honesty. She smiles a little.

"Your brother's kind of a screw-up," she says, "but he's also nineteen, and who wasn't a screw-up then?"

"You weren't," Val says.

"Right," she agrees, "and look where it got me. I really have nothing going on in my life. Or I didn't before."

"Eh," Val says, "you have a hundred grand, which is about a hundred thousand times what I have saved."

She nods.

"True, but it's nothing, and it's not for me," she says and stands up, pacing beside Val's bed.

"Being nineteen, Randy is also kind of a blank-slate, do you know what I mean? I don't know, that sounds manipulative, but that's not what I mean. I don't want to turn him into whatever it is I think I want. I want him to be the opposite of all that, the opposite of me," she says.

Val hears this but is focused on what Charlotte said just before.

"That money's not for a house, is it," she says, not bothering to make it a question, knowing it's true as soon as the words leave her.

Charlotte hugs herself impulsively.

"It's for my baby," she says.

Val stares at her. She's a completely different person than the one she's known for twenty years. She starts to say something like "Are you fucking crazy?" but Charlotte sits back down and puts her hands on Val's and repeats "I know" over and over until Val calms down. They sit there silently for a while.

"My mom had a hysterectomy when she was thirty-four, just after having me," Charlotte says.

"That used to be so young," Val says.

"It still is," Charlotte says and nods.

After a minute, Charlotte speaks again.

"I've always wanted a child," she says, "I've always wanted to make a better version of me, and it's the only way I know how. I'm too…stubborn to change, you know that."

"Yeah," Val admits.

"So, you know I've been thinking about this for years, and nothing's going to stop me," she says and sounds more like herself.

"And Randy?" Val asks.

"It's not Randy, stupid," she says. "It's you. I want a reason for you to be involved in my child's life."

"Christ, Charlotte," Val says, failing to keep the smirk from her face. "You know I never wanted any fucking kids."

They laugh and talk a little more, none of it earth-shattering, but it feels more important in its banality. Randy comes back with coffee and snacks. Not from the hospital but a Starbucks down the street. Charlotte gives her a look that means he doesn't know about any of these grand plans yet. He can always refuse to cooperate. But the way he looks at Charlotte… Val knows he can be talked into anything. His hair is even combed, and his clothes are a step above his usual unemployed slacker outfit.

They ask her when she's being released, and she lies and says she doesn't know, and they promise to check in with her later and she gets hugs from both before they depart. Her mom texts her and asks when they're letting her out and she says tomorrow—also a lie—but her mom wouldn't have stood for an "I don't know" and would have made her own inquiries. She has a few missed calls and unopened texts from Warren and she'll forgive him eventually but not now.

A couple nurses and the main doctor treating her come in a half an hour later and give her a once-over and she's free to go. She gathers her stuff and they make her ride down to the ground floor in a wheelchair. She pretends to look at her phone and claims her boyfriend is in the parking lot. The orderly nods, totally bored, and leaves her on the sidewalk. She thanks his back as he walks away, all her excuses for where this "boyfriend" parked go unused.

She's outside and alone and that's all she wants. She begins to walk.

She has a new cell phone, and her mother also brought her purse and wallet and keys. Her apartment's maybe two miles away but she walks anyway. She needs to do something under her own power, under the power of her own body, her own two legs.

She needs to move through the world.

Val walks down the sidewalk, vaguely in the direction of her apartment, and will most likely go inside once she reaches it and reclaim the life that's been paused for a few days. For now, though, it feels good to walk and pretend that she might keep going, that she might walk right out of her life. That she might keep walking and never stop.

# THREE

# THE OTHER SIDE
# OF THE TREES

**B**illy finds his little brother sitting in the grass with legs crossed, hands in his lap, staring into the trees.

Billy sits next to him, like a basketball player on TV—pitched forward resting his elbows on his knees. He looks over at his brother.

Who continues to stare at the trees.

"What do you think's in there?" his brother finally asks, having yet to look at him.

"More trees?" Billy hazards. "What do you mean?"

"The Woods," his brother says, a weird hushed quality to his voice like the trees can hear him. Like he's talking in church or something. "What do you think's in the Woods? Why won't dad let us go in there?"

Billy pulls a fistful of grass from the earth, raises his arm straight out with hand fully extended and lets the blades sprinkle back down to the ground. He does this absently, mechanically pulling a fresh clump when the previous has expended.

"I don't know," Billy says. "I think there's hunters out there. And bears."

His brother looks at him with that seriousness only small children possess.

"Do you really think it's bears?" he asks, the awe in his voice dialed all the way up.

Billy sighs.

"What are you doing out here, dumbass?" he asks.

Joey shakes his head slowly.

"You're not supposed to say that. Dad says."

"Well," Billy says, pushing him on the shoulder lightly, "Dad sent me to 'go get the dumbass,' so I guess he changed his mind."

He pushes Billy back, starting to smile.

"No, he didn't. He didn't say that."

"He did, Joey," he says, nodding emphatically. "I'm sorry, but the doctor called, and your ass is one-hundred percent dumb. They did a test and everything."

The smile drops from Joey's face.

"It's Joseph," he says. "My name is Joseph."

Billy waves him off, disgusted.

"Ah, you ruined it," he says. "We were having fun, and you ruined it with your Joseph crap. What eight-year-old goes by Joseph? Maybe you really are a dumbass."

"I'm almost nine," Joey says, "and Joseph is my name. Mom told dad—"

He stops, horrified, realizing he's broken the one unbreakable rule.

Billy pushes him over on his side before he can speak again.

"What the fuck did you say?" Billy says through clenched

teeth.

"I'm sorry, Billy!" he pleads. "It just slipped out!"

Billy jumps up, goes to kick him, but ends up kind of just pushing him with his foot. His heart isn't in it. He tries to be mad about it. He is mad, but it's harder to stay mad lately. It gets easier every day, which means it gets harder every day, too. Like seeing her face when he closes his eyes. He can barely remember what she looks like, which makes things easier but worth less.

"She's not your mom, you never met her," he says. He doesn't add how Joey killed her, but they both feel it.

"I'm sorry, Billy," he says again.

Billy sighs and squats down on his haunches. He extends his hand. Joey hesitates—he's fallen for this before. He takes his brother's hand and Billy pulls him up.

"C'mon," he says, "we're supposed to go home."

They walk out of the empty lot, both eyeing the path into the Woods where a few long bicycle tracks extend out from the dirt onto the street.

"Why isn't there a house here?" Joey asks, referring to the lot they'd been sitting in. A few chunks of concrete are scattered around, but it's mostly overgrown grass. Houses loom from every other part of the street.

"It burned down," Billy says.

"Did you see it?" Joey asks. "Did you see it on fire?"

"Nah," he says, kicking some loose dirt as he walks. "I don't think I was born yet. Mom and Dad told me about it."

He thinks about this. Being only eight, Joey's used to the idea that things occurred before he was alive. People remind him of it all the time.

"Why didn't they build another house?" he asks.

Billy shrugs.

"Who knows," he says. "Maybe they were afraid of bears."

Joey laughs.

"You're teasing me about the bears," he says, confident now that the Woods are a few houses away and are less menacing with every driveway they pass.

They turn down the sidewalk that cuts between houses and come out on a different street at the top of a cul-de-sac. They call this sidewalk The Secret Passage even though everyone in the neighborhood knows it's there.

"I gotta take a piss," Billy says. "Wait for me at the end of The Secret Passage."

"Where are you going to go?" Joey asks, fascinated. He's one of those weird boys who never pees outside.

"Just over behind that fence," he says. "I'll only be a minute. Wait at the end."

He pisses freely and fiercely on the stranger's fence, abandoning an attempt to write his name after he messes the B up spectacularly.

He skips back to The Secret Passage and sprints out onto the cul-de-sac and Joey isn't there.

"Little shit," he says, imagining his brother tearing ass down the street and arriving home before him.

He's about to take off himself when he hears something over to his right and sees a commotion of small bodies trying to hide behind a tree.

"Dammit," he says and trots over, faking to the right and then double-timing around the left side of the tree. There are three of them, plus Joey. He's behind them, and can see Joey struggling. He thinks he recognizes them from the neighborhood maybe. They're somewhere between the brother's ages, so maybe ten or eleven. He doesn't know any of their names, so they must go to the public middle school. Somebody has a hand over his brother's mouth.

He reaches up and grabs the biggest, thickest branch he can reach and breaks it off with ease.

"Shit," one of them says. A girl? Filthy and dressed like a boy but yup—girl.

He snaps the branch over his knee and smiles at them.

"I start breaking arms next," he says, feeling like a total badass.

"Get away from us, faggot," one of the boys says. They shove Joey away from them towards Billy. He passes the longer half of the broken branch off to Joey as he stumbles into him.

Billy takes a step towards them still smiling. He's inches taller than all of them, even the girl.

They take a tentative step towards him.

Without breaking eye contact, he raises his stick and then swiftly kicks the closest one squarely in the dick.

The kid drops hard, moaning and comically grabbing his junk with both hands. The other boy backs off, half turns, ready to bolt if Billy so much as breathes on him.

But the girl doesn't move. She stands up straighter.

"Try that one on me, asshole," she says.

He blows her a kiss.

"What'd they do to you, Joey?" Billy asks without looking at him. He's hiding behind his older brother, but grips the stick firmly in both hands.

"They were just saying mean things to me," he says, trying his best to keep the tremble out of his voice.

"Hmm. I figured. What'd they say?"

Joey says nothing.

"What'd you say to him?" Billy asks, louder than he'd

been talking to Joey.

The boy he hadn't drilled in the nuts takes off, finally. Billy whips his stick-half at him. It twirls heroically through the air, but spins wide and skips along the street. The other boy sits up now, panting. Billy's impressed the kid hasn't shed any tears over it. His face glows red, though.

"Pussy," the girl says to the kid's retreating back.

"They said…they said I was a mother-killer," Joey says, flinching at the forbidden word, muscle-memory for all the times Billy's hit him.

"That's what I thought," Billy says and takes another step towards them. He doesn't seem to remember that he almost said the same thing minutes ago.

The girl helps the boy up and they jostle, each trying to get behind the other one.

Billy laughs.

"You're all pussies," he says cracking his knuckles. "Next time, bring more friends. Maybe a few who don't run away or get kicked in the nards so easily."

"We will," the girl says looking into Billy's eyes with a ferocity he's only ever seen in the mirror.

He's about to tell her to name the place and time, when a screen door bangs near them. A fat, balding man in a stained, sleeveless white t-shirt barrels out with a rolled newspaper in hand. He's immediately followed by a woman in light blue jeans.

She jumps in front of him, between him and the kids by the tree, putting her hands on his chest. She's taller than him by a few inches. She says something to him. Billy can't hear her words but understands her tone. She's trying to calm him down.

The kids stand frozen.

"I don't care," he says to her in a thick accent. "Move, dammit. I said I don't care!"

He pushes past her. She throws her hands up and retreats into the house with another screen door bang.

"Hey! Fucking kids," he yells and points his rolled newspaper at them. His accent makes the swear sound like fookin. "What you exactly doing to my tree?"

The spell breaks. Billy scoops Joey up and runs. The other kids rabbit in different directions from Billy and each other.

He thinks he hears the girl yell "Next time!" over her shoulder but it's probably just his imagination. The fat guy keeps yelling and gesturing wildly with his newspaper as Billy rounds the street corner and catches a final glimpse of him. The other kids are already long out of sight.

"Next time!" he thinks he heard.

Yeah. He hopes so.


When safely out of sight, two houses up the cross street from the fat man, Billy sets Joey down in somebody's grassy front lawn and collapses next to him, suddenly spent.

They laugh, Joey following his big brother's lead.

"Shit," Billy says between chuckles. "Did you see that dyke trying to act tough?"

"What's a dyke?" Joey asks.

"Forget it," Billy says standing up. "Come on. We really have to get home."

They trudge along the last blocks to their house.

"Why were they so mean to me?" Joey asks.

"You know why," Billy says. He feels the annoyance in him stir into anger.

"But I didn't do anything," Joey says, not recognizing the change in Billy as the topic creeps back up.

"You killed my mom," Billy says, "so they called you mother-killer. Makes sense to me."

Joey shakes his head.

"I didn't!" he shouts, "I didn't! I don't remember it. How can you do something if you can't remember it?"

Billy shoves his hands in his pockets to keep from hitting him in full view of the house.

"I remember," he says.

He presses his hand on Joey's chest and stops him.

"Wait here until you see me get inside the house," he says. "Then you can come home."

"What?" Joey asks.

Billy leans in close to his brother.

"Learn to shut the fuck up," he says. "Or I'll leave you to those kids."

He walks to the house without looking back. He hears the front door a minute later after he's inside and upstairs in his room.

"…Then he said, "'Your legs are next!'" Joey exclaims. "Isn't that great?"

They sit at the dinner table with their father, having just finished tonight's Hamburger Helper and slices of white bread with butter, a meal all the boys in the house can happily agree on. Their father sits with his chair, tilted back against the kitchen wall, a leg propping him up against the table and a bent arm resting on his elevated knee. His chin is on his knuckles, and he looks down at Joey with a bemused smile. Every so often, during a particularly good detail, he'll glance at Billy. He hasn't said a word to interrupt. Joey loves telling stories.

"Wait. You kicked a kid in the balls?" Dad says, but still

smiles.

Billy shrugs, fails to keep his own smile from showing.

"He had my brother hostage," he says.

His father nods.

"Shock and awe," Dad says and turns back to Joey. "Continue."

"And then the girl," Joey says, tripping over his own words with excitement. "She, um, what did that dyke say, Billy?"

Dammit.

"Um, the girl," Billy says, feeling his face flush. "She said 'Try that on me, next time,' or something like that."

Dad looks at him again. His smile's gone, but his eyes are still playful.

"That's not a nice word, Joey," he says, still looking at Billy. "Where'd you hear it?"

"Uh," Joey panics. "TV? I think?"

Dad looks at Joey, who's redder than Billy by now.

Their father laughs, a big abrupt sound.

"Good answer, Joey," he says. Joey never pulls that "My name is Joseph" bullshit with Dad.

"Go wash your hands, son," he says, easing himself out of his chair. "Billy's gonna help clear the table."

Dammit. Shit.

Billy goes to the sink and turns the hot water on. He pops the dishwasher open. Dad stacks the plates, places the silverware on top and brings it all to the sink. Billy rinses the dishes before loading them into the washer, filling from back to front.

Dad collects the glasses next and then the balled-up napkins. He uses them to wipe any crumbs from the table into his hands. He throws them in the trash and dusts the crumbs off. Lastly, he gathers the salt, pepper and toothpicks from the table and returns them to their spot on the stove.

He strolls over and stands by Billy, who busies himself. He's quickly running out of dishes to distract himself with.

Dad lets him finish before speaking.

"I'm proud of you for watching out for your brother," he says. "You can't put all your violence into videogames, can you?"

"No, sir," Billy says while drying his hands.

"Jesus, Billy," he laughs. "Cut the 'sir' shit. I hate all that stuff."

"Sorry, Dad. I know," he says.

"Look," he says, putting a hand on his son's shoulder, "you're a good kid. You're a tough kid, I know that. I don't want you picking fights just to get in a fight, understand?"

He nods but doesn't really get it.

"But you do have to watch out for your brother. He's…not going to be a scrapper like you or me," he says. "He's more like your mother. He's thoughtful."

Billy feels his face blush again, rolls his head around on his shoulders and smiles at his dad—anything to keep the blushing in check.

"I get it Dad," he says.

"I know you do," he says. "You watch out for him, I'll watch out for you."


He tries playing videogames. He tries watching TV. He tries reading comic books. He tries sitting in his room.

He tries everything he knows, and nothing works.

He finds Joey in the basement, at the bottom of the steps, playing with G.I. Joes and using the bottom stair as a cliff or a high-rise or something. He's making machine gun noises with his mouth and toppling Cobra soldiers, flipping them over the edge with a flick of his middle finger.

Billy kicks him over and clamps a hand over his mouth before he reacts.

He feels his brother's breath heat his palm.

He whispers harsh words to him. He isn't entirely sure what he says, but it's at least as bad as whatever those other kids had said. Probably worse.

He punches him once, in the side, but not hard. The hardness leaves him with whatever foul words he says. Before climbing off him, he releases his mouth and wipes his hand on Joey's shirtfront.

He leaves him on the basement floor, his legs wobbly as he pulls himself up the stairs.

Joey slips into his bedroom in the middle of the night, waking him from some formless, structure-free dream.

"I can't sleep, Billy," he whispers. "Can I stay in here?"

Billy scoots over and holds the blankets up for him.

"Don't tell Dad," he says. "You know he wants you to grow up."

Joey climbs in.

"I won't," he says. "I won't tell."

Billy rolls onto his side and faces the wall. He feels Joey lying there, opening and closing his mouth, trying to figure out how to say or ask him something. He never does.

Billy shuts his eyes and concentrates on his own heartbeat until it lulls him asleep again.

Billy swings at a pinecone with the rake. Whiff. He tosses the useless thing away, but carefully. Too hard and he might hit the house. His dad doesn't really care if he rakes the yard like he asked him too—he just wants him outside while preferably not bouncing garden tools off the siding. Well, Dad never said not to do that, but Billy knows that'd be no excuse if he's caught doing it.

"You can't shit a shitter," Dad would probably say. It's what he usually says when Billy or Joey try to wiggle out of trouble on a technicality.

He smiles.

He likes that phrase, and not just because it has swears in it. He likes the economy of it, he likes how you understand it the first time you hear it. It doesn't need explained or translated—it's exactly what it sounds like.

He picks up the rake, the broom from the sidewalk, a few other things and stows them in the garage. He hasn't been out here that long, probably not even an hour. He exits through the back door in the garage and into the backyard. He'll have to find something to do before enough time's passed and he can safely sneak back into the house for a glass of water followed by a casual slip into his room for some quiet videogames.

He makes his way to the back fence gate. There's no lock on it, but he runs at the gate in a full sprint, places one foot halfway up the fence onto a diagonal beam, wedges his hand onto the top support and smoothly vaults himself over the fence. He lands on the grass beyond, like an action star, tucks his legs, rolls and everything.

He springs up in the weird no-man's land of overgrown grass between his fence and the neighbor's. The area that Joey and he and all the neighborhood kids called The Tunnel, for reasons Billy can't remember or never really knew. Whatever—you got to call it something.

The Tunnel is L-shaped, starts at his next-door neighbor's

side yard and stretches behind his house to another few houses down where it dead-ends into another fence meant to keep kids out of that house's yard, but doesn't. Billy can't even count how many times Joey's scaled that chain-link fence to gain access to the other street, let alone himself.

All the kids use The Tunnel and the other borderless stretches of the neighborhood. Billy goes days without ever leaving International Waters—as the older kids call it—for the street proper.

So, Billy isn't surprised to see another kid back there, but he jumps. A personal no-no—never let anybody see you flinch. He runs his fingers through his hair, pretty sure the kid doesn't register his shock at not being alone.

The kid's Billy's age, maybe a year older, and vaguely familiar. From the neighborhood or school, maybe both. He wears a faded t-shirt with some cartoon karate character Billy doesn't recognize, a backwards baseball hat, dark sunglasses and jeans, weirdly. There're still a few weeks left of shorts weather, especially in the afternoon.

He sits on a ten-speed and looks past Billy, over the fence and into his backyard. Even in the dark glasses, Billy knows the kid looks past him and it pisses him off. Like looking at Billy is beneath him.

He stands up, extends to his full height and walks over, closing in on the kid. When he's practically on top of him and blocking most of his sunlight, Billy dusts his hands off, making sure to scatter some grass and dirt onto the kid's shirt. The kid lowers his sunglasses an inch to stare at him, opening his mouth to speak.

Billy cuts him off.

"Who the fuck are you?" he asks, like he's asking the time.

The kid ignores the question. "I'm looking for the asshole that lives in that house," he says, motioning to Billy's house with his chin.

Billy shakes his head slowly.

"No assholes living there," he says. "Just me."

He hears a slight rustling behind him and to the right. Did this kid bring backup? He smiles. If he thinks he needs help, then Billy's already won. The kid doesn't react to the noise, so Billy doesn't either. Let them think he doesn't know they're here. See how an elbow to the face feels when they make their surprise entrance.

The kid shakes his head, matching Billy's slowness.

"Nah," he says, "I'm looking for Billy The Asshole. She said you lived here."

"Ah," Billy says, "I get it. The dyke sent you for round two. What are you, her girlfriend?"

Billy hasn't backed off an inch. He sees the kid's eyes flash and watches his skin redden a shade before he controls himself.

"Yep," he says, looking in Billy's eyes now. "You're the asshole all right. She wants you to get a couple friends, like two or three, and meet somewhere at midnight tomorrow, and we're gonna kick all your asses."

Billy's smile threatens to split his face.

"Midnight," he says with mock shivers. "Spooky."

The kid says nothing.

"All right," Billy says. "Tell your boyfriend, midnight. In the Woods."

He hears the rustling again. This time the kid glances around, acting confused by the sound. Billy chuckles at his commitment.

"The Woods it is," the kid says and readjusts his

sunglasses. He hikes himself up to pedal off. Right before he takes off, Billy gives him his exit line.

"Tell your boyfriend I haven't forgotten," he says. The kid pauses, curious. "I owe her a swift kick in the cunt."

The kid makes an uncomfortable face, then takes off, his ten-speed gaining easy traction on the overgrown grass.

Billy watches him tear from The Tunnel out into the street and careen out of sight.

That rustling again. He's forgotten about—

"Is he gone?" Joey asks. "Who was that?"

Billy lowers his fists. Joey doesn't notice.

"You know as much as I do," Billy says.

Joey looks at him seriously.

"You said a bad word," hc says.

Billy sighs and shrugs.

"You said the baddest word there is," he says.

"I didn't know you were here, Joey," he says, like that's what makes it bad.

Joey shakes his head.

"But you're never supposed to say that," he says. "Not even to yourself."

Billy shrugs again, starts walking away from him. Joey follows at his heels.

"It already happened," he says. "What do you want me to do? There's nothing to do about it now."

"You gotta say you're sorry," he says.

"Sorry? To who? You?" he asks.

"To God," Joey says.

He stops and looks up to the sky, spreading his arms out.

"I'm sorry, God," he says. "I'll never say c—"

Billy sneaks a peek at Joey, relishing the way his eyes bulge and his mouth droops.

"Um, I mean," he says, "I'll never say the baddest of words again."

He turns to his brother.

"There, OK? Now leave me alone."

Joey keeps pace with him. They leave The Tunnel and cross the street, ducking through a neighbor's yard.

"You'll have to do confession, too," he says when they pause.

"Jesus," Billy says. "Go home."

They reach the entrance to The Trough, this street's section of International Waters. This fence is too tall and gnarled for Joey to make it over on his own. Billy leaves him on the ground and scales it.

"Wait!" Joey says. "Billy, are you really going to fight those kids in the Woods?" He asks, those last two words hushed with reverence.

Billy hops to the other side of the fence, leaving his brother. They can see each other through cracks and holes in the wood.

"Yeah," he says. "It's just some trees, Joey. I've been in there a hundred times. It's no big deal. You saw what wimps those idiots were."

They stare at each other through the fence.

"Can I go with you?" Joey asks, "To the Woods?"

Billy laughs.

"There's hope for you yet, Joseph," he says. "we'll see. You might have to punch some people."

"I can do it," Joey says, nodding his head forcefully.

Billy looks at his little, serious brother.

He puts his index finger through one of the cracks in the rotting fence at his younger brother's eye-level. Joey grabs it.

"I know you can," he says. "but you don't have to. It's

what I'm here for."

He pulls his finger back through and they're separated once more.

"Go home, Joey. I'll be back in a little bit."

He turns and runs.


He stands at the mouth of the Woods, feet on the earth of that weird, burned down abandoned lot. Unbroken, overgrown grass sways in the late summer breeze like calm waters barely lapping to the shore. The broken concrete pieces of foundation poke out here and there as if bobbing up like flotsam and jetsam in the green surf of the yard. International Waters.

He lied to Joey, a little. He hasn't been into the Woods a hundred times, but he has a few. Enough to not get lost, not enough to trust himself to win a fight at midnight. Not without better familiarizing himself.

He hops over a small concrete chunk and strolls right in.

The tarmac of the road gives way to the dirt of the forest floor without preamble or ceremony—one stops and the other starts. Not even a change in elevation, like the asphalt just melts into the dirt.

Calling it a forest is a tad grandiose. It's barely wider than the street, including facing lots, and maybe twice as deep. Less than a quarter of the total volume of Billy's own street.

The path diverges immediately in the trees. The left path, he knows, curves gently to the north and exits onto a similar street in an abutting neighborhood.

The first time he'd been here he'd followed a couple older boys and in five minutes they'd emerged on a street so similar to the one that led into the Woods from his part of the world, he was completely disoriented. Totally turned around, he thought they'd circled completely around and left the Woods in the same way they'd entered it. Then it got Twilight Zoney as he noticed small details of the street had changed. The empty lot was no longer empty—a ranch-style house took up most of the property. The streetlights seemed a different hue, and there were no sidewalks on this street, that side of the neighborhood being older than his.

When he realized he was in a different place, a street so close to where he was but full of houses and people and cars and other children he didn't know—his mind ran wild. He pretended he'd teleported into a different world, traveled to a different dimension or gone back in time.

He stumbled around, gawking at the stupidest shit. The older kids grew tired of laughing at him and bailed further into the Bizarro-hood and left him stranded on the wrong side of the trees.

He wasn't worried. It was just dusk and that was his favorite time of day. Plus, they'd taken one path in, one single arcing dirt path. How could he get lost going back?

But he went left again, instead of right, the weird mirrorness of the other neighborhood still playing with him and turning him about.

The path split and split again, and it was very dark by the time he realized he didn't know where he was or how to get out.

His parents found him later—it hadn't been long. A neighbor on his side of the street had seen him follow in those troublemaking older kids and called his parents. They'd called for him, bobbing flashlights around, making their way to the sound of his echo-like callbacks.

He'd cried a little, when he first realized he was lost and had tripped to the ground, but when he heard his parents' voices and saw their beams sweeping the trees, he wiped his eyes carefully. He didn't want his dad seeing he wasn't tough.

He could tell his dad was proud of him, secretly, but his mom was so worried. She'd forbidden him and, patting her belly, his little brother or sister, from ever going back in the Woods.

He'd obeyed her until she died when Joey was born, his spoken promise to her negated by the breaking of a larger, unspoken one to him.

He veers to the right, further into the trees and away from either neighborhood.

It's cooler in the trees, and quieter. All the leaves and branches muffle the sounds of the neighborhood. It's louder, too, with insects, with rustling and snapping. He takes the left in the next fork, then a right, which abruptly opens to a small creek and old farmland beyond the neighborhoods.

He looks around. This is the spot.

The lowest branches hang taller here than in the Woods proper. He doubts whoever the dyke and her girlfriend bring with them can reach them as easily as he can to break off for weapons or swing himself for some face-level kicks. He'll lead them back here, get behind them and knock one of them into the creek. That'd shut all of them up.

Maybe he should break off a couple of branches and secure them around the bases of these trees. Ugh. He doesn't want to get all *Home Alone* with it—he wants to punch some kids in the face. He wants to get hit, too.

But he also doesn't want to lose.

He spends a few minutes measuring the layout of the clearing by paces—the distance from the path to the creek, the square footage of the clearing and some of the larger gaps between the trees. He'll need to lead them in by the path, but get behind them and emerge from somewhere else. He breaks off two good baseball bat-sized branch chunks and props one against a tree close to the entrance and secreted with leaves and grass. The other one he hides by the creek, under the drop-off from the main forest floor, right up against it. It can't be seen unless you're in the water already.

He practices retrieving the sticks, swinging them in wild, flailing windmill gestures, changing his attack arc on a dime and slicing through the air, then ultimately kicking at his make-believe opponents. He wishes he hadn't had to kick that kid in the balls. They'll probably be over-protective of their nuts. Oh well. That'll leave their heads unprotected.

He stretches, hops slightly and catches an overhanging branch, swinging a massive kick out. The tree holds his weight without complaint.

Satisfied, he gives one final glance around and leaves the clearing, winding back through the Woods. He checks over the rest of the terrain, considers obstacles for some of the paths and then thinks better of it. It'll be hard to remember where they are in the dark, and he'd probably just fumble over them since he's one hundred percent going to be here before midnight.

He wanders around the Woods, earmarking possible alternate sites or paths, but these kids are dummies so he won't need them, and his heart isn't really in it. Now he's decided where to stage the battle, a significant part of him feels done with it. He'll have to psych himself up later if the darkness of the Woods at midnight doesn't already do it for him.

He knows the kids are stupid. If they weren't, they'd be here now like him getting ready for tomorrow. Besides, they should have just picked the place—he would've showed no matter what. They should know that about him, they should be able to tell. Either they don't or can't.

The kid on the bike said bring two or three friends. Which tells Billy how many kids will be there. Four, if they're overconfident, or five if they want to win. The dyke will be there—no doubt she's sharpening her fingernails and stuffing her crotch right now. The kid on the bike, surely, sans bike. The kid that bolted won't show. He might want to, might try to talk himself into it, but the girl isn't that stupid. He'd run once, he'll run again. She'll cut him out if she hasn't already.

That leaves the one he'd booted in the dick and one or two mystery kids. The one at home icing his nutsack right now will be there—revenge is a strong motivator and so is wanting to look like a tough guy in front of your friends.

Billy mentally files through his various enemies from the neighborhood to discern the mystery kids. He can't settle on any definite candidates, so he stops thinking about it.

Probably nobody he knows anyway, certainly not anyone he's beat up previously. They'd know to stay the fuck away from him.

The mystery man might be a scrapper, or even a good fighter, but it seems unlikely it'll be anyone older than Billy. He's twelve and the other kids are the same or close enough anyway, and even the thirteen-year-olds are teenagers and act like it makes them a different species.

He emerges from the Woods, blinking away the daylight as best he can and weaves over into the empty lot. He sits down on some of the exposed concrete.

He has them figured out—you can't shit a shitter.

He toes at a few smaller chunks of cement littering the yard. Maybe he'll load his pockets up with some on his way into the Woods. That'd definitely give him an edge. So would calling some of his friends and getting them out here to help him. He can think of a few that'd be up for it, some he'd even like having his back. But he never seriously considers it.

He'll go in alone and he'll come out alone.

"Billy, what are you doing, man?" his dad says waking him up. He's standing in his door while threading a tie through itself, still pantsless but with dress socks and his shoes already tied. "Didn't you hear me? Time for church."

Billy rubs sleep out of his eyes.

"Hurry up, we're leaving in five," his dad says, retreating into the hall and talking to him over his shoulder. "Brush your hair. No shorts or jeans, and if I find videogames on either you or your brother I'm having the priest send you straight to hell with no supper."

Billy finds mostly clean churchy clothes on his floor, probably the ones from last week, and dresses quickly. He checks on Joey, who's fully dressed and sitting on his bed, reading one of Billy's comics.

He snatches it out of his brother's hands without a word and goes back into his own room. He finds a clip-on tie, grabs his brother and bolts downstairs. He hears his dad in the bathroom.

"We'll be in the car!" he yells from the garage. Joey sits in the back, playing with Billy's old Nintendo.

"Dad comes out, don't let him see," Billy says.

His dad gets in the car exactly one minute before church starts. They floor it through the neighborhood. The lot's pretty full and he drops them near the door with other perpetually tardy families pushing their kids in front of them, and dashes off to park.

Billy lets Joey pick their seat this week, grabbing a pew towards the back on the far right of the church near the

Sacristy. Joey's fascinated by the goings-on behind the scenes, the backstage of anything, but mostly church because that's most of his experience. He likes how from this seat he can see the priests, the altar, the altar boys sitting off to the sides, and back into the Chapel which is like a smaller, mirrored version of the church. But he especially likes seeing the priests exit the Sacristy with the altar boys in tow, winding their way back through the church to begin the procession up the center aisle. He's entranced if something goes wrong during the service, like they don't have enough Eucharist or wine, or Father's microphone battery fails, or anything that requires the altar boys or one of the choir to run back there and grab whatever needs grabbing.

The only thing they don't have a view of is the choir, specifically the organ. That section is on the opposite side of the church, the extreme left. Billy catches glimpses of the choir director's hands as she flints them up and down, directing the singers. But what Billy can't see at all is his favorite—the organist playing.

He loves watching them hammer away on the three-tiered keyboards, stomping on the pedals, spreading out the music sheets beforehand and pulling the stops and levers to get that perfect combination of sound they're always chasing. He loves when the song's too long or too complicated and all the sheet music can't be held at once. The organist needs to either keep playing with one hand and hurriedly flip pages with the other or, if the organist has children, make them stand patiently, nodding at them to turn the page.

When he was much younger, Billy told his parents that he wanted to be a page-flipper for the organist when he grew up. His dad had smiled and laughed, telling him that wasn't a real job, but his mother had told him she'd see what she could do.

Nothing ever came of it, like everything else his mother had ever said to him. He probably would've been too entranced by the way their hands moved over the keyboards to catch their increasingly frantic nods at him anyway.

Still, if he'd picked where to sit, it would've been on the side with the choir and organ.

Dad slips into the row next to Joey and soon they stand and parrot the remembered words. Billy has no thought or feeling behind them.

They sing, shake hands with everyone sitting near them, say "Peace be with you," and soon Billy, Joey, and Dad line up for communion. They sit back down, sing again, then it's over and they leave the church. Dad stops to chat up various people. Joey solemnly follows him around and smiles politely, but weirdly vacantly, at them, acting like he doesn't understand the concept of other people, people who aren't himself, his dad or his brother.

Not that Billy does much better today. The whole mass blipped by. He's only half aware of spying a friend or two among the Sunday best of the adults, of seeing cute girls from school looking away and giggling, of being surrounded by these familiar others, but none of it sinks in. He can't pay attention. He's in church but it's like he never left the Woods.

They veer right towards the school gymnasium instead of left towards the parking. Billy shakes himself out of it just enough to wonder what they're doing. He's out of it, sure, but there's no way he would miss a "Coffee and Doughnuts Sunday" announcement at the end of mass. He has a sudden, irrational fear that school has started a few weeks early (and around 10:30 a.m. on a Sunday, no less) and Dad's dropping them off for class.

They enter the gym where most of the space is taken up

with large, foldable picnic tables. The same ones Billy eats lunch at during school months, only configured differently. Along the left side of the gym/cafeteria are several long, white tables, completely covered by huge, open doughnut boxes.

He knows that, technically, midnight will be tomorrow, but the idea that he gets to sneak out of the house and into the Woods to beat up some losers and eat doughnuts that same morning? Well, it might be the best day of his life.

He smiles.

The foggy distraction of the impending melee lifts completely.

As always, Joey picks a doughnut selection that mystifies Billy. Why not one filled with something, or lathered with a thick crust of icing or at least one of the long-johns for sheer volume? But no. Joey picks a wimpy looking cinnamon and sugar ring-shaped one and a carton of plain milk.

Dad has a large, steaming coffee and an apple fritter—Billy's least favorite variety, a fact that seems like more than coincidence as if Dad picks it, so he won't have to share.

Billy negotiates for a third doughnut and, surprisingly, Dad consents without much fuss.

The first choice is easy, a Bavarian cream-filled long-john with chocolate frosting, easily the single greatest food item ever created or consumed, and indisputable proof that the God the priest had been droning on about for an hour actually exists.

Second, not so obvious, even counter to his usual grumblings about Joey's poor doughnut skills, he picks a classic—a glazed yeast doughnut. Not boring, like his brother's inevitable letdown of a selection, but a timeless pick. Celebrated throughout history for a reason. These particular glazed are larger than your average at a Dunkin or Krispy

Kreme—slightly hexagonal in shape with a perfectly round center hole, not that crinkled butthole of lesser confections. Now, the classic glazed can go south quickly but Billy does a quick check and the glaze cracks when he pokes it gently but doesn't flake off onto his fingertip, and—this is the most important—there's no sweating or wetness to the bottom of the doughnut or surrounding box. That's always a killing blow.

The last selection, the bonus. Billy thinks of this third one as a wild card, a way to sample a new potential favorite without quite the risk of when he's only allowed two. On these rare instances when he's allowed the fabled Third Doughnut, he always makes himself pick one he's never tried before. He still has his first and second draft picks after all and they can easily override his disgust if it comes to that. Usually, like with a lemon-filled powdered sugar one he'd tried a few months ago—the creamy tartness of the pudding-like lemon custard balancing the usual pukey-sweetness of the powdered sugar—was pleasant enough that he'd had it again when the glazed weren't up to par. Or the crumb-cake—he usually disliked cake doughnuts, but the crunchiness of the crumble and the subtle cinnamon in the batter swayed him. He'd looked for it since but not seen it again.

Hmm. The crumb cake gives him an idea and he selects a small but heavy for its size blueberry cake doughnut. He doesn't like cake or fruit, but he loved those previous wild-card selections he's thinking of now.

He sits down next to his brother with his doughnuts and his chocolate milk and starts with the glazed, a risky gambit if the blueberry's awful, but he's feeling pretty good. He eats the glazed in four or five bites, the crispness of the glaze perfect, the soft insides of the thing almost dissolving in his mouth.

He opens the chocolate milk and takes a few sips, only after the first doughnut is entirely consumed. Dad dunks his doughnuts in coffee sometimes, and this horrifies Billy. Coffee is a bafflingly gross drink, so he'd tried dunking with chocolate milk once with disastrous results.

He looks over at his younger brother while he sips his drink, and is amused to find Joey breaking up his doughnut into tiny chunks and consuming them one at a time. Billy did this himself as a little kid, explaining to his parents that it "made more doughnuts" obviously. He's pretty sure he'd grown out of that practice before Joey was born, but here he is emulating it anyway.

He eats the blueberry cake. He has a brief panic right before he bites into it. Most of the wild-card doughnuts have been passable, if not downright delicious, but what if it's like the coconut one he'd tried a year or so ago? That had been pandemonium. Absolute chaos. Even the taste of a glazed jelly-filled couldn't wash the foul taste of that putrid thing away. He found little evil slivers of coconut in his teeth for days, no matter how much he brushed his teeth.

He pushes these thoughts aside and soldiers on.

The blueberry cake is good—very good in fact. The glaze is subtler than on the yeast and adheres better to the cake. The denseness of the cake is still moist, and squishes pleasantly in his mouth with a pleasingly fake blueberry taste, more like candy than fruit, and there are little surprise pops of tart blueberry hidden in there, but no seeds or skins to sour the experience.

Billy finishes the blueberry cake and sits back, savoring the taste in his mouth before washing it down with sips of chocolate milk. He'll have to remember that one.

And, finally, the Grand Finale.

Billy looks at his brother's paper plate full of large chunks of doughnut insides. Joey tends to eat the outside of a doughnut first, somehow, then gives up when the task of finishing the center proves too much. He does the same with cupcakes. He's opposite from him in a lot of ways—Billy always saves his favorite part of a meal or snack for last, his brother eats it first then gives up.

Billy locates the hole on the end of the long-john where they filled it with cream, and turns the doughnut around to start from the other end. It's a wise move as his first bite has no filling at all. This happens often, but does nothing to curb his excitement. If anything, it ratchets up his anticipation another notch.

He hits pay dirt with bite number two.

The Bavarian cream oozes and fills his mouth, the amazing, impossible buttery texture of it, like vanilla pudding flavored Cool Whip or some other product that's never existed. The best, lightest and fluffiest pudding ever created. Inside a fucking doughnut. The cream mixes with the savory, unadorned fried dough and the thick smear of chocolate icing. Perfection. They mingle in his mouth and he savors every bite, trying to make it last all day, forgetting about the church service making him fearful and afraid for himself and everyone he loves, forgetting the impending fight and his assured victory and the doom of his enemies making him feel more powerful or in control than ever really can be. He forgets everything. He just sits and chews with his eyes closed.

He ignores his surroundings—the adults chatting and laughing, the kids screaming and running around, the old-fashioned cash register clinking and clacking. Now all of it fades in slowly, as if it's been there the whole time he's been eating doughnuts. Which of course it has.

Billy becomes aware of Joey looking at him, his dad chuckling, their breakfast long finished.

"What?" Billy says.

His dad takes a last sip of coffee.

"The way you eat doughnuts, Jesus," his father says, quieting on the blasphemy and shaking his head. "Well, when you discover girls. That's going to be trouble."

The drive home flips by uneventfully. Billy waits in the car while Joey and Dad go into the supermarket for a few things, retrieving his old Nintendo from where Joey stashed it. He plays haphazardly, with one eye looking out for his dad, so he can return it to its hiding place.

At home the boys and their father disperse, the forced containment of automobiles and churches necessitating freedom from each other.

Billy finds the Sunday comics, but nothing even makes him chuckle. He grabs a couple favorite Batman comics, rolls them up in one hand and goes out to the patio. His father is on his phone, sitting in a deck chair. Still in his tie, looking weird like he's stepped out of a commercial or a magazine ad, and Billy leaves the concrete slab to get away from the sound of his voice, finding the one-sided half of an overheard phone call one of the most irritating things in the world. He lies down on his stomach to read comics in the grass.

He keeps finding himself having to flip back a page or two, realizing he's been skipping dialogue balloons, instead focusing on Batman kicking ass, imagining himself as the Caped Crusader, spinning around warehouses and sweeping crook's legs out from under them. Never Robin, though. He never puts himself in brightly colored hot-pants. He's not even sure why Robin exists. Batman doesn't need him, and Billy sure as hell doesn't want him. One of the kids at school says it's a "character kids can relate to, someone they can see themselves as" but why would they want to do that? Just be Batman—fuck Robin. It's like all his friends that like Spider-man. He can't understand it. Peter Parker's life is shit, just like real life. Why the hell would you want to read that?

He reads comics in the grass for a while and then goes inside and has some chips and salsa. When they have Coffee and Doughnuts Sunday, since it's so late in the morning, they usually skip lunch, but Dad doesn't care if they have a snack or two during the day.

He plays some videogames, watches TV. It's dinner then, not Hamburger Helper, shockingly, but tacos, which are Billy's favorite, but he's back in that fog he'd been in during church and it just sort of carries him throughout the meal and into the evening. More TV and videogames maybe. He can't say for sure. It's Sunday and they usually hit bed early, even though school hasn't started yet. Dad has to work in the morning and he has some theory that when school does start they'll be more ready this way.

Billy's never prepared for school. If he prepares for it then he thinks about it, and then he dreads it.

He isn't dumb or too smart or too poor or rich or not good at sports or too good. He isn't a nerd or a jock or a loser or preppy or a smartass or a tattletale or anything really. Mostly, he's just bored. He doodles in his notebooks and kind of half-listens to the teacher, but she's just reading from the book they all have anyway. The same when she fills the blackboard up with things for them to copy. It's either the same words that are in the book, or that are coming out of her mouth or, often, both.

He gets pretty good grades. He takes tests well and can't

remember to do his homework. Mostly, he stares off into space waiting for it to be over.

Ugh.

He shakes his head and slaps himself lightly on each cheek. Quit thinking about fucking school. You'll make it come true.

He floats on through his nightly routine, brushing his teeth, showering and tucking his brother in.

"Are you really gonna fight those kids in the Woods tonight?" Joey asks.

He's forgotten his brother overheard that conversation.

"No," he lies. "They aren't going to show up."

"But what if they do?" Joey asks.

"They're not," he says, the lies coming so easy. "I heard that they're not."

"From who?" Joey asks, wanting to believe him but still cautious.

"Remember how they wanted me to bring friends?" Billy prods him, "Well I called a couple dudes and Chris said they were asking around about me and abandoned their plan cuz they heard how tough I was."

"You promise?"

"Yeah, Jesus," he says. "I'm not even going to go. I'm going to bed."

It takes a little more cajoling, but Joey's pretty much convinced. Billy's even sure his brother's lightly snoring already as he slips out of his room.

He goes to bed himself, turning off all the lights and getting under the covers. He knows his dad will be by to make the rounds in a few minutes and he doesn't want anything out of place.

He feels tired, weirdly, so he slips his digital watch from

his nightstand onto his wrist. He can't remember where the watch came from, but he almost never wears it.

By the dinky green light of the watch, he sets the alarm for eleven, then makes sure his arm's tucked under his pillow and firmly out of sight.

He hears his dad peek into his room a few minutes later but only partially. He's half asleep, but kind of still aware of his room. The walls and ceiling move in time with his slow breathing. The trees outside his window sway and dark nighttime clouds roll by with a sliver of a bright blue moon poking out here and there when the clouds part. So shiny they appear wet, cars slide by noiselessly on the streets, weaving in and out of lanes, never stopping or colliding but dancing. His school looms a few miles away, not breathing with him, not moving or alive like the rest of the world but cold and dark and solid. And his mother watches down from somewhere, from everywhere at once, and he can remember her face and smile now—he can remember her laugh and her smell and the way it feels to be picked up by her, to be hugged. Everything.

The alarm on his watch goes off. He's positive he set it wrong.

But no. He looks at his bedside alarm clock—it's eleven.

He slips quietly out of bed, still dressed, and sneaks downstairs. The TV's on softly in the backroom, but he hears nothing else. Dad's asleep on the couch like usual.

In the garage, he finds some old shoes and leaves through the back door. He hesitates and then backs into the garage. He fumbles around in the dark on Dad's tool bench until he finds the pocketknife. Not a Swiss Army one, although there are plenty of those around. This is a single, locking blade which his father keeps razor sharp and tests on the hairs of his forearm every so often. Billy drops it into his back pocket.

He doesn't like weapons, not weapons that are supposed to be weapons anyway. He likes making his own from rocks or nails or tree branches, but mostly he likes fists and feet and heads. The knife is just in case they bring knives.

In the backyard, he opts not to vault the back gate, instead opens it with as much care as he can and leaves it ajar.

In The Tunnel, he glances back at his quiet house. Blue light from the TV flickers in the back windows but otherwise it's as if no one's home. As if no one's ever lived there.

He could've made noise leaving. He could've given his dad a reason to catch him and ground him for sneaking out. He could've called friends for help. He could've come up with worse lies to tell Joey. He could've gotten out of this and it wouldn't be any less tough. Everybody gets caught, everybody gets grounded. Everybody falls asleep.

Yeah, no.

He knew as soon as he saw that fucker on the bike back here that he was going to have to beat some asses all by himself. Must keep it fair for the other side. It's how your legend grows.

He leaves The Tunnel for the street. It's risky, but easier to hide and less suspicious if someone sees him. He's big enough to pass as a teenager or small adult from a little distance—especially in the dark.

He's careful all the same. He avoids street lights, darts across the street to stay away from houses with lights on and ducks behind trees or into ditches when cars approach.

It's only quarter after and he's halfway there.

He skips The Secret Passage for the same reason he sidesteps International Waters. Taking the long way around will add an extra half of a street, but he's way ahead. There's no way they'll beat him there. It probably won't even occur to them to get there early and, if it did, they have too many people in their group. "Too many cooks in the kitchen" he heard once from a teacher or somebody. It doesn't have the word shit in it—twice! —but it's still a useful phrase.

He encounters no more cars or lit up homes and arrives at the Woods in ten. He stops in the abandoned lot and scoops up a couple fist-sized chunks of concrete. He touches his back pocket to make sure the knife's still there.

The dark—memories of being lost and the mirror world on the other side—makes him stupid and nervous, so he loads up on obvious weapons. It'll get better once he's inside the trees and at his chosen battleground.

That's how he works. He dreads shit and over-prepares, but when it starts he's suddenly calm and cool.

He opted against bringing a flashlight. He figures it'll freak them out more this way. They'll have one or two, undoubtedly, and that'll help decide who to target first. Smash them if he can, or kick them into the creek if not. Toss them further into the trees as a last resort.

He stops near the entrance, a few feet onto the path, and listens. Nothing but nighttime forest noises. He heads straight to the clearing by the creek.

In the clearing, he realizes the moon is fuller than he thought. The clouds have all rolled on. He would've liked more darkness, but the moon's spooky and that might help freak them out.

After secreting his concrete grenades, he pulls himself up into a tree with his pockets loaded with small pebbles.

He sits in his tree and zones out. He thinks of nothing, sees nothing, listens to his own breath join the surrounding woods and is perfectly content.

When he hears them enter the Woods, he checks his

watch. Not only aren't they early, they're ten minutes late.

God, they're making a lot of noise. Why aren't they coming in? Do they think he'll meet them at the entrance and then walk with them inside? Like he's stupid enough to show them his back so they can sucker punch him and run off to tell everyone how they kicked his ass.

They're talking louder now—feeling bold, secure in the knowledge that he isn't here and that he isn't going to show.

He closes his eyes and concentrates. He can just barely hear them. The night carries their voices as if on a lake. He can snatch single words here and there. His name. Woods. Ass. And, finally, the word that tears it—pussy.

He clears his throat comically loud. They continue to talk, all of them, right over it, but he hears a shush in there and the volume of their voices dials down. He waits for the briefest of pauses and then at full volume says:

"Cunt."

There will be no doubt as to who it is, or his intentions.

There's silence and then a quick, whispered argument and finally the rustled, snapping sounds of them entering the Woods.

His Woods.

He can't tell yet how many there are, but they sound like an army barreling through the trees. They're heading in his general direction, but he tosses a pebble whenever they pause to get their bearings.

There.

Two flashlights. Like when his parents found him all those years ago. There's no meaning to that. They simply have two flashlights. Joey's still young enough that he thinks everything has purpose or meaning. He thinks if something happens to him or Billy or Dad that there's some evil force fucking with their lives. Billy knows the real, horrible truth. There's no evil force and so there's no good either. Nothing means anything. It's all just luck. He knows this. He pretends to blame his brother for his mom's death, but he knows it was random meaninglessness. He blames Joey to remember his mom for as long as he can, to keep her in his thoughts, even if only in dreams now.

There's no symmetry between that night in the Woods and this one. Two nights spent in the same place. That's it. There'll probably be many more.

They're close now.

They're on the path that leads them past the clearing to the creek. He starts lobbing pebbles into the water. The sound of it's unmistakable, and the direction clear. He shifts as silently as he can to the backside of the tree, away from the direction they're approaching, in case they get lucky with one of the flashlight beams.

Their footfalls and mumbled swears are beneath him now.

They enter the clearing.

He counts as they pass below him.

The kid on the bike from The Tunnel is first, and followed quickly by the dyke. Two more boys, one of them surely the kid he racked in the balls. The other might be the kid that booked it, but he's not sure.

That's it.

Just four of them.

The first and last kids have flashlights. The more Billy looks at him, the surer he is that the last one is the kid that bolted. Low on recruits it seems.

Instead of fanning out, they clump and get in each other's way.

"Where the fuck is he?"

"I heard something in here."

"Guy's a fucking weirdo."

They're trying to get their nerve back. Before long, one of them will grow brains and look up. Imagine that, geniuses. Hiding in a tree in the Woods.

It's now or never—can't lose the shock of swooping out of the fucking air.

He leaps out of the tree like he's about to belly-flop at the pool and takes the back two down with him hard. The kid that ran glances over his shoulder at the last moment, long enough for Billy to positively identify him and for the kid to register total panic. They grunt as he hits them and pushes them all the way to the ground. The kid drops the flashlight and Billy kicks it into the creek as he springs up to face the other two.

They spin around, holding on to each other for a moment before composing themselves. Billy lashes out first before they know what he's doing. He smashes the flashlight in the kid's hand to splinters with one of the chunks of concrete.

"Fuck," the kid says, shaking his hand in the sudden darkness. The moon shines and, somehow, the flashlight in the water still shines.

"I think he broke my hand," he says.

"I'm gonna break your fucking face next," Billy says. "After I stomp the shit out of your boyfriend here."

The girl comes at him then, much faster than Billy would've thought, flailing her arms around at him wildly. Something sharp connects with his arms. Girls and their stupid fucking nails.

Billy leans back and sticks a leg out. Her momentum plows her into him and she topples onto the ground by the other two. This is risky because he has no intention of hitting the girl. You don't hit girls, everyone knows that. He will let her hurt herself by tripping all over him. She turns back towards him and gets up. Something metal flashes in her hand and Billy feels that blood's trickling down his arm.

"Did you fucking cut me, you bitch?" Billy asks, trying to control the anger in his voice and seriously weighing the fact that you aren't supposed to hit girls. There must be exceptions like if she has a fucking knife. Maybe she'll get that cunt-kick after all.

"Yeah I cut you," she says. "We're gonna kill you. You should've brought help."

She stands there, chest heaving from the effort of standing up from a simple tripping. Her girlfriend still shakes his busted flashlight hand and the other two haven't gotten up off the ground yet.

Billy laughs. Real, maniacal laughter. Almost in tears, laughter from these pathetic losers. Of course he came alone. Batman doesn't bring friends.

Four against one and they are still hopelessly outnumbered.

Billy laughs, and they glance at each other, uncomfortable. He doubles over with laughter and puts a hand out in mock surrender. They get annoyed. The other two scramble off each other at last and dust themselves off. Billy moves his outstretched hand in the moonlight. The blue glow catches his pale palm and causes it to glow as if it radiates light, where her dinky blade merely reflected it. They're easily distracted by it, and he calmly snakes his other hand behind and grips one of the tree branches put there this afternoon. You don't hit a girl, but you don't let her swipe you with a knife a second time either. He might have to break her hand to get that thing away from her and into the creek.

They're getting antsy, so Billy ups the ridiculousness of

his laughter, clearly faking it now, goading them into doing something stupid like attacking him one at a time without coordination.

Even if they know Billy's egging them on, it doesn't matter. The one that ran the day before comes at him, desperate to prove he isn't pansy. Billy stands his ground, waits for the kid to telegraph his shot and chucks a chunk of concrete onto the kid's foot. It connects with a crunch and his face contorts into a shocked grimace. He's already committed to the punch, but he's lost all the force behind it. Billy considers dodging or knocking his arm away, but instead he punches the fist full force—knuckles on knuckles. The kid howls and falls to his knees. Billy swings the thick branch they now realize he's holding into the kid's ribs and he falls to the mud, moaning and pushing himself back into the trees with his feet, already in full retreat again.

"I can't believe you let that faggot come with you," he says, sounding more out of breath than he would like. His hand does hurt like hell. He followed through with that punch and practically hammered the kid's fist into his wrist, but his adrenaline is pumping at maximum. He can ignore the pain.

Besides, he hasn't gotten to kick anyone yet, not properly.

The kid pushes himself out of the clearing and out of view of everyone. The rustling grows more intense as he struggles through the overgrowth.

"Once a pussy, always a pussy," he says.

He makes like he's lunging for the kid from the bike but pivots and shoots his right leg out full force, going straight for the other boy's nuts again. His foot hits something solid with sickening pops, and pain piggybacks up his leg. He feels the pain coming before he feels it, like his brain can see it traveling up his body before the hurt can get to him. He swings out with the branch at the kid, but misses his smiling face by an inch or two. The pain hits him then and he staggers backwards into the trees, drops the stick and tries not to step on his broken toes.

"Wore a cup this time, genius," the kid says, and bends to retrieve the stick. Billy screams and the other two jump at the ferocity of the sound as his fist comes down fast on the side of the kid's head. He makes a "gak" sound and stumbles sideways and tilts like he's been spinning around to make himself dizzy. He falls off into the trees somewhere and stops moving.

Billy tries regaining his balance with his bad foot and bites his own tongue to keep from screaming like a girl. He goes down hard, lands on his left arm and feels it go instantly numb.

One or both kids left kick him now, but they're firing wildly in the mostly dark and miss more then they connect, kicking the dirt or each other at least as many times as his legs and back.

One blow glances off the side of his head and he sees stars for a second, but he shakes it off, pushes himself off his face and rolls away from them—away from the trees and towards the creek.

"I got his beater," the boy says. At the same moment he brushes his fingers over the other one he hid under the drop-off to the water.

He pushes himself up onto his knees and puts his good foot under him, ready to use the branch as a crutch to stand himself up before he beats them with it. Both of them. Maybe he'll stop when they beg for mercy or stop breathing. Maybe he won't. Maybe he won't stop until he's pulverized them, beaten them into the ground until they become part of it, until he's just punching wet earth.

He knows this about himself suddenly—that he could murder them. He could do that. He pushes it away like his brain pushed the pain of his broken toes away until he could deal with it. He knows, but does not know. How long can his brain keep this thought from him? The pain of knowing this about himself is worse than broken toes he knows without knowing.

He thinks none of this, but is aware of it in the way he's aware of breathing or the ground he stands on. It's deeper than knowledge.

They're almost on top of him now.

Time continues at its sluggish pace. No, that's not quite right. It's like he's falling asleep between blinks, between breaths. Between heartbeats. It's taking forever for them to get close enough. Billy wishes they'd hurry up, so he can finish passing out or whatever's happening to him.

Finally, the kid pulls back the stick to take a huge swing at Billy's head. Billy leans, hopefully out of reach, and swings his other branch, the one they still don't realize he has. It connects with the kid's knee. It's like they're moving in slow motion. Maybe he isn't Batman—maybe he's the Flash.

The kid's knee buckles slightly. Billy hits without much force, no more than his weight behind the blow, but it throws the kid's aim off and his stick arcs down into the dirt and sticks there. Billy brings his body down on it and it cracks. He pokes the kid in the cock with his stick and the kid starts to retch. Guess all of them didn't get the memo to wear a cup.

He looks for the dyke, but she's gone. Poof.

He feels something and realizes she's behind him, straddling him and plunging the knife into him over and over. He has no idea how many times she slices him, but his skin feels hot and wet.

He elbows backwards with two quick jabs, and connects both times.

He rolls over, off his stomach and sees her slump back into a tree. The leaves and small branches encircle her, hold her up and appear as if they're pulling her into the trees and winding around her body.

His Woods.

She has both hands to her face, the knife abandoned, and blood pours from her nose and fills her cupped hands, runs over her fingers and onto her shirt. It looks black in the moonlight.

Billy's been hit in the nose before and he knows it loves to bleed, even when it isn't bad. She's crying freely like a girl scared of a little blood. A technicality maybe, but he hadn't hit her—he'd elbowed her.

As he crawls out of the clearing, he tries to find the knife to kick it into the creek with that flashlight that had finally died at some point, but has no luck. He'll hope she's too worried about her sprung leak to come after him.

He hears her and the boy talking in raised, panicky voices back by the water as he crawls along the path. He doesn't pass either of the other kids, so they must have ducked out while the rest of them were trying to kill each other.

At the main path, he goes opposite of the way they'd all come, back into the trees, deeper into the Woods. He doesn't want them coming across him when they leave.

Plus, he has this funny idea that he won't go home, that he'll go into the Mirror-hood, that if he can loop his way through the forest and out on the other side, he'll be OK. If he can come out where everything is a little different, he'll be better. The Mirror-hood doesn't have a house that burnt down and wasn't replaced. The houses there are all fine, their cars are newer, their kids well-behaved and friendly. He imagines meeting himself on the other side, the version of him that stomped the other versions of those kids and came out on top without a scratch on him. They meet and smile, shake and merge. Refreshed, he strolls back through these familiar woods and home for dreamless sleep.

Dreamless, but with his mother there all the same.

He wakes in the empty lot, on the wrong side of the trees, when his dad finds him in the early morning, when the sun's not quite up, not understanding how he made it out of the Woods or how his father found him.

Billy's dad keeps him out of school when it starts a few weeks later, even though his foot is mostly healed. He's off crutches and in a walking cast. He had a broken rib as well, but they taped him up and told him to try and not laugh or cough too much.

His knife wounds were hardly that, and were cleaned and bandaged. Not even any stitches required. There were only four cuts. It seemed so brutal at the time, but was entirely superficial. They hadn't kept him in the hospital overnight.

Joey had woken and went into his room to sleep and found him gone. Billy isn't sure, but he probably wasn't passed out in International Waters for long before his dad found him and took him to the hospital.

He does have to talk to the cops.

The other kids are in a lot more trouble. None of them had to be admitted to the hospital. Billy doesn't know any of their names and pretends he doesn't know what they look like, but Joey's more corporative. He can't tell but he thinks his dad's proud of him for not giving the kids up. They give up on each other fast, each one blaming and painting each other as the mastermind.

The cops seem more than a little impressed with Billy, that he'd taken on four kids all by himself to protect his little brother, but mostly they're impressed that he hadn't used the girl's knife, or the one in his back pocket.

"You tried to fight fair," one of them tells him.

He doesn't admit that he'd completely forgotten he had it.

The four all get pulled out of school as well. His father promises he can go back when his cast's off, but Billy doesn't care. He's doing better this year, way ahead on his homework and tests now that it's simply up to him to read everything and do the workbooks on his own.

School in bed or on the couch is much better than inside a school.

He gets his cast off on a Friday and he's going back on Monday.

Joey seems different, having started school himself. Dad tells Billy there's only one third grade class and only twelve students Joey's age. There are three classes in Billy's grade— 91 students. He wonders how few there are in the first grade. It feels weird to think about it.

Joey asks their father and Billy about their mother openly now. Billy never reprises him for it. He even finds himself volunteering memories, though she seems so distant in his mind, like he can't focus on her quite right.

But he remembers better when he talks about her.

He realizes when he recalls these memories they're partially wrong. Sometimes he pictures Joey there, even though he hadn't been born, or he pictures their dad with glasses, even though he only started wearing those two or three years ago. And he pictures himself as he is now, tall and lean. He can't see himself as the kid he was, and can't see his mother at all, as if he's seeing the memories from her eyes. He can feel her there, but never see her.

Family albums and framed pictures make their way back out into the house from wherever Dad had secreted them. New ones are added, with Billy and Joey as they are now and Dad in his glasses. These are more painful for Billy to look at than the ones with mom in them.

The kids from the fight come by to apologize. Billy's dad never told him to, but he says he's sorry too. His dad's face tells him he's made the right call.

They look different in the light and out in the open. Smaller and weaker—a lot like his brother.

It's a Sunday and they're finally back from church—no doughnuts today and it was a real long one.

Billy's returning to school tomorrow and he finds he doesn't dread it and maybe it'll be nice to get out of the house and go somewhere besides the doctor.

He's still in his church cloths lying in the grass out back and wiggling his mended toes while Joey is playing nearby and talking non-stop, which seems to be his new default setting. Billy isn't really paying attention, instead he lets the kid yammer on and on. It's his ninth birthday today. Billy can start pounding him again for these minor infractions tomorrow or the next day.

Joey says something that perks him up.

"What did you just say?" he asks his brother.

Joey jumps, startled, like he thought he was talking to himself the whole time. Like he's forgotten Billy even existed.

"The Woods?" he asks.

"Yeah, dummy," Billy responds impatiently. Now that he

wants to hear him, the kid has nothing to say. "What did you say about the Woods?"

"They're gone," Joey says like it's the most normal thing in the world. "I thought Dad told you."

Billy stands up with no problem, no stiffness or soreness in his foot.

"Nobody ever tells me shit," he says and reaches a hand out to his younger brother. He takes it and pulls himself up.

"Show me," Billy says.

No sneaking—they walk straight there with purpose. They take the normal streets to get there and it takes no time at all. Faster than International Waters and faster still than the last time Billy's been here.

But there is no there they've walked to.

Joey's right. The Woods are gone.

Workers in neon vests and hardhats move around barking orders at each other. Large earth-moving machines growl and beep. Some lay motionless, their purpose unknown as they sit in the once abandoned lot. A trailer with a screen door is plopped in the middle of the lot at a crooked, haphazard angle. The screen door squeaks and bangs as men go in and out. There's a dumpster, a bright green one, at the far edge of the lot, closest to where the Woods had been. Branches and leaves stick out from the top of it.

Some trees are left standing, most of it really, probably including the clearing and the creek, but they've carved a path that slopes to the left and arcs into that other neighborhood. They've connected the two streets that had once melded into the forest floor. Now a two-lane hard-packed dirt road joins them like a pale patch where a wristwatch was left on a sunburnt arm.

Even that won't stay, Billy realizes. On the other side, on

what had once been the other neighborhood and is now just another part of his own, a cement truck sits churning, slowly spinning its contents to keep them from solidifying until the proper time.

The loudest part of the work is happening by the cement truck, funneling the liquid concrete onto his forest floor.

"It's so short," Billy says mostly to himself. "The path seemed so much longer in the trees."

He doubts it will take a car, turning slightly up the street's new elbow, a full second to traverse the new area once it's complete.

He sees the other neighborhood, even from here. He sees the houses on their side, and there's nothing magical about them at all. They're just houses. They look likc thcy've always been part of the landscape.

"Are they doing something in that old field, too?" he asks.

Joey nods. "Yeah. More houses. It's another part. What do call it?"

"Addition. Haven't you started math yet?" Billy teases.

Joey pushes him lightly.

"Dad says they were supposed to do all this years ago," Joey says. "Like, when he was a kid."

He says that last part with his patented Joey wonderment, marveling at the fact that Dad had ever been a kid like him.

"Why'd they wait so damn long then?" Billy asks. He hates that there's a street where there had been trees. If it must be that way, if it must be a street, he wishes it'd always been that way, so he would've never known the difference.

He wishes he had nothing to miss.

Joey shrugs.

"Dad says money, probably somebody ran out of money. Everything's money, Dad says," Joey says, kicking at a rock near the sidewalk. "He says the neighbors here? They're all pissed because they're gonna have more cars going by their houses all the time. But they couldn't do nothing about it cuz they didn't have money, or somebody else had more moneys, or something."

Billy nods and turns to walk back home.

"They left some trees, Billy," Joey says, trying to help.

"Sure," Billy says, "but not enough."

# FOUR

# WE COULD BECOME
# EACH OTHER SO EASILY

**G**wen smiles. She smiles back at the nuns with the same fake smile they give her. They don't like her, and she doesn't care. Half of the faculty in the school is secular now and she's the sixtieth—the one that splits them right in two.

They hate her and so what? Next year, or maybe even next semester, they'll have to hire someone else and the balance will tip the other way. Then it'll be their time to be the others.

She chuckles inwardly.

So grandiose and she's playing right along. It's fun somehow.

She'd first applied for a job at Our Lady of the Sacred Heart—or Our Lady of the Sacred Fart as a creatively D-vandal had put on the side of the gym last year—when she was first out of college a few years ago, but they'd informed her that the school was still entirely staffed by nuns and clergy, one of the last of its kind in America, and certainly the largest.

She thought that was pretty stupid, but had shrugged and said "Oh well" and began subbing around town until finding a permanent gig.

This had been five years ago, so only five years into the disaster, when church attendance was still way up and new nuns and priests had seen their numbers peak like never before.

But now, days before the beginning of the new school year, it's just over a decade since the disaster, and with God remaining his usual quiet self, people have been leaving the church in droves. The number of nuns and priests leaving the church even outpacing the simple churchgoers.

So, a couple years ago they started hiring laypeople (as they called them) and now, in just two short years, Gwen is the sixtieth layperson hired, marking the Rubicon.

She smiled at the thought of dressing as a line in the sand for Halloween,

If you count janitorial staff and cafeteria workers, she thinks, the nuns' days are past numbered.

Maybe it makes her a bad person, but Gwen can hold a grudge. That she works here now, years after them claiming they'd never have secular teachers let alone ones who aren't even Catholic… Well, it makes her smile.

She gets up from the table and goes to the sink, carefully washing her mug and placing it back in her cubby with the few unopened pieces of mail—all dumb shit like insurance and 401k stuff.

She takes the long way out of the lounge and slips into her classroom, leaving the lights out and working by the daylight slanting in the windows.

It's a full day of bullshit—meetings and inspirational crap and she's going to cross her fingers and try to get away with skipping a few this afternoon.

She skims over her first few lesson plans, but doesn't really glean anything new, having gone over them a hundred times already to change as much as she can from the retired Sister Genevieve. Knowing the old bitch still came by, Gwen won't be surprised to see her sitting in the back of the class come the start of classes on Monday.

She hears a few teachers talking freely as they clamor past her room, unrestrained without any children present. Gwen sinks down into her chair and pushes herself into the murky corner of the room to remain hidden if they peek their heads in here.

The footsteps never slow as they zip by, and she's safe and alone in her darkened classroom.

She tries refocusing on her tasks, but is easily distracted. A weird sound from the ventilation system, traffic noise from the street, the squeak of desks and chairs getting pushed and pulled across the linoleum of a distant classroom down another hall—all of it's fascinating to her because it isn't the work at hand.

She wishes she'd made another cup of coffee and brought it back with her; even the single serve pod machine crap they have in the lounge is better than nothing. But she'd liked slowly and carefully washing out her cup in front of the nuns, her strict compliance with rules being its own special brand of defiance.

A previous employer had chastised her for wearing sneakers, even though there was nothing in the employee handbook forbidding it. She wore a dress and heels every single day afterwards, smiling at him manically whenever she clicked past him.

She looks longingly at the door, caffeine beckoning. No.

She'll get caught out there and shooed into whatever bullshit meeting she's skipping right now.

She sips from a bottled water on her desk and pretends to gag and choke on it for her own amusement.

She stands up and stretches, steps to the windows and no longer pretends even to herself to do any work. She stands at the extreme right of the wall of windows, entirely out of the line of sight from the door. She watches the lawn crew finish up around the playground and the side of the cafeteria she can see. The jutting corner of the building is in the way, or she would be able to see the old public grade school across the street, now closed due to lack of attendance. There are only going to be fifteen kids in her class this year and that's the only class for the whole fourth grade. Here in the middle school, in its own separate but attached building, they used to have ninety plus kids per grade split over three different homerooms.

She sighs. Just tell yourself how much easier it will be. Just think of how focused you can be with each individual student.

She shakes her head. It doesn't help.

She thinks of all the parks and playgrounds she passes on the drive to get here every morning, overgrown and unused. The schools and churches closed for noncompliance or lack of attendance. The remodeling of play areas into more seating at fast-food joints. The lack of kids' menus in restaurants. The strangeness of missing kids crying in the grocery stores, or the hushed awe of seeing them occasionally. Most of these developments springing up during the last year or two as the people's defiance has evaporated along with their faith. She doesn't know if she can ever get used to this new world.

She has, though. That's the worst part.

They all have. The emptiness she feels thinking about these things now is bottomless, but she doesn't think about it all the time. How could she? How could anyone? Those people that could—they're long gone now, another statistic to pile up with all the rest. No one can hold out forever when being tortured.

In a few days this classroom will be half full, and the kids will misbehave and learn and cry and laugh and everything that is normal, and Gwen can forget for a few moments now and then what it cost for them to be here.

Until a parent teacher conference, where it will strangely be all fathers, or clear step-mothers or grandmothers. And the sadness. The unbelievable cruelty of it will press back onto her with force.

And next year, how many students will she have? More or fewer? Women are still giving birth, of course. You can't stop them if they're determined. Each and every one of them dies from it—dying to bring a child into the world.

It's hard to know what to believe, she admits, but she reads many articles that in the first year of the disaster birth rates actually went up—increased—in spite of the terror of certain death. Some women were already too far along in their pregnancy to do anything but hope and pray. Laws changed quickly as the wives, daughters, granddaughters, the sisters and nieces of elected officials began dying in droves. There was a defiance to it, then either a naive "It won't happen to me" or a ballsy "I am special". None of that panned out of course. Urban legends and internet bullshit. Internal hope and religious belief are all crushed under the weight of fact—No woman who's given birth in the last ten years has survived more than a few hours.

Where are all the kids, then? Gwen wonders. If birthrates

had increased at first and she teaches the fourth grade, then she should have too many students rather than too few. Maybe because Our lady is a parochial school? Jesus. Will she have any students at all in another year or two when the stats plummet? She knows many places have severely cut the requirements for home schooling, those that had any standards to begin with.

But she also knows that the rates for kidnapped children has exploded. She's watched more than a few terrifying Netflix documentaries on the subject—the skyrocketing prices people are willing to pay for children all over the world intensifying the black-market trade, even as stricter laws and harsher punishments are handed down. Sure, you can be put to death for kidnapping a child in most places now, but you can also make ten million for a single one.

Eating disorders are up, drug use is at an all-time high (if that's really possible to measure), crimes of passion are up and violence against children is up, too, somehow, because humanity is the absolute worst.

It's overwhelming.

Church and school attendance are way down. College enrollment has also nose-dived with graduation rates even farther down. Voter participation is at an all-time low and so is confidence in elected officials, especially those who ran on gaining more funding and finding a solution to the problem, because they ultimately failed, haven't they?

It's barely been a decade and the world is giving up on itself.

Gwen can't blame them, any of them, for any of their destructive or self-destructive behaviors. What is the point anymore?

What's the world going to be like in another decade? In

two? How long until civilization is unrecognizable? How long until it's gone? Fifty years? A hundred?

She sighs and checks her phone.

Talking herself into depression was always her special talent, even prior to ten years ago. She'll have to swing by Walgreens after work. Otherwise it'll be the weekend and she won't want to go, and suddenly it'll be the start of the new school year and then she won't have the time. She needs to make the time, she needs to keep taking half of the pills every night before bed to help her sleep and cut back on her anxiety or depression or whatever the hell it is. The pills that let her know intellectually that, yeah, we're all fucked and there's no point, but keeps her from feeling it too acutely and doing something self-destructive.

She hasn't been rescued but keeps treading water instead of slipping her beneath the waves.

She hasn't signed up for therapy, though, and her primary care doctor knows that, or will know it soon, and then she'll call in another refill on her prescription and they won't fill it. She'll have to find somebody new, somebody unaffiliated with her previous doctors, somebody she can cajole and con into some more Trazodone, a drug that is so lowly dosed— and that she also snaps in half on her bathroom sink—that nobody really abuses it. So, she could count on six months, maybe even a year, with a new prescription from a new doctor before they became wise to the fact that she isn't doing everything they told her to. That she isn't trying to get better, not really, she's just trying to maintain.

She isn't sinking but she isn't swimming to shore either.

Gwen has never tried to kill herself. Not really. She's thought about it a lot and planned it once or twice and even written a suicide note here and there, but most of that is in the past.

"So, you're better?" a friend or relative will ask.

No, of course not. Once certain doors are open, they can never be shut again. Of course she isn't better, not in the way they mean.

It's like a seal was broken to open that door and you can shut the door again, put your shoulder into it, but it will never be airtight the way it had been.

This might seem scary to some, but it's comforting to Gwen knowing that her death, her suicide, is always with her if she needs it. If things get really bad and she needs out, it's there like a warm embrace waiting for her.

She supposes everyone's death is like that for them, even if they run or fight or do whatever they can to avoid it.

She saw a gravestone once and has forgotten the name on it, but the epitaph read "He tried everything" and it made her smile. Maybe it was intended to mean that he had a full life, but Gwen thinks of it like a person who tried everything—diet, exercise, religion, money, having a family, helping others—and he winds up dead like everyone else.

No matter how long you live or how well you die, you are dead for the same amount of time as everyone else. Forever.

There's no reason she should find this comforting, she knows, but she does anyway. Maybe it's the great equalizing of it.

She had a science teacher, the first teacher that made her want to become a teacher herself, and on one wall in his classroom he had a huge, blown-up star chart. A mere fraction of the spiral arm of the Milky Way galaxy, and you could barely make out the earth's sun among the tens of thousands of stars, let alone earth itself. He said he liked to be reminded of how truly little we mattered.

She wonders if he's still alive and what he thinks of nothing mattering now that the world is finally starting to agree with him.

He would probably smile his smile that was more of a smirk than anything else, adjust his glasses slightly even though they didn't need adjusting and continue with his lesson or whatever he had been talking about before.

"I have no answers," he used to say. "hopefully we can come up with some good questions together."

She shakes her head, realizes she's been staring out the window and not seeing anything, and turns to go back to her desk when she sees a young boy, alone, standing outside and hidden in the shadow of a tree near the cafeteria.

She blinks and turns away and then back.

Yes. He's there.

She checks the clock on the wall. It's twenty till, so the nuns and teachers and faculty will be safely tucked away in the classrooms or the gym or wherever the hell it is they are, watching slide-shows and PowerPoints and listening to each other drone on and on. She can probably sneak out.

There's an exit to the outside across the hall from her classroom and down a few feet. It would put her in the courtyard and she could either hug the building from the outside or stalk across open an area to get over to where the child is. It'll be easier to not get caught this way rather than zigzagging around the halls inside until she can come out by the cafeteria, near one of the entrances by the playground. If she's caught inside it'll be hard to talk her way out of getting sucked back into whatever mind-numbing bullshit everybody else is attending right now, but if somebody sees her traversing the courtyard she might get in trouble later if they can identify her and if they remember. She can always come up with an excuse on the fly, or pretend she doesn't remember. Who remembers all the reasons they zip around in the hectic days before school starts?

She scoops her keys up from the desk in case any of the doors are locked along her way and opts to hold on to them tightly in one hand rather than let them jangle freely in her pocket. There are a dozen or so and they won't help her if she needs to avoid a fellow faculty member—she can't keep them straight. She even made little notes on pieces of masking tape, but the marker smeared, and some have been lost in the infinite recesses of her purse already.

Tuesday, she found a small piece of tape stuck to her ass that said BOILER so that grand plan was abandoned.

The only one she knows for certain is the key to her own classroom, but that won't help her out here in the rest of the school.

She slips into the hall and closes the door behind her silently. There's a small indentation for the classroom door, probably so when you open it you open it into a wall instead of a child's face, she only now realizes, and she presses herself as flat as she can in that little alcove and glances out into the hall.

Nothing in either direction.

The restrooms are well within her field of vision from here, and certainly the most pressing concern. If anybody is out and about in the halls, they are in there or on their way to or from.

She darts across the hall and away from the restrooms, ducks into Mr. Jimenez's door/alcove thing and knows that buttoned-up, straight-laced guy won't be in his classroom, but at whatever mandatory mission statement enforcement hell she's playing hooky from right now.

She peaks her head out again.

The angle's worse from this side of the hall but she's closer to the exit doors. She hears, or thinks she hears, a toilet flush and abandons her careful plan to hop to the next classroom and look around before heading to the exit. She explodes from the alcove and sprints to the exit, no longer concerned with checking her blind spots or even being seen.

Outside, she turns immediately to the left. Going right would be faster, but if the kid's hiding, as he certainly appears to be, she'd have to walk straight up on him, over almost entirely open ground, and she doesn't want to spook him. She hugs the side of the building as best she can while still walking with some pace in her step.

She does her best not to hum the *Mission: Impossible* theme song as she traverses the grounds.

She feels a little silly. The kid is obviously one of the ground crews' and came with his daddy to work today for whatever reason. But he does seem to be hiding from them as well. Kids do stupid shit like this all the time, though, don't they? Turn everything into a game?

It doesn't feel right.

It feels like the kid shouldn't be there, and he knows he shouldn't be there. He's trying to remain hidden, and not for a lark.

Gwen rounds another corner of the school into the courtyard. This will be the trickiest section of ground to cover without being seen from the inside, but she's come too far to chicken out now. Besides, even if someone sees her, getting to her before she loses them will be difficult for them as they'll need to step away from the windows to get to any exits and will lose sight of her.

She enters along the left wall—is that East? She's terrible

at cardinal directions—then she beelines across the open area and makes as if she's headed back inside via the double doors. When she passes under the shadow of the building, however, she cuts further to the right and though a propped open single door that cuts between the classrooms and the main hall in front of her.

She comes out on the far side of the school and, if she took the time, she could pick out her classroom windows from here, but she doesn't.

She's past the playground and well behind where she's seen the child hiding and, unless he's frequently checking his six, she'll be able to grab him before he can skedaddle.

Her heart sinks and she almost slows her pace a little as she approaches the spot where he was. She's pretty sure he's moved on, but then sees a slight rustling and maybe the white of a tennis shoe, a child-sized one, poke out from behind the greenery.

He's more well hidden from this side, which makes sense, she supposes. He can be seen from the street in this direction, and who's looking out from the windows of a school not even in session yet?

Ah, you have underestimated my laziness and day-dreaming flights of fancy, young one.

The grass is freshly trimmed and short and she hardly makes a sound as she approaches. When she gets closer she sees he's crouched with one foot beneath him and ready to explode into a full sprint if discovered.

He wears a t-shirt and shorts and appears to have nothing else with him save pieces of grass he pulls from the ground, absentmindedly letting them tumble from his hand as he surveys the school. He seems to be counting to himself as his gaze moves down the row of windows.

Gwen, still unnoticed, gently kicks his extended left foot under his propped up right foot, tangles his legs together and tumbles him to the ground. He rolls over, panic in his eyes, but she smiles at him with her best friendly teacher smile and he seems to calm down almost immediately.

She sticks her hand out and helps him stand up, subtly blocking his exit unless he plans to trip himself up again, battling through the brush.

He brushes loose grass from his shorts. It doesn't seem likely.

He doesn't say anything, so Gwen points towards the school.

"I saw you from my window," she says, making her voice as cheery as she can. "I'm a teacher at the school. What are you doing out here?"

He shuffles his feet and shrugs, avoiding her eyes.

"Nothing," he says. "Just looking around."

"How old are you?" she asks, making a show of looking around. "Are you out here by yourself?"

Besides the extra layer of cheeriness, she adds to her voice, she speaks to him as if he's an adult, as if he's the same as her. She finds children respond best if you don't talk down to them. Maybe for younger kids you can, but he looks to be nine or ten, and around that age most of them want to be taken seriously, or at least not treated like little babies.

"I don't have to," he begins, then stops himself and takes a breath. "I mean, I shouldn't talk to strangers."

She smiles at him and nods.

"Very true," she says, and sticks her hand back out. "I'm Ms. Tsukuda."

He has his hands in his pockets, and noticeably flinches when she goes for the handshake, willing himself not to cooperate. His face reddens, and he seems more and more flustered.

"C'mon, Bailey," a voice says, approaching from the right. "It's rude to leave people hanging."

They shake, and she says, "Nice to meet you, Bailey."

"Yeah," he says.

She lets go of his hand and turns to face the incoming voice. It belongs to a man in shorts, a Hawaiian-type shirt and mirrored shades. He's trying his best but is rapidly losing his black hair. He's in his late thirties and he strolls towards them at an easy pace, hands in his pockets, with an animal grin on his face.

"Wondered where you got to, Buddy," the man says when he arrives at last.

The boy recoils from him slightly, but the man reaches in and ruffles his hair and the kid relents. "Hope he wasn't giving you any trouble, Miss."

"No, I just saw him out here, and well, you know how unusual it is to see a child by himself nowadays," she says.

"Well, he's not by himself," the man says, still smiling, "he's with his dad."

Something about the man's smile doesn't match with the rest of his face. The mirrored shades don't lessen the unnatural effect, for sure.

"He's starting school here on Monday," the man says. "We had to move this summer, so we're checking it out. Kids are always weary of a new school."

"Where'd you move from?" she asks, directing the question to the boy.

"Ohio," the man says.

"What grade are you going to be in this year?" she asks the boy again, as if the man isn't there.

"Fourth," they say simultaneously.

"What luck," she says, turning to smile at the man in the shades. She can see her ridiculous expression distort in his mirrored lenses, the fish-eye ghastly warping her reflection. "I'm the fourth-grade teacher."

"Huh," the man says. "What a coinkydink."

This homespun nonsense is as out-of-place as the smile he says it with.

She turns back to Bailey and leans down, getting on his level.

"Is this your father?" she asks, more quiet, but probably not quiet enough so the man won't overhear. She doesn't care. She doesn't like this man, and certainly doesn't trust him.

"Yeah," Bailey says and brushes past her to stand near the man in the sunglasses, but still out of reach from him.

"Well, we better head out, buddy," he says to the boy while continuing to look at her. "See you later, Teach."

When she doesn't return his smile or acknowledge him, his smile drops, and he turns and walks away without another word or gesture. Bailey follows him.

"See you Monday, Bailey," she calls after them. The boy attempts to look back at her, but the man in the mirrored shades yanks him by the arm and pulls him away and out of sight.

She's hot and agitated from the encounter, so instead of walking back around the wing of the school and entering near her classroom, she walks into the closest door near the cafeteria and feels a rush of relief as air conditioning settles on her like a fog.

She walks with purpose through the halls. As she rounds the corner, able to see the door to her classroom—it's right there—two nuns materialize out of thin air, blocking her path.

Not knowing what else to do, she nods and smiles at them, widening her circle to walk past.

"Sisters," she says. Walk with a purpose.

"Miss Tsukuda?" one of them says.

Dammit.

She stops, turns around, and hopes her smile doesn't seem as fake as it is.

"Sister?" she asks, not remembering either of these nuns' names. They'd worn nametags for the first few days, but most everyone has abandoned them by now. Damn habits make it impossible to tell them apart, but Gwen figures that's probably the point. "Do you need something?" she asks, doubling down on playing dumb even though she knows her face is flushed from the heat and her clothes smell of the outdoors.

The nuns glance at each other. Hopefully they're convinced by her ruse.

One of the nuns, the slightly shorter and slightly fatter one—Sister Eleanor, maybe? —opens her mouth tentatively and then falters. Her mouth wants to interrogate her before her brain's formed any questions.

"Thank you for helping me with that, Ms. Tsukuda," Mr. Jimenez says, doing his best nun impersonation by coalescing out of the mist to stand right in front of them.

He smiles at her and places his hand out, palm up. She instinctively drops her keys into his hand and he puts them in his pocket.

"Sisters," he says, smiling and nodding at them. He immediately turns back to her. "Would've taken me all afternoon to load that stuff into my car."

He winces and puts on a show of rubbing his shoulder. He winks at her with the eye that's just out of the nun's line-of-sight.

"Old basketball injury," he says.

The nuns glance at each other once more, conferring telepathically. They either believe Mr. Jimenez, or they don't, but ultimately, they decide not to question them. They're both lay people in the eyes of the clergy, but Mr. Jimenez went to school here, was a volunteer and the first lay person hired. He's no Jesus, but is well-regarded among the priests and nuns.

When the nuns round the corner of the hall and are safely out of earshot, they break into a brief chuckle.

"Thank you," she says, and does a serviceable imitation of a nun's curt nod of dismissal. They chuckle some more. "But you probably didn't earn any brownie points with them."

He shrugs exaggeratedly.

"Eh, by next year we'll be able to out-vote them. Besides," he drops his voice to a whisper. "I have a secret weapon to use against them."

"Oh yeah?" she asks, playing along.

"Yeah," he says, and wiggles his moustache.

She laughs, covering her mouth.

But he points to his wiggling mustache and makes the rest of his face entirely serious. Too serious—the result is absurd.

"Sincerely," he says. "The nuns at this school cannot resist a good 'stache."

She calms down enough to ask, "OK, why? How do you know this? Did Jesus have one?"

He stills his mustache and smiles broadly.

"In my volunteer days, I had to run stuff over to the convent for them, and they have a gym in there. Did you know that? Anyway, on the wall of that gym they have a Magnum P.I. poster," he says.

"What?" Gwen says, completely baffled.

He nods, and then tucks his bottom lip out of sight under his mustache.

"I shit you not. Tom Selleck," he says. "When I found out they were finally going to start hiring lay people, first thing I did was grow a mustache."

She shakes her head at him. Who is this bizarre maniac who just saved her from the wrath of the nuns?

"I guess I have to believe you," she says. "You saved my bacon."

He waves the comment off.

"Anytime," he says.

"Well," she says, "a Tom Selleck poster doesn't explain that part away. Why get in their way to help me?"

He absently checks his watch, balking at what he sees.

"That story will have to wait for another time," he says.

He excuses himself and heads for his classroom. When she gets to her door he calls her name. She turns, and he sails her keys at her. She snatches them out of the air one-handed. He nods his approval and disappears into his classroom.

Gwen hangs around until 3:30, but accomplishes no more work. She locks her door and slips out.

She encounters several other teachers and nuns, but simply nods or waves or says "bye" and refuses to get drawn into any conversations. She doesn't see Mr. Jimenez or his mustache, but she can thank him again a different time.

She drives home and stops by the grocery for a few lunch things for next week, so she won't have to go out on the weekend, wasting an afternoon running errands. Why do that when you can waste your evening?

She gets home and lets the dogs out and checks her email

and the news and none of it really sinks in. She does some yoga, following along to a YouTube series she likes, but still can't focus. All she can think about is nuns working out to a Tom Selleck poster and eyeball-fucking him from a sweat-drenched treadmill.

She has a few texts, still unopened, from two different guys and one lady she went on first dates with recently, but they were too serious for her—all looking for a "relationship." She'll need to dip back into the more casual hookup apps during the school year as her focus blissfully splits into other directions.

Her mom and aunts used to sit around the kitchen table drinking sugary cocktails and spinning yarns about their misspent youth. The men and women they had screwed, screwed over and been screwed up by.

It sounded so weird and wonderful when she was a child or teen eavesdropping on them, although she suspects they knew she was there. Then the world changed just as she grew up. Everything became so serious. There aren't pregnancy scares anymore—there are pregnancy death-threats. Sex is sacred in a way it's never been before. Or at least was never talked about where she could overhear. But this is more of a joke. It can't possibly be this real and this dangerous, especially to only half the population. Think of how disposable women are in certain men's minds. Now, talk a woman into sex and she's literally taking her life into her hands and giving it away.

She exhales when she realizes she's been holding her breath.

None of this matters, of course.

There's always tragedy and, also always, people adjacent to it. They live their lives. Some a more solemn life and some heightened to another extreme. Some more desperately meaningless. Most just move on like nothing's different. What else can you do? Still gotta go to work and still gotta feed yourself.

Gwen had her mom sign the forms, and got her tubes tied a couple weeks before her sixteenth birthday and never looked back.

She thought teaching would blow those doors back open, bubble up any remaining biological needs to the surface, but it's remained walled-off in an air-tight seal from the rest of her. If she ever had it in her at all.

So why stop there? She's an only child and is perfectly happy being alone both then and now. There's no real reason to get married, so there's no real reason to date seriously. This casualness doesn't always work and some people—usually women, it bugs her to admit—become fixated on her simply because she isn't interested in being with them in any intimate way beyond the physical. For a while she only went after people already married or in serious committed relationships. They're eager for the purely physical, but they're also stupid and get caught and the spurned partners put the blame on her. As if that makes sense.

It took her much too long to realize it isn't worth the headache.

She doesn't have weird quirks or fetishes, so that eliminates ninety-nine percent of apps and sites for casual hook-ups. Twenty-six is a strange age. Most of her peers are pairing off for at least the next few years. She can pass for younger and has better luck with those her own age when she fudges her age a little. She hasn't gone for anyone younger yet, finding their casualness doesn't stem from self-knowledge but lack of maturity. She hopes this trend doesn't keep pace with her as she ages. She thinks when she crosses that thirty mark it'll be easier to line up younger people than ones her own age as everybody will be married off. Until they all crash through a midlife crisis or whatever's going to happen in this new nightmare world of theirs.

Huh. She should Google articles about that. Someone must be studying it.

She briefly considers that Mr. Jimenez's apparent interest in helping her is out of some pervy creepiness but dismisses it. She knows he's married and has a couple kids—sons, maybe? —and with his general goofiness it just doesn't jive with a seduction angle.

She's been wrong before but that mustache… No thanks.

She fucks around on her phone for a while after eating dinner, pursues a few apps, but nobody does it for her and so she goes to bed early. Saturday, she goes for a run and has a smoothie for lunch at the new place down the street, then matches up with a guy that seems all right. They meet for drinks later, but he's what Gwen calls Too Far In The Other Direction—checked out, watches other people, looks at his phone, oblivious in his own body—so she thanks him for the drink, and bolts. His expression runs the gauntlet from confused to acceptance in the few seconds she glimpses him in the mirrored wall of the bar as she exits. He'll be fine. She still isn't hungry, even though meal replacement smoothies usually make her hungrier, so she mentally adds the place to the rotation. She zips across the street and down half a block to another bar. It's a dive-bar, or at least in the neighborhood, but she's had luck here before. Tonight's thin—the pre-dinner and dinner crowd still somewhere else—so she has a gin and tonic and throws in the towel. She picks up some Thai food on her way home. She eats on the couch, watching *Charade* and then to bed. The whole day gone in a series of blinks.

Sunday is the same, only faster and she watches *The Glass Bottom Boat* instead, then suddenly it's Monday and she's smacking the snooze button on her alarm. No matter how much sleep she gets, she always feels tired and hits snooze once or twice. So why not stay up late watching old movies?

She realizes she's forgotten to do laundry all weekend even though it's the only real chore she had to accomplish. Oh well. They dressed casually last week since the kids weren't around, so this coming weekend she'll have to remember. Or maybe even sooner, she thinks, looking in her closet and feeling woefully inadequate. At least the kids have uniforms to wear—it'd be a terrible thing to have to compete with ten-year-olds.

She showers, dresses, has tea and a single piece of toast. She hasn't prepped any lunches either, of course, so she grabs a few handfuls of things she hopes will appear appetizing later and stuffs them into her purse.

She miraculously leaves a few minutes early and decides to reward herself with a fancy coffee from Starbucks rather than single-serving swill from the teachers' lounge.

She arrives on the nose, an hour before the students, and wonders if she should keep track of how long that will last into the year, but figures seeing a graph chart of her slipping into tardiness will just depress her. Not a real positive way to start the new year. It's strange to think of late August as the start of the year when, if anything, it's winding down. She knows it's a holdover from farming days and they couldn't start school until after the harvest. Oh well, it isn't any stranger than bitter cold January being the new year.

Two of her aunts live in Arizona now and that place has winter figured out for sure, but that summer heat? Nope.

Some kids are already at the school a full hour before classes starts, but that is common. There's always some miscommunication or parents that have to work early or other circumstances, and the school has the cafeteria open and a few tables set up for kids to waste time. She sees that this used to be the old gymnasium—the faint ghosts of old basketball lines still dot the highly glossed finish, and thousands of buffings haven't erased the past of the place. She thinks that it still smells somewhat of a gym, but that might be her imagination mixing with the unpleasant scent of kids running through here all day long.

She gets into her classroom without dropping her stuff, spilling her coffee or resorting to setting anything down. She kind of wedges everything between her body and the door as she blindly tries keys until one works. She then runs, or mostly falls, as the door clicks open and she embraces the momentum to dump everything onto the surface of her desk.

She has everything set up and ready to go. Her name is printed neatly on the whiteboard, the kids' books and tablets are stacked on their desks in alphabetical order, her coffee is drunk, and she still has half an hour before they show up. Longer, now that she thinks of it, since it's the first day the faculty will be corralling them into the auditorium for a ten- or fifteen-minute welcome that—thank God—she isn't required to attend.

She walks across the hall to Mr. Jimenez's room. He teaches the fifth-grade class, which is about the size of hers, maybe even smaller. The seventh and eighth grade classes have three separate home rooms each, so they're in for a rude awakening with some forced early retirements or layoffs in the next couple of years. It's already happened to all previous grades as the Orphans grow and move from grade to grade.

To their credit, it's mostly nuns that have retired from teaching to focus on their commitment to Christ, or whatever, but those remaining? They're holding on the tightest.

Mr. Jimenez's at his own whiteboard, writing away. He fills it with all kinds of information about the rules of his classroom, how to turn in assignments and when they can do this or that. It's intense, overwhelming and color-coded.

He nods as she enters, finishes what he's doing and steps back to admire it.

"Pretty intimidating, I hope?" he asks, his eyes sweeping back and forth across the nearly inscrutable field of text.

"Very," she says, her eyes glazing over as they pass over it.

"I like to hit them with a lot of shit in the first few days. Becomes easier to figure out who's going to be trouble and who's going to need extra help," he says.

She lets out an exaggerated sigh.

"I'll be sure to warn my class about you," she says. "Maybe they'll opt to be home schooled."

He puts a hand over his heart in mock-wounding.

"You'd attempt to put me out of a job? Then who would keep the nuns from your door?" he asks with a straight face.

"All right," she says. "I guess I owe you one."

He waves it off—no, no. Then smiles and makes a few quick changes here and there to the board.

"Just tell me what time it is, and we're even," he says, that goofy smile still on his face.

She looks above the whiteboard, then quickly around to the other walls, and finally gets the joke.

"You don't have a clock," she says stupidly.

He steps back from the board again and dusts his hands off on his pants as if he's using a chalkboard or gearing up for a gunfight at high noon.

"I do not," he says. "It's supposed to keep them focused and keep me from losing my temper when I see them staring at the clock. It sort of works. The daydreamers are always going to daydream, distracted kids are always going to see stuff out the windows and the creative ones are always going to doodle. And they all have tablets and phones anyway."

"So, it doesn't really work?" she asks.

He spreads his arms out wide and shrugs. He lowers his voice to a whisper.

"I'm not sure any of this works," he says. "But I guess we should probably keep doing it until we know for sure."

She laughs.

"I'll have to use that line on my therapist the next time I go in," she says.

"It's yours to keep," he says.

"I guess I'd have to get a therapist, first," she says, foolishly walking her own joke back.

Why doesn't she want this man to think she's in therapy?

He doesn't seem to notice, care or even possess the ability to judge her.

"Anyway," she says, trying to dig her way out of it, "what do you have against nuns?"

"Nothing," he says. "Or specifically, anyway. That's not why I helped you last week."

"Then why?" she asks.

He smiles and shakes his head.

"Ah, c'mon," he says. "It'd be more fun if you guessed. But you're out of time; the bell's about to ring."

She opens her mouth to ask how he can be sure of that without a clock, and the bell sounds at that exact moment, as if the sound emanates from inside her.

"Touché," she says, because it's slightly less stupid than "saved by the bell," and gives him one of her imitation nun nods, and leaves.

The kids are quiet that first day as if unsure of how they found themselves back in this place. Some try to be good and others try to figure out how to be just bad enough. She knows these first few weeks will be the all-around best behavior of the year for everyone.

Not one of them has a mother that's alive.

She hasn't had an all-Orphan class before. When she subbed, yes, but those kids weren't hers. She'd been like a wacky sitcom neighbor who strolled in without knocking, not a teacher. And most of those had been normal, not Orphan.

She cringes inwardly.

But the Orphans are normal, too, of course.

She has yet to figure out if that's better or worse—how boringly normal the Orphans are. Maybe in a decade or two they will be different. Maybe the children of the future—the children of these children—the second-generation Orphans will be unrecognizable…

Some believe the kids will be better than fine, that they'll give birth easily without dying, but Gwen doubts. They're the same, just smaller—why would they be any different? Others think that all the children will be sterile—unable to even conceive—and the final nail in humanity's coffin. That seems too easy as well, somehow. She figures, like anything else, it will be more of the same.

She looks out at them, and they have no idea yet of the responsibly placed on them, of the burden they'll carry. Some of them can feel it, as she can feel it emanating from them, a sense of sadness or loss that wafts palpably off them. It'll be years, she hopes, years and years before they must deal with it in a real way. At least they'll all be in it together. They're all motherless—boy, girl, black, white, rich, poor. No matter their country or race or heritage or beliefs—no matter anything—they are exactly the same on this fundamental level and she hopes it'll be enough to bind them together.

But again, she has doubts. She hopes they'll band together and help each other find a way to live with it, but they probably won't. They'll find a way to squabble and divide and hate and blame each other like people always do. What tragedy could ever change that?

There's one empty chair, one student's face she doesn't see. The only face she was expecting.

No Bailey on that first day.

She goes over some rules and other maintenancc-type things and has the children stand up in turn and introduce themselves to the class, and they do and are mostly awkward or coy with it.

There are more boys in her class than girls, by a large margin, but she's read studies that this is the way of the world now. In world birth rates, males account for as much as sixty percent of new babies brought to term, if you can believe anything anymore. Woman seem more likely to carry an embryo to term that won't have to make the same painful decision about sacrificing their life for their child's when they become old enough.

After the class intros, it's about time for lunch. Because it's the first day, she walks them to the cafeteria before letting them loose. She stops by reception and inquires about Bailey. It's an excused absence—the boy's father called in.

"Did he give a reason?" Gwen asks, and when the old nun in the coke-bottle glasses looks at her strangely, she explains. "I bumped into them last week, and he seemed fine, is all."

No, he had not been forthcoming with the reason for the boy's absence.

She tries to forget about it, but keeps returning to the way the boy had acted—flinching away from his father, the man in the sunglasses and phony, shark-like smile.

The kids have art after lunch, so she gets a longer break than normal on Mondays. She'll need it later in the year as she tires of these tiny monsters.

The rest of the day zips by quickly as they familiarize the children with things already learned in past years and prepare them for all the new horrors they'll have to cram into their brains next.

Bailey's absent the second day as well and Gwen makes a mental note to ask Mr. Jimenez what he thinks she should do about it. As if there's anything she can do. He's not around after the last bell. Must've taken off like a shot after his kids left. She'll ask him about it in the morning or lunch time since their classes have the same lunch period.

But Bailey's there at the beginning of the third day and he does appear sick. He even provides her with a doctor's note without prompting. She scans and files it away. The note's as devoid of explanation as his father's calls.

He's a distracted student, not seeming to pay attention in class, but usually has an answer ready if she calls, and will perform tasks she assigns him without complaint. He continues to look sickly, too, having trouble getting over the mystery illness. She's known plenty of students like this, and none of it's strange, especially for the new kid to the school. He does seem to fit in with other students rather easily, which is good. Unusual for the new kid to make so many friends right away given his quiet and reserved attitude in class, but she sees him chatting or playing with almost every other kid in the class at one time or another. Even most of the girls. She doesn't know what to make of it, and is more baffled when Mr. Jimenez approaches her about the same thing, only in his grade.

"Is that Bailey kid a good student?" he asks her out of the blue.

"What?" she jolts. She was thinking about Bailey and is now suddenly sure telepathy is real and Mr. Jimenez is a seasoned practitioner. "He's OK. Why?"

He shrugs.

"I don't know. Mrs. Ocampo, from the third grade? She thought he was one of my students and was concerned that he was fraternizing with the younger kids, going out of his way to do so," he says. "But I told her that no, he was a fourth grader and that was it. But then I noticed him hanging out with some of my kids too, older kids. Do you know why he left his old school?"

She admits that she does not.

"I met his father briefly, and he said they had moved from Ohio, but I don't really know the circumstances," she says.

"Hmm," he says. "Notice anybody else acting weird?"

"No," she says. "What do you think is going on?"

"I don't know," he says. "I just don't want it to be drugs."

She's appalled. It's quite the conclusion to jump to.

"You think it's drugs?" she asks, lowering her voice.

He shrugs again.

"Well, I hope not," he says. "Maybe he's a budding politico or something."

Gwen gags and makes a pukey face.

"I'd rather have it be drugs."

Weeks pass, and then months, and everything is normal and falls into its patterns and routines. The teachers find their ruts and kids find their grooves and they jostle around each other and everything is as normal as it can be. She guesses at Mr. Jimenez's—Thad, please, he insists after a month or so— reasons for interfering with the nuns when she can, but never guesses right. So before the holiday break, Thad takes pity on her and tells her.

"I went to school here. You probably know that," he says. "I've gone to church here my whole life, and I know all these people and they are good people, mostly, but they talk about things they, at the same time, profess ignorance of have steadfast opinions about. When I got married I had priests, Catholic priests, give me marriage advice, something they cannot possibly understand. And, a few years ago, in church, one of these priests was talking about sin. Sin used to be something you acknowledged that you did, that you had, and that you lived with and tried to be better about. It was a struggle, it was not something you could ever overcome, and that was the point. It was always something to strive to be without, yet something you knew you would die having committed. There's a power in that, an honesty in it that I admire, but somewhere, sometime recently, it became something maybe you didn't have, somehow, which is ridiculous. Completely absurd that a human being could be perfect. And this priest talked about sin this way, as if perfection was a real thing, not just some ideal to strive for, as if it could be attained here on earth, as a human being. And everybody nodded along with him, complacent in this lie. Lying is a sin of course, and they were all lying to each other and to themselves, and knowing they were lying and knowing the others were lying and they just kept nodding and smiling and lying right through their faces. And I'm sitting there, completely shocked, downright livid, and he segues into strange territory, talking of unforgivable sins, of which any good Catholic could tell you there's only one. Do you know it?"

"No," she says.

"Suicide," he says. "The thought being that you never have a chance for forgiveness with suicide. I have my doubts about even this. I don't really know how you could be in the right mind and kill yourself, and if you're not in control of your actions, well, then it really isn't a sin, is it? But that's beside the point. Suicide is the one unforgivable sin. The church teaches this, it is true, and I'll do my best to accept it at face value. But is that the unforgivable sin he is talking about?"

He pauses, and she answers, not knowing what else to do.

"No?" she asks hesitantly.

"No," he says. "He said being gay is one of those sins and that's not true. That is not taught, and something about it really pissed me off. Before you ask, no I'm not gay."

"I wasn't going to ask that," she says, wincing inside at having thought this about him sometime in the recent past.

"I have known plenty of gay people and they have no agenda other than to live their lives and be left alone," he continues. "Maybe it is a sin, I don't know, it's not for me to say, but I know it isn't unforgivable. After that—I don't want to demean the word sermon by calling it that—I just couldn't tune-in during church anymore. It isn't God's fault, I know that, but these people need to be challenged. They need to be fought and questioned at every turn. They need to be embedded and battled from the inside, so that's what I'm doing, in my own small ways. I had no idea what you were doing outside of the scheduled meeting, or why you were outside, but I saw your  disdain for these holier-than-thou types that run this place, and I figured you were a kindred spirit."

"Wow," she says, "that's, I don't even know how to respond to that. That's amazing. I was just ditching that day because I couldn't bear to sit through another meeting. I never really liked school, which probably sounds crazy."

He laughs and tells her it doesn't seem crazy. They wish each other happy holidays and depart.

Gwen spends two weeks in Surprise, Arizona, with her aging and cranky aunts. She sits in the sun and drinks too much and eats too much and heads into Phoenix after they've gone to bed to find some companionship and otherwise neglects her duties and tries to forget she still has the entirety of an Indiana winter to get back to in just a few days. The only thing she misses are her dogs, and she has an app on her phone where she can look in on them at any point in the place where they're boarded, and she knows they don't miss her at all and will be reluctant to leave all their new best doggy friends. She finds an app for her aunt's TV where she can bounce whatever she's watching from her phone up to the big screen, and they spend many quiet evenings watching her dogs play and eat and sleep and her normally chatty and bickering aunts are subdued by the cuteness of the dogs. Soon the weeks are over, and her bags are packed and she's saying her goodbyes. They all agree she'll just bring the damn dogs out here next time, and she's flying through the air and staring at the clouds below her and trying to ignore whatever the person next to her is trying to talk about.

And she's back at school and everything has started up again. Four kids are absent on the Monday school resumes. It isn't too unusual for a few missing kids after a holiday break. Parents schedule things incorrectly or kids fake illness to extend the break just one more day. Bailey is one of the missing kids in her class, which is also no big deal—he's been absent from school more than most in the first part of the year. Thad mentions he's missing quite a few kids in his class as well and the second grade teacher overhears them and says, yeah, she is too and Gwen has this awful thought that it's only the Orphan grades that are speaking up, that the seventh and eighth grade teachers aren't missing children, when cops start streaming into the school and the teachers' lounge and it's no longer curious, but downright extraordinary.

The cops corral all the staff and students into the auditorium and have the teachers take attendance to make sure everyone is accounted for. Then they begin taking the staff and faculty out three or four at a time to talk with them.

Gwen has no idea what's going on, nobody does, but it has something to do with the missing students. It has to. Barring a few exceptions, their absences aren't excused she's learning through hushed rumors. Some of the children were reported missing yesterday or this morning.

They seem to be selecting facility alphabetically by last name, so it's taking them forever to get to Gwen and it's driving her crazy. She was never one to put something off that is going to hurt. She always volunteered to go first, but this doesn't appear to work that way.

Thad is in the second or third group to be called back, but they're keeping them separated when they return so Gwen can't ask him what the hell is going on.

But his face looks grave.

Mrs. Ocampo is in the group before they call Gwen back, and as they pass each other in the hall outside of the auditorium she mouths "Bailey" at her. But as to what this means, Gwen has no idea.

Once she's called back, they sit together in a waiting area and then are called into a closed room, one at a time.

"Ms. Tsukuda?" one of the cops says, not one in uniform but a detective or something. He tells her his name, but she forgets it as soon as she hears it. Her brain has no room for anything save one question: What is wrong with the kids?

He smiles at her kindly and she follows him. He has the slightest of limp in his right leg when he walks, and he doesn't sit on the edge of the desk so much as lean into in, wincing as he does so.

"You OK?" she asks automatically, looking at his leg.

"Hmm? Oh, yeah," he says. "That's an old one. The cold just bothers it, you know?"

She doesn't, but nods anyway.

Another man enters. He's younger than the detective, but seems to be the one in charge.

"I'm Special Agent Raj Singh," he says.

"Special Agent?" she asks as her fear ratchets up another degree.

"Yup," he says, and sits down across from her. "DPEA."

Drug and Pregnancy Enforcement Agency.

Oh God. It is drugs and her students are dead and she didn't do anything and—

"Are you all right, Ms. Tsukuda?" Singh asks her. "Would you like Lieutenant Dixon to get you a glass of water?"

She takes a breath.

"No," she says. "What is this about, please?"

The older one leaves to get her a water anyway.

After he returns, they go over the briefest of her background and Singh asks a few questions here and there but seems distracted and impatient to get to the point, so he soon pulls out a single sheet of paper and slides it across to her, facedown on the desk. Dixon observes them, but says nothing.

"This photo—" the agent begins, but Gwen cuts him off.

"Oh, Jesus," she says and slumps into her seat. "What is it? Just tell me. Is it one of my kids? I can't look at it if it's one of my kids."

She feels sick.

They see that she's close to tears, and although they betray panic with their eyes, they form tight smiles and Dixon places a reassuring hand on her arm.

"It's not, I assure you," he says with a voice practiced in teasing real information from distraught women and shattered men. From victims and from killers. He continues, somehow even more soothing, "We just need you to tell us if you've seen this person."

She wonders why one of them doesn't hold the picture up to her, or at least hand it to her face up. What bargain-basement psychology effects are at play here, making her pick the photo up and turn it over? Is this supposed to invest her more in the process? Maybe something like jump-starting her brain and getting the wheels turning about any suspicious people or instances that have occurred recently, priming her for whatever is on the other side of the photo.

She turns it over in her hands and is surprised to discover that it's a developed photograph, or at the very least, printed on glossy photo stock. She was expecting a smudgy fax or something else simultaneously modern and archaic. It's also upside down.

"Most of the guys and gals would have just run it off the printer," Singh says, reading her mind, "or probably just pulled it up on their phone to show you. But everybody has their quirks. And Dix lets me share his office when I'm in town, so I indulge him."

"I do my best thinking during menial tasks," Dixon justifies, "waiting around for stuff like photos to develop. Connections are made in the in-between, when nothing's going on."

Singh makes a *Can you believe this old timer?* face at her, but there's no malice in it.

She's about to tell them that no, sorry she can't help and that she has never seen this man before in her life, but as she rotates the photograph 180 degrees the features morph into a face she recognizes.

Of course, it's the man in the sunglasses with smile like a hungry predator.

No mirrored shades are allowed in mug shots, so she can see his dead, black eyes. If only she could have seen those before, she would have known. She could have stopped whatever has happened. She would have known with one look in those eyes.

Singh and Dixon see it on her face and hear it in the catching of her breath that she recognizes him, and they drop their acts—the put-upon hotshot and the slow-moving detective—and get down to business. They make her go through the scenario of her one and only meeting with Bailey's "father" and Bailey's subsequent behavior in school.

After she finishes telling it for a third time and they've exhausted all their questions for her, she finally asks one of her own.

"What is this?" she asks. "What is going on?"

Singh sighs. Dixon smiles, but not from happiness.

"We don't know, but it's bad," Singh says. "The children are alive. There's no reason to think otherwise. They are worth nothing dead so that's in our favor."

"Oh, Jesus," she says.

Singh shoots a quick, uncomfortable glance at the crucifix on the wall next to the clock. Dixon keeps his compassionate eyes on her.

"Yeah," Singh says, and picks the photograph back up.

"This man," Dixon says, "is into ransoming children, or selling them off into the sex trade, or holds elaborate child auctions with a cabal of foreign billionaires."

Gwen looks completely distraught—not an ounce of blood in her face.

"Well," he says, walking it back a step or two, "maybe not that last part. I dunno, it's a theory, anyway."

Singh pulls another photograph from a manila envelope and holds it up to her. They know she knows this one without any prompting. It isn't a mug shot, but a capture from a candid security camera, freeze-framed and blown-up.

It's Bailey.

"He usually works with this kid," Dixon says, "or so we've been able to discern from other departments. You must have caught them off guard with some of your questions; we're pretty sure the last school they hit was in Ohio."

Why did he tell her that? Or had Bailey? It's so hard to remember tiny details from many months ago.

"Why weren't we warned about these people?" she nearly shouts, suddenly very angry.

"About what? A new kid acting strangely at school? And who do we get the word out to? They've been hopping around the country, seemingly at random. As far as we know, you're the first person at a school to actually see this guy in the vicinity. Besides that, this isn't the only person or persons doing this around the country. And, well…" Singh trails off and looks away.

"And what?" she says. The anger builds inside her.

"School attendance is down," Dixon says. "I don't have to tell you this, I'm sure you know, but dramatically down all over the country. There are whole cities, good sized cities, where there isn't a single school open."

She shakes her head slowly as the anger tussles with the depression that lives in her. They merge and become one emotion. It pushes itself back onto her, into her and makes her feel bad about herself. All emotions angle inward, as they always do. She's never mad for long because eventually she's mad at herself.

And any emotion directed at her becomes sadness.

"I know it's bad here," she says. "I know the public system is doing worse, and I heard it's even worse in other areas, but you never know. You never know what to believe. You never know why somebody's telling you something, for what purpose. Everyone's lying to you all the time, and you never really find out why."

They sit silently for a minute and she tries not to believe what she just said. She tries to feel different, but she can't.

"Is Bailey involved?" she asks. "I mean, how involved is he?"

"We don't know," the DPEA agent says, "Well, he's sent into the school and scopes out and finds kids nobody's going to miss right away, and then over a long weekend or holiday break they scoop them up. The schools become aware and they get ahold of us."

It sinks in and pulls the rest of her down with it.

"Is it usually this fast?" she asks. "I mean, it's early Monday afternoon. How'd you figure this one out so quickly?"

"You should be the detective," Dixon says and smiles at her. "They went off script a bit this time, varied their M.O. a tad, and grabbed a few kids who were missed, far ahead of their usual timetable."

She sits up straighter in her chair.

"Do you think that was Bailey?" she asks. "Maybe he's trying to get caught, giving them bad info?"

They exchange a glance. Singh shrugs.

"Anything's possible," he says, humoring her. "But it's not like we know where they are or anything."

"Well, he couldn't be too obvious about it," Gwen says, starting to get into the idea. She stands up. "Let's go search his desk."

The detective shifts his weight on and then off his bad leg. Singh busies himself shuffling papers.

"Humor me," she says.

"Go ahead, if you want," Singh says, without looking at them.

She zips out of the room. Dixon follows her at a slower, stiff-legged pace.

She stops and waits for him at the door to her classroom. She unlocks it and holds it for him. The role reversal doesn't seem to bother him.

There's nothing in the kid's desk. Not a scrap of paper, not a pencil shaving, not a used piece of chewing gum.

"Is that strange?" he asks. "It seems strange."

She nods. Super weird and not helpful.

"Life's not like the movies," he says.

They finish up and he leads her back to the gymnasium. He hands her Singh's card.

"I scribbled my number on the back," he says. "He has a large territory and isn't always around or reachable, but I'm local."

She's penned in with the other teachers who've already

been seen. There are only a handful left that haven't yet been spoken to. School let out while she was back there and most of the kids have cleared out. Only a few stragglers remain— children of faculty or those whose parents are chronically late. It instills her with a palpable sense of unease. When she left they were all here. Now, they've all vanished like Bailey and the kids he helped that cold-blooded maniac kidnap. She knows the man in the sunglasses will be put to death when they catch up with him. He knows it too, she realizes, and that's part of where his smile comes from. She'd taken it for an *I'll eat you before you can eat me* smile but now she thinks it's worse than that. It's a *Fuck you, try* smile. A nothing matters smile. A nihilist's smile of pity that you believe in anything.

They talk to the remaining teachers and nuns, dismiss everyone and Gwen walks straight out of the gym, not bothering to go back to her classroom and retrieve anything. She has her purse anyway. She might never come back, she thinks. That's absurd. More than losing a third of her class to a kidnapping ring?

She'll see in the morning.

She exits on the opposite side of the grounds from her car because she must get out of that building. She needs fresh air. She walks around the outside walls of the school, almost there before she realizes she's tracing the route of the first time she saw Bailey hiding out in the bushes. She's disgusted with herself. Why hadn't she been more suspicious of his, and his "father's" behavior? Could she have stopped them? Even appearing more suspicious might have scared them off to another school, or out of the city entirely. She makes a mental note to appear less trusting. Maybe this act will make her less trusting like a forced smile that makes you happy as it sits on your face and worms its way through your head into your brain. Well, that's how she heard it works anyway.

She rounds the other side of the building and, instead of simply walking across the front expanse of grass to the teacher's parking lot, she tightly hugs the corner and crisscrosses through the courtyard like she had that day she met Baily. It's significantly colder now, and the going much more difficult. All the snow that fell over the break still blankets the ground, and the top layer has melted into a nearly impenetrable crust. January in Indiana.

She'd gladly live in this winter forever to get all the kids back safely.

She walks towards the side of the cafeteria and the tree she'd rounded months ago to block Bailcy's escape. The leaves are long gone and the bark of the thing's become smoother and grayer. The bushes and ground below are the same, only white and gray with snow.

She looks at where the boy was and tries to picture him there, or at least tries to picture him as she had then—a hopeless, lost child. Not a monster with an agenda as she thinks of him now. He's ten. How responsible for his actions can he be? How much does he know about what they're doing?

The church, she knows from teaching here, believes seven is the age when a child becomes responsible for their own actions, but it isn't that simple or black and white. Sure, a kid knows when they're lying to you, but do they know why it's wrong? Can they understand the gray areas? What if they're intentionally mislead by an adult or even a parent—do they know it's wrong to follow bad advice?

They're still coming on-line as people. They can't be expected to understand all the subtle nuances of bad behavior.

Gwen shudders and not just from the cold. What's the youngest a child has ever been charged as an adult? Fifteen? Fourteen? She has no idea. What if Bailey and the man in the shades get away? They won't just stop. What will happen if the cops don't catch up to Bailey until he's in his teens? Will he be put to death for years of doing this all over the country?

God. Should he be?

She makes a quarter circle around and approaches the tree much as she had months before. There's no child hiding in the bushes this time, looking for weak points in the school and trying to glean some sort of hidden knowledge from the structure of the building itself, so he could help steal his peers.

No child here—just dead trees and frozen earth and snow and bits of garbage.

Wait.

Garbage?

She sweeps her eyes around. Everything is pure snow, not even footprints, save her own. Why does it look like someone overturned a trashcan right here in this exact spot?

Most of it's wadded up paper and plastic packaging from some snack or another. Tiny broken, unrecognizable chunks of wood or cloth or whatever it is poking through the frost. But right there in the middle, where Bailey would've been crouching is a pencil sticking out of the snow—sticking straight out with its eraser up. She bends down and wriggles it free. Dirt clings to the broken tip. It was stuck in the frozen ground.

The pencil is embossed with ST. MARY'S on the side. A different Catholic school from a different part of town that's been closed for years.

She doesn't call Lieutenant Dixon or Special Agent

Singh. She gets as far as getting the card from her purse, but she looks at it without really seeing it and slips it back into her wallet to get lost among frequent shopper cards.

Hell, they're probably still inside the school finishing up less than a hundred yards from where she stands right now looking at this pencil. She doesn't have to call him, just march back inside and present him with this earth-shattering clue. If it is a clue. If he'll take her seriously. If all this isn't her fault and she should've done something sooner.

Stop. Feel shitty later, push it aside. Think it through.

If the pencil's been placed here on purpose, as the way in which she found it certainly seems to suggest, then it must have been placed here by Bailey, right? Only he, besides herself, knows about this exact spot.

Well, that's not entirely true, she admits.

The man with the smile like a skeleton knows. If Bailey's being coerced, then he's being watched. He can't just leave her a note. He must leave a message without words.

The pencil has teeth marks on it, chewed-up on one end.

She glances around nervously. She feels exposed, but feels no eyes on her, nor sees any. She gets onto her knees and digs around in the snow and hard dirt, but there's nothing else.

The pencil is the message.

Is he there? Are they all there? Using an old shuttered church and school to keep the kids before…

Before.

Gwen has an idea—dozens, really—of what comes after this before, but it's so big and so terrible that she can't bring herself to confront the thoughts. Her mind skips over it like a stone on a lake. Like when she lies in bed alone at night and grapples with her own mortality; she thinks around it to avoid thinking about it as if that will save her. As if that will be enough.

The audacity of these kidnappers hiding in plain sight, under everyone's nose, scooping the kids up from one school and locking them in another.

She falters.

Are Special Agent Singh and his partner right? Is it too fantastical, too movie-script perfect? Would a ten-year-old boy send her secret messages to help foil a ring of child kidnappers? It sounds completely insane.

She grips the pencil tighter and runs an index finger over the impossibly tiny teeth marks on the end near the eraser. She walks straight to her car never glancing back towards the school.

Either the man or the boy put this pencil here, and that man's never chewed on anything nervously in his life.

It's up to her. It must be her.


St. Mary's is located on the corner of two rarely used residential streets, deep in one of the town's oldest neighborhoods, a few blocks south of downtown.

It's not in one of the nice neighborhoods, not the ones with the big old Tudor and Victorian houses that get passed around amongst the self-described movers and shakers of this medium-sized Midwest city. It isn't located in one of the neighborhoods that clutch to the outskirts of downtown, the once-fancy homes now divvied and cut-up with cheap walls plastered in and rickety stairs slapped on the sides of the houses to accommodate college kids and shiftless twenty-somethings looking for the cheapest conditions possible. It isn't located in the streets just past these areas which cling like static to the check cashing places, Laundromats and hyper-specific foreign groceries.

No. There's nothing here anymore resembling much of a functioning society. The old church and school are the nexus of this dead zone and radiate its shabbiness in all directions. The nearest streets and blocks are devoid of anything living, homeless or otherwise. No strays, predators, squatters or thrill-seekers.

The last time Gwen drove this direction she took a wrong turn out of downtown and slowed to a crawl. Not out of any traffic congestion but a morbid fascination, as if she were moving slow-motion through the debris field of a train wreck. She double- and triple-checked her door locks as she scanned the streets.

She sees vehicles this time. Not the abandoned toilets that usually dot the landscape, but functional, working automobiles. Even a van in the church parking lot, mostly hidden by the overhang of an outbuilding. She would've missed it if not looking closely for signs of activity.

She speeds up, rounds the corner and finally pulls over to the side of the road three blocks later near an open cantina and taco house. She curses herself. She saw the van and maybe another vehicle near the church, but how many did she miss? Who saw her? She didn't see a single person, or signs of people, but surely they're there, and noted her presence.

If any of them is the man in sunglasses—she is rightly and truly fucked.

This seems unlikely. It'd be beneath him. He'd hire it out. Maybe delegating most of the dirty work to the children.

Unlucky and direction-adverse drivers cruise through these streets all the time, night and day, and they probably ignore most of them, but she can't go back, not now and not in this car. They'll recognize her, or at least her vehicle. Nobody wanders around in here unless they're looking for something. What other choice does she have? On foot, she'll be slower and more exposed. Besides, she doesn't know the layout enough to set out through the tangle of fences and junk in the backyards of these supposed vacant houses. She gets her cell phone out. What other choice does she have?

She inputs Singh's emergency number from his card and is about to thumb it open when two spots below she sees "Thad" in quotes. She did this as a joke a few months ago when he insisted she call him by his first name.

She calls before she can think much about it. He answers immediately.

"Gwen?" he says, his voice loud and wobbly. He's in his car. "Everything all right?"

"No," she says, and throws in a fake nervous chuckle for good measure. He probably can't hear it over the ambience of the street. "My car died. I just wondered if you could give me a lift?"

He says, "Sure, of course" and "Where are you?" and "That's maybe ten minutes away" and "Be as quick as I can." She tells him she'll be in the taco place, thanks him again and hangs up.

She's starving, she realizes. The cops cut her lunch short earlier and she hasn't eaten anything since. After a brief game of charades and a back and forth of broken Spanglish from both sides, she sits down in a window booth with a plate of steaming carne asada with cilantro and onions, beans, foil-wrapped corn tortillas and a bottle of Mexican Coke.

She's half-finished her food and is trying to figure out why soccer blaring from a TV in the corner seems exciting when in Spanish, rather than any other time, when she sees Thad pull up outside. He gives a little wave and comes inside.

He walks straight to her table, looks down at her food and

then looks over at the counter. He hooks his thumb over his shoulder.

"Are we, uh, in a hurry?" he asks.

Yes, but she can't tell him that without telling him everything, so she shakes her head no. He bows and goes and gets his own steaming plate.

"Try it," he says and points at one of his tacos.

"Thad, I just ate three tacos," she protests.

"Not like this," he says. "Just have a forkful of meat."

She spears a piece. It's thinner and pinker than the steak. It's also more flavorful—buttery even. It falls apart in her mouth without chewing, dissolving as her tongue touches the meat. Flavor explodes as the meat evaporates.

He laughs at her expression of bliss and takes a huge bite of taco.

"Wow," she says. "I've never been so out-ordered in my life." She cranes her head to see past him to the chalkboard menu near the counter.

"Lengua," he says, as if that means anything.

She sees it printed there in pink chalk and nods, but he still has this shit-eating grin on his face. She matches his smile.

"What?" she says.

"Lengua is tongue." he says and takes another bite.

She knows he's telling her the truth and trying to shock her at the same time. It's something he loves to do, but she isn't going to fall for it.

"Well," she says, "that's some of the best tongue I've ever had."

He smiles and hands her a spoon.

"Try the beans," he says.

She doesn't reach for it. It's a pet peeve of hers to be

handed things unsolicited. She attempts to push her revulsion aside.

"I had beans," she says.

He nods.

"You did pretty good," he says. "I see that you got your tacos traditional with just onions and cilantro, and even squirted lime on them. And soft corn tortillas, thank God. If you'd been eating flour tortillas with cheese and shit on them, I probably would've swiped your whole tray into the trash. Now you've tried the lengua, so you know I'm not full of shit. You had refried beans. Try the charro beans and you'll be ordering like a real pro."

Perhaps somehow sensing her discomfort at having a utensil pointed at her, he relents slightly and sticks the spoon into the small crock of beans with the handle cocked slightly her way. She takes a spoonful of beans but, thankfully, he's focused on his tacos, so he doesn't sit there and watch her eat—another pet peeve.

It's more like bean soup than what she thinks of as a side dish for tacos, but they're delicious, with a deeper, more complex flavor than the refried beans, which are already pretty good. The beans are rich with that melt-in-your-mouth texture without being complete mush—a delicate harmony. The broth is peppery and well-seasoned with little chewy chunks of bacon and crunchy bits of vegetables and herbs giving the whole dish a nicely balanced feel and a savoryness her beans did not possess.

"All right, two points for you," she says.

He shrugs like it's no big deal but his smile's still full.

"You picked one of my favorite joints for tacos," he says. "Now, if you want enchiladas or a good mole, well. I'll have to show you where to go. Next time."

Gwen uses this as a segue into why they're here at all. She was practicing lies in her head before he arrived and opts to be as vague as possible, a simple passing through scenario and some kind of known issue with her car. She really hopes he isn't a car guy and doesn't ask to take a look it.

"I'd ask to take a look at it," he says. "But I don't even know how to change a tire, let alone anything under the hood."

"I've got a guy coming," she says, the lie easy with her relief that he isn't an armchair mechanic. "Old friend of the family, but it's going to be hours before he can get here, so."

He nods, not interested in any further details, simply taking her at face value. She feels shitty.

"I'll take you home. It's not far out of my way," he says.

She nods and says thank you again. This is going to be the hard part. How to convince him to not take her home, but drop her off two miles or so in the other direction and not wait around or insist on coming with her.

The man from behind the counter comes out to their table with a to-go bag and hands it to Thad, who thanks him in Spanish, and they bump fists. The counter man smiles at her as he leaves. Maybe she's passed from gringo to valued customer by being in Thad's presence.

"For the wife and kids," he says holding up the bag. "If they found out I was down here, well, you know the rest. Ready to go?"

"Yup," she says, and suddenly checks her phone as if it vibrated. She curses when she looks at the screen.

"Everything OK?"

"Yes. Well, no," she says. "I feel stupid asking you to come down here now. I had this appointment down here and they won't let me cancel without charging me. I should have walked the rest of the way, and worried about my car later."

"Walk?" he says, "it's freezing. I'll drop you off. Where is it?"

He says all this in good humor, but there's a hint of doubt in his voice and the way he shifts his eyes. They've become pretty good work friends over the last six months. They see and talk nearly every day. She's been to his house and met the wife and kids. He probably knows when she's full of shit, even if it doesn't consciously register. She's certain she's a terrible liar and an even worse actor.

They put on their winter coats, hats, gloves and scarves, complete with the required bitching about January weather in northeast Indiana.

He starts the car, blasts the heat and leaves her in the passenger seat while he wipes away the light dusting of snow accumulated during their time inside.

"I can do that," she says, "as payment for the ride."

"Yeah right," he says, like it's the craziest idea he's ever heard, and yanks the snow scraper she holds from her grip with one confident tug.

The snow accumulates as soon as it's wiped away. It's really coming down.

"OK," he says, getting back in, "Where we going?"

She gives an intersection. He cocks his head, tries to picture it. Fails.

"I'll direct you," she says.

He nods and they're off. She worries that cock of his head isn't confusion, not an act of jumpstarting his brain into parsing mental maps of the city, but one of judgment. She worries he's picturing exactly where they're headed and can't understand why she'd go there. She barely understands what she's doing herself.

She half-heartedly rehearses lies as they drive. She takes

pride in honesty and, Jesus, the last half-hour or so… Lies of omission are lies all the same.

They arrive far too quickly, she realizes, as Thad says "Here?" with such disbelief that she almost breaks down and tells him what she thinks is going on. Does he suspect? They avoided talking about the missing children during tacos because why talk about something so horrible and recent when you can eat your feeling instead?

She has to look out of the car window as she answers him to keep the doubt swelling inside of her from turning into vomit and erupting from her.

"Yes," she says, facing the window. "The only therapist I can afford."

Her hand's on the door handle, but is having trouble steadying enough to open the fucking thing already. All that doubt finishes its growth and takes up full-time residence inside her. It snakes permanent roots into her biological systems. Her head echoes with reasonable questions. Why are you doing this? Why can't you ask for help? What are you going to do if the children are really here? What are you going to do if the kidnappers are? What would stop them from murdering you and the children if they're discovered?

Miraculously, the car door opens and she's standing on the sidewalk.

"Gwen," Thad asks from directly behind her but miles away. "Do you need me to hang around or come back for you later?"

She puts a smile on her face that in no way reflects a real feeling.

"Nope," she says simply when all her half-formed lies evaporate. She tries to give him a look that says *I'll explain later* but fails.

She shuts the car door, gives him a friendly wave goodbye and heads straight for the building on the corner. Thad hangs around for a second and then leaves. She continues towards the building until he's out of sight, then cuts across the street without looking, and heads for the backside of the church's lot. She picks this location carefully. If Thad doubles back or something he can't be sure where she's gone. The snow's stopped and she's mortified to see nothing but her boot prints corrupting the fresh, white powder on the ground.

The cold air feels like a relief after the stifling heat of Thad's car. She left her hat and everything intact for the short drive, not because she needed them, but as a disguise if anybody was watching.

She walks at a casual pace and hugs the inside edge of the sidewalk which she notices is cleared of all snow. Not merely shoveled, but most likely blown. Would kidnappers do that to maintain appearances? Was it someone from the diocese? Could they clear all this yet not notice a strange van on the premises?

When she's nearly past the church, she crouches, jumps towards the building, lands and moves swiftly around the corner. She stops for one moment to catch her breath, then double-times it the rest of the way around the wall and comes out near the van parked between the church and the school.

Now she has a choice to make. Left, or right? She puts that off for the moment to decide what to do with the van itself.

She contemplates slashing the tires to keep them from escaping with the children, but what if she needs that van to make a quick getaway herself? A small part of her mind nags *What if this isn't the place? What if they aren't here and this is a huge waste of time?* You want to throw slashing the tires of a random church van on top of that?

The passenger side of the van is closest to her and angles away from either building with facing windows. It's unlocked. The keys are in the ignition. She reaches over, slides them out and into her coat pocket, thinks better of carrying the noisy things, and places them inside the inner wheel-well of the driver's side of the van. She moves as quickly as she dares, and hopes no one sees her.

It feels like an hour has passed since Thad dropped her off. She knows this isn't right, but she's moving slow and the sun's rapidly dropping. She'll have to get inside soon as the temperature is dropping fast.

She picks the school over the church to explore first for simple, logical reasons. The school's been closed longer than the church, and is neatly divided up into smaller rooms. Easier for keeping the kids separated. Plus, there'll be kitchen facilities, more bathrooms and smaller windows.

The church takes up nearly a whole block, situated right on the corner. The school is a long, squat single-story. The long side runs perpendicular to the street, so the part of the building facing it is only as wide as a pair of double-doors.

She wants to check the windows from outside, but it looks as if shades are drawn over most of them and there are no lights on in the building. The power probably isn't even turned on.

She steps as lightly as she can, crossing the few feet to the side of the school, but her boots crunch all the same. She can't imagine making that much racket as she circles the building and peers through dirty, covered windows. The door it is.

She steps back to the van, rummages around in the cluttered center column for a second and comes up with a clipboard. She smooths a couple paper-sized receipts for special diet dog food from her purse and clips them to the board with a pen. She lets out a long, slow breath, rights herself and walks up to the school's front door while looking around and checking her clipboard. "Acting!" she hears some mostly-forgotten sketch rattle around in her head.

She pretends to knock on the door for any passing cars or pedestrians' benefit. After a second of standing there in silence, she tries the doors. They're both locked but, feeling emboldened by her new persona as official clipboard lady, Gwen rounds the side of the school without hesitation, looks in all the windows and checks all doors. She hopes she won't have to scramble in ass-over-tits through a window.

Finally, when nearly back to where she started, she finds an emergency exit not entirely shut. Without bothering with the pretense of keeping up her flimsy façade, she wedges the end of the clipboard in between the doorjamb and the door and levers her entire weight into it. The particleboard creaks and strains in the process. The door pops open at the same time the clipboard cracks and splinters. It doesn't break into two pieces, instead stringy fibers of the wood cling to each other like interlocked fingers. It reminds Gwen of the wiggling fingers of children saying "The church, the steeple, open the doors, here's all the people."

She stuffs her right arm into the darkness behind the door and wrenches it open far enough that she can squeeze in and out of it, even if she has to turn sideways to do so.

It's dark inside. The only light comes from the door she left ajar. She stands waiting for her eyes to adjust and inhales stale breaths of the place.

There's no one here, she knows once inside. There can't be. There's nothing living here, nor has there been for years.

She's suddenly and completely unafraid, at home in this

dark, musty place. She searches the school, front to back—every classroom, office and closet. She never gets her cell phone flashlight out as she planned to. It would've felt like a violation somehow to light this place up, as if it's sacred or as if it's ancient ruins and she's passing through as an accidental observer. She tries looking at the place with an archeologist's gaze, but it's impossible. This had been a building much like the buildings she's spent most of her life in. The equipment and things left behind are all the tools of her trade, so the walled-off magic of the place wears off and it becomes a chore like any other to search the rooms. She's less thorough as she goes, merely peeking her head into the last couple of rooms.

Nothing. No one here. No kidnapped children were ever here.

She exits and shoulders the door closed. She struggles for sound footing on the snow-slick pavement until she hears a satisfying click and the door is entirely flush with the wall.

She still holds the clipboard and tosses it into snow. The sun's set and it's time to shed her disguise. Wouldn't make much of a weapon either.

She doesn't have the same luck gaining entry into the church, but there's also no light; she hears and feels neither heat nor power running to the building. There's nobody here. Not interstate child kidnapping criminal fugitives and their captives. This is stupid and a waste of time.

She turns to trudge back to her car and notices something about the sidewalk. It was snow-blown, yes—she noticed that on her first trip past here in her own car which she wished to God she had right now—but only the throughways, only the parts of the sidewalks that the city will cite you for if they get around to it. All the paths and walkways leading up to the church or the school, any steps or patio areas, are still snow covered and, from the ice-crusted dirty gray of them, they haven't been cleared off all winter.

Except one.

One of the outbuildings, closer to the church and back along the trees by the parking lot, has a clear and recently shoveled path from the sidewalk and street. It's a low, plain rectangle of a building, like the school it mirrors in miniature. Gwen knows what it is. The convent for the nuns, or whatever they call the equivalent structure for the priests. Rectory—that's the word.

She smiles.

Rectory sounds like rectum, and one of Thad's racier dad jokes comes to mind. *Rectum? Damn near killed 'em!*

It's perfect, she realizes—a dozen or so modest rooms with beds and a simple kitchen. It's situated farther from the street than any other building.

She walks towards it. There's condensation on the windows. There's heat going to this building.

She notices another vehicle parked behind it, one she didn't see on her drive through the neighborhood. No repeat of her plan with the van—all the doors are locked up tight. She removes all the valve caps from the tires and tosses them in different directions. She hopes that will be enough to at least annoy them.

She has no real expectations of catching the kidnappers or rescuing the kids or even leaving this desolate place alive and it doesn't seem to bother her.

Shouldn't this bother her?

She pushes away her unease at not feeling unease and giggles to herself.

This all seems very wrong, but like TV wrong. Like she watches somebody else on an unfolding crime drama. There's a sense of dread, as she's grown to identify with this plucky heroine playing amateur sleuth, but she's really on the couch in her PJ's snuggling with her dogs and a big bowl of stovetop popcorn.

And it must be stovetop. Not this microwave crap or, what's the other kind called? It's a word Gwen hasn't thought of in a long time… Air-popped. Right…air. It uses hot air like this air is freezing or would be if she was truly here and not really at home and snug on her couch with this buttery, crunchy, salty popcorn…you must use coconut oil and skim the foam off the melted butter so things don't get…soggy…

Gwen stands there on the porch to the convent. She's so cold she sweats inside her winter clothes. She comes out of it all at once like descending a hill and emerging from a cloud of fog. Or, like when she was a kid, her grandma's old TV turned off but didn't turn all the way off—it kind of froze a negative afterimage on the ancient gray screen and then shrank to a dot, eventually dying out like a candle. It's like she's inside the static between radio channels and somebody finally tunes her right and suddenly she's here, coalesced from the ether to find herself fully formed and standing on snow dappled concrete.

What had she been thinking about? Popcorn? Why? Jesus, had she said that shit out loud? Is she going into shock or something?

She tries the door, but it's soundly locked. In fact, the lock looks out of place. It's a flat nickel-plated thing of brushed metal when all the other fixtures she's seen around here are brass. This seems important.

She shakes her head and fights the fog as it attempts to descend again.

No. This is important. It means someone replaced the lock with their own. It means they might still be inside.

She circles the building, but finds herself daydreaming and doesn't take it in. She's suddenly back at the front and on the porch. If she ever left it.

What did she babble about this time?

She takes her car keys and squeezes them in her left hand until it shoots real sparks of pain up her arm and across her brain. It's like that first shot of alcohol or intake of smoke. She moves the keys to her right hand and does the same. She leaves the keys there after the desired effect and squeezes them every so often, rhythmically, like there's a heart beating in her hand.

She counts things as she rounds the building again. She counts steps and windows and cars she hears passing by on some street close by. The counting and the squeezing focus her, and she takes in her surroundings—her actual, real surroundings and not the tangled landscape of her brain.

She's three windows down on the side of the building facing the parking lot and she hears children's voices.

She stops and stoops and counts forwards and backwards. She squeezes the keys in one hand and then the other. Yes, children's voices. They are right there behind a single pane of glass. They are right here.

They're speaking quietly, but not whispering. There's nothing conspiratorial about their tone. Nothing hushed or scared in their voices even if she can't quite make out the words. She's fairly certain she hears girl and boy voices, but it's hard to tell at that age and the muffling of the glass doesn't help. She hears laughter and giggles.

She hears no adult voices—none at all.

She pulls her scarf down and her hat back and tries her

best smile. It feels funny on her cold face, like trying to drink from a straw after having a cavity filled. She's pretty sure she's using the correct muscles in the correct way, but there's no feedback to tell her anything. Just cold numbness.

She must get inside, and not just for the children, she realizes. She must warm up. She must sit down.

She taps on the window with her right hand, but her giant glove muffles the sound so much she isn't sure she can even hear it. She risks removing her glove, tucks most of her hand down into her sleeve for warmth and leaves only her index finger exposed. The window is warmer than anything else out here. It radiates the heat from within. It's possibly warmer than anything she's ever felt. She gets closer to it and resists the overwhelming urge to press her whole face against it. She settles on her forehead and taps with her index finger and then her whole hand. She wants to feel the warmth, wants to bring it inside her, to commune with it through touch, through osmosis. Somewhere in the back of her conciseness a tiny voice warns her about making too much noise, but she can't help it. The warmth.

She's about to remove her other glove and start slapping the window with both hands when she hears a couple children shush the rest, and the talk in the room drops off. She still has the presence of mind to revert to a quiet, rhythmic tapping with one finger and pull her face back from the window.

The shade flutters and she squints the sudden light away. She hears a small gasp and, when she opens her eyes, one of her students is staring at her in disbelief. She also sees a few tiny hands holding the shade up and more shadows passing beyond it. Another tiny face pops up next to the shocked one, registers her and retreats. She distinctly hears him say her name to the rest of the kids in the room. Other tiny voices pick up her name and send it forth like a chorus or the world's simplest game of telephone.

"Marcus," she says, trying to speak loud enough for him to hear her and understand but not loud enough to be overheard by any malicious entities. "Can you let me inside? Can you get to the doors?"

He shakes his head slowly, never breaking eye contact. His expression is a little sad.

"Marcus," she tries again, "it's very cold out here. Can I please come inside with you?"

His expression changes from sad to uncomfortable. He doesn't seem scared at all. Like there's really nothing he can do and he's truly sorry she must stay outside in the cold.

"The doors don't open," he says and turns slightly, listens to someone out of her field of view, returns to her gaze and nods thoughtfully.

"Or the windows," he says.

She shuts her eyes and rests her forehead against the warmth of the window. It will be so easy to fall asleep right here. At least her face will be warm.

How can she convey her need to get inside into the warmth without panicking the children? How can she explain to them in as few words as possible that she will die if she does not get inside this building and that they all might die if they don't immediately leave? How can she tell them this without losing control of the situation?

She smiles, and it feels as if she's cracking the skin from her face. What control of the situation?

She reluctantly pulls her head back from the window and is about to try again when she hears a scraping noise to her right, and she sees one of the windows further down open and tiny hands motioning for her. Two girls, not from her class, appear at the window and look at her.

She scrambles over, pulls, jumps and falls in through the window. She hits the floor with a soft thud. The air is so warm it's stifling, and she begins shaking and shedding her outer clothes at once. The other children pile into the room to look at her, but nobody talks yet. She attempts to stand, but her vision tunnels and crackles with a reddish blackness at the edges. She falls back to her hands and knees and reaches out in ever-increasing blindness for something soft, for anything when she passes out. She manages to say "Pillow," or at least thinks she does, before the world blinks out and then things like pillows don't matter anyway.

She gasps awake on the threadbare carpet covered in blankets and a pillow under her head. She's so very hot after being cold for so long that it feels like drowning. As if the warm air has become so thick as to become water, and it fills the room and her lungs and gently pulls her beneath.

She kicks at the coverings until free of them and rolls over to press herself into the floor, which is still cold from the freezing temperatures, outside leaking in.

She sits up and looks around in the dark. The hallway light is on and she blinks towards it. Alone in the room, she listens hard but can't hear the children.

"Kids?" she says and forgets to whisper. They're probably not alone here.

She gets up from the floor. Her boots and socks are gone. She doesn't see them anywhere. Her coat, hat, gloves and scarf are all missing.

It isn't blankets that covered her as she dozed, she realizes, but dozens of hand towels and washcloths.

She pads slowly across the cold floor in her bare feet and

leans against the door frame when she reaches it.

"Kids?" she tries again, but quieter.

She pulls herself through the doorway and launches her body with her arms, as if from a slingshot, into the hallway. She stumbles into the opposite wall, glances off it and ricochets down the hallway. like a forceful but poorly shot billiard ball, towards the room where she saw the children. The lights in this room are off and she stumbles into the room, flails about wildly for the light switch and scrapes her hands on the rough texture of the unadorned walls.

The light pops on like a camera flash. The room is as empty and motionless as a photograph. She blinks and tries to will the children to be there, somehow, to be hiding just out of sight and playing some ill-advised game with her.

But no. The room is empty.

As she turns to leave and check all the remaining rooms, the door behind her closes softly.

The man with the grim reaper smile stands in front of the door with his hands in his pockets. He isn't wearing his sunglasses inside in the middle of a winter night, but his eyes are as dull and lifeless as lenses.

He nods towards one of the two bare-mattress beds in the small room.

"Sit," he says.

She's so wobbly on her feet that she's afraid she might fall over and wants no more than to sit, but she feels obligated to defy him and remains standing. She sways, hobbling in a tight square like a drunk. What her college roommate called a land-shark—if they stop standing, they'll drown.

"Fine," he says, "stand."

He jerks his torso towards her and she flinches. He steps towards her and does something with an extended leg, sweeps behind her suddenly tangled legs, which feel as if she has an extra one or two now and she falls backwards onto one of the beds. She nearly bounces off it onto the floor.

She sits up on the bed and looks at him with as much hate as she can muster. He stands by the door, not appearing as if he moved at all.

"Who'd you tell you were coming here, Tsukuda?" he asks, looking at her. His tone is like he's completely bored by the whole thing.

"Where are the children?" she asks.

He sighs, mostly for her benefit she assumes, and removes his left hand from his pocket, holding a small, matte-black gun.

He takes one step towards her and holds the gun, so she sees it. He doesn't point it at her, but shows her that the ugly thing is in his hand and that it is very real.

"I'm going to ask the questions," he says. "You're going to answer the questions. When I run out of questions or if I don't like your answers I'm going to shoot you in the face. If I like them, then maybe I'll fuck you and leave you tied up in here for nine months and let nature do its thing."

He smiles his sharp smile at her. She does her best to throw it back at him.

"I've had my tubes tied," she tells him.

He shrugs.

"You're not leaving this room alive," he says. "We both know that, but I can make it painful for you. I can rape you into the cold floorboards and I can do it in front of your students. I can do it for weeks or months. I can bring in some of the other guys here and have them do it. I can break your arms and legs before I fuck you, I can pull your tongue out or your eyes. I figured out all the horrible things that can be done to one body and I can do them to you while you're still alive. I can figure out all the things you're afraid of, all the things you don't want done to you, and then I can do them all, over and over. Or I can bring the kids in here, one at a time and do things to them. I haven't lied to you yet, and I won't start now. Those children are valuable, and the better condition they're in, the more they are worth to me and my associates, so I won't break anything on them, probably, and I wouldn't want to leave a mark, well, not many, nothing too bad, but go ahead and take a moment, use your imagination and think of all the things I could do to these children, right here, in this room you are never going to leave alive, things I could do to them that wouldn't leave any traces. Not on the outside."

She was wrong about him. He isn't a shark. Sharks aren't evil. They're just an animal. They simply are what they are. An animal just survives. She thinks about a cat her parents had when she was little and how it would torture smaller animals it would drag squealing into the house.

Fine. So maybe this guy isn't a shark. Maybe he's a fucking cat.

But why do they do that? Do they gain some sort of sick fascination from it or does it stimulate some other need? Does it make them feel as if they're hunting and they need the hunt to survive?

No, he's not a cat. Not even that lowest of low creatures. Is that why she dislikes felines so much to begin with? Are they too human in all the worst ways?

None of this matters. Certainly, none of this matters now. Now, she must figure a way to get past him and get out of this room.

He stares at her and waits patiently for a reaction. He doesn't prompt her to hurry. What does he care? He has all the time and she has none. She has nothing. Not even shoes or a belt. He's, what, twice her size? She isn't going to overpower him. She isn't going to overpower anyone. Not in her half-hypothermic state and not barefoot in an abandoned convent in a neighborhood classified so far below desolate there aren't even squatters here. *In here* is a better description. She's near the heart of the city—a disused and forgotten chunk of it.

But her mind wanders again, and this is not the time.

She finally worries that maybe there's something really wrong with her. Maybe she was colder longer than she thought. Why else does her mind wander and zip into useless tangents? She instinctively feels the back of her head. Had they hit her or done something to her? Does her skull always feel this weird through the back of her scalp?

Stop.

Stop, stop, stop.

Shake it off. The children. Your mind has to function properly, so you can get out of here with the children. You don't have fucking time for brain damage.

Time. Your weapon has to be time. He thinks it's his, but the longer he keeps you alive here, the more time you have to get the kids and get the fuck out.

"How long have I been here?" she asks, breaking a silence that seems incapable in its length.

"I told you," he begins, but she cuts him off before he can repeat himself or brandish his firearm again.

"You ask the questions, yeah I remember," she says and rolls her eyes, so he can see it. "It was rhetorical. Do you know what that means? Think about it. If I told anybody I was here, wouldn't they also be here by now?"

He stares at her and tries to keep the wheels that are

turning in his brain from showing on his face. It's a valiant effort, but she can tell her condescending got to him. How far can she push him?

She mulls over what to try on him next when there's a soft knock on the door. No. Not just soft. One louder knock, a pause, then two soft knocks in quick succession. She burns the pattern into her brain.

He takes half a step backwards, then reaches behind him and unbolts the door. It opens a crack, and someone attempts to whisper something. He shows real impatience and anger in the moment and barks at the person to just come into the fucking room already.

A short, fat, balding man enters, glances around nervously and tries to look at Gwen while not looking at her.

He quickly shuffles over to the man with the jagged smile's right side and whispers into his ear. There's something funny about his shuffle. He never quite picks up his feet. It reminds her of something the nuns scold the children for.

The fat man's amusing waddle distracts her from something important, but she can't grasp what it is as she strains to hear what the man whispers.

"What?" the man says and they both glance at her for a split second. "Check her coat and things."

She knows what it is. They're planning to leave, but the keys are missing. She glances around absently for a clock she knows isn't there. The drawn window also reveals nothing. Has she been here long enough to drain significant air from the other vehicle's tires?

The shorter man makes one brief moment of eye contact with her before leaving. There isn't dull hate or contempt the way there is in the other man's gaze, but a frantic sort of nervousness. Things are not going as planned. She keeps her smile and observations to herself. Time is her weapon, but only until they leave this place. She has no illusions. They have no reason to take her with them.

The children. She must figure out where the children are.

She has no misconceptions about killing any of these men. There's no part of her that can do that. She can die for her students; that would be easy. Well, not too easy, but she can do that. She cannot kill for them. Deep down inside where she knows and accepts herself, she knows she can never kill anyone. Not even these horrible men. Not this monster with the almost-human smile. Not if he does the things he threatens to do. Not even then. Not even if he hurts the children in ways they can't come back from or kills them in the process, by accident or design.

"I pity you," she hears herself say, before she can think better of it.

"What?" he asks, even though he clearly heard her. He takes three huge steps and he's right on top of her.

There's no going back now.

"I pity you," she repeats, raising her voice and slowing her cadence as if he hasn't heard her, as if she believes him to be foreign or a dullard. "You think the whole world is full of people like you. You think the things that motivate and frighten you are universal. You think we're the same, that there's this thin margin that separates us and we could become each other so easily. You think that if we switched places, if I got that gun away from you, I would use it. But I don't even want it. Not even now. If you dropped it or set it down, it would never occur to me to touch it. I'm here for something greater than me, I'm here for the children. You don't even believe in anything greater. That's how completely different we are."

He pulls the gun up, but not to shoot her with it. To pistol-whip her. She braces for the impact and smiles a genuine, sweet smile at him. A smile she would give a tardy child for being on time or a forgetful one for turning in his homework. A shy child for answering a question. She gives him her finest *You're doing your best, I know that and am proud of you* smile.

That same knock on the door—loud, pause, soft, soft. He hesitates with the gun in his hand and she thinks it's because of the knock, but he instead seems to be thinking about his retort to her. When the knock comes again, and he still doesn't notice it, it clicks into place. Why he had the flunky come in and speak to him and not just whisper through the door. Why he walked all the way around to far side of him to whisper. Why he has that weird flatness to his voice.

He has hearing problems. Most likely he's deaf in his left ear.

"We are different," he says. "The difference is I have the gun."

As he finally brings it down to smash her smile, the person on the other side of the door tries the knob and bangs on the door much harsher—strikingly loud. He finally hears it and takes his eyes off her as the swing enters the bottom of its arc. She shifts to the side and he brings the gun down hard onto the ancient bed frame and misses her completely. She feels the wind from it.

She knows nothing about guns, has never touched one and will venture to go her whole life without doing so, but even she sees that there's something wrong with it now. It's bent in some deeply wrong way. He brings it up eye level, stares at her in shock that her face is still in one piece. Looking at the gun, he notices that it's distorted and examines it in both hands, forgetting her at once.

She swings an arm with all her force, pushes herself from the bed as she does so and connects perfectly with his good, right ear.

He screams and pitches forward, grabs for his ear. Maybe he hopes to fall on top of her and stop her with his body, maybe he's forgotten her again. Either way, it isn't going to work. She spins away from him before he lands awkwardly on the bed. She's at the door.

She throws the bolt and yanks it open. The fat man stumbles in as if it's a trap door and he was standing on it. She steps over him and hears a gun go off.

She turns to see the man with the tombstone smile drop something metal and smoking, his forearm's an insane bright red. He doesn't scream this time; he stares at his blackened, ruined claw in wide-eyed disbelief.

She isn't quite ready to believe Sister Eleanor's "miracles happen every day," but clusterfucks sure do and she sends up a silent prayer of thanks to whoever the patron saint of that might be.

She pulls the door shut behind her, glances to see if she can lock the door from outside—sees nothing—and runs down the hallway, yelling for the children.

She hears them in front of her somewhere down the hall, in the direction she heads. Their voices are raised in alarm and terror. She runs as fast as she can and covers the hallway so quickly she isn't sure her feet touch the ground.

The door's locked and she screams something like "Back!" and throws herself into it. It pops open with a crack very similar to the clipboard earlier, which seems like it was months ago.

They're clumped together near the window. One of them

has already forced it open somehow. They stare at her with impossibly wide eyes. They're all barefoot and with no winter clothes. It doesn't matter. Winterize later.

She shoulders the door shut as best as she can and screams at them to jump out the window. They aren't sure, and with her ear to the door she can hear feet running down the hall, so she screams "Fire!" because that's all she can think of, and the children scramble through the window two or three at a time. Her heart sinks as she realizes she hasn't seen Bailey anywhere. They must be keeping him somewhere else, but this is the last room at the end of the hall. Where else can he be? She's distracted enough worrying about Bailey that she's almost caught off guard when a body slams into her from the other side of the door. But her feet are planted, her stance is wide, and she pushes back with what feels like more weight than she's capable of. The door jerks and a gap appears momentarily. Warmer air burps in from the hall, but she closes it immediately and hears cursing from the other side. It doesn't sound like the man with the sharpened smile. She risks a look back at the children as the last two pull themselves out of the window. When she feels the mass from the other side lift from the door for another try, she waits a beat, swings the door open wide and sticks her left leg out. The fat man falls for her tricks again, trips into the room and sends something shiny flying from his hands and under one of the beds. He slides a few feet across the floor on his face. She reels back with a foot to kick him in the head, but intense pain flares in the leg she tripped him with and she nearly falls over. She regains her stance enough to grab onto the window ledge and pull herself out into the snow.

She might have passed out.

Either way, she feels funny and slow as she pulls herself

up and limps towards the street where she hears the children and other familiar noises, and she notices the snow all around her strobes from red to blue, and has been since she got back up and the cops are here and her chest feels like she's exhaling a breath she's held since this afternoon or maybe her whole life and she feels so much better without it. Feeling empty is such a relief. She has an image of a tomb opening after being sealed for centuries and that puff of gas that escapes and blows the dust out and across, and she wonders briefly what a horrible smell that must be.

Something bites her hard in the right side and she reaches down and it drags its teeth across her hand and she holds up her palm to look at it and is pretty sure it's her blood even though the blue light make it appear nearly black and in the red light it vanishes almost entirely.

It stabs her again and again as a blackened hand clamps over her mouth and barbequed human meat fills her lungs. But the hand is so much weaker now than it was before it became charred and leaking, and she wriggles her jaw free and sinks her teeth into it and pulls and twists and puts as much pressure into the bite as she can and she hears an insane animal howl very close to her—right behind her—and feels more frantic stabbing at her back and side, but shallower as most of the fight has been taken from them and she hears something else even louder in front of her beyond the hand she's eating— sharper and louder sounds than the dying thing behind her but they are also voices, maybe.

The hand and the knife and the whimpering animal they belong to pull free from her and she only hears the gunshots after she's standing there alone on the snow and she tries to turn and see what shape the man with the bone-shard grin has become in the end, but her legs give out and she tunnels down into blackness.

She wakes up in the same spot and it must be only seconds later and Special Agent Singh is leaning over her and he doesn't have a coat on which seems funny in this weather and he barks orders and there's blood on his shirt, lots of it, and she knows it's hers as if it calls out to her. Like it misses her.

He glances down at her and sees that her eyes are open, and he smiles at her and then quickly turns to shout some more.

Unseen forces lift her from the ground and into the air quickly but gently and it's as if she floats there. Her eyes flutter open and she sees the man who will never smile again crumpled and discarded and in probably more pieces than a person should be, lying in the red snow completely forgotten.

She comes to on a stretcher in the ambulance with strangers working on her calmly but quickly. She tries to ask for Thad, but Singh's face appears.

"We got all of the children," he says. "They're OK."

She coughs and rasps and tries to get the taste of seared hand from her mouth. She tries to speak but there are all kinds of foreign tubes and things stringing out from her face.

"Bailey," she manages at last.

He glances away briefly and the darkness that passes over his face is like nothing she has even seen, like a single enormous rain cloud blots out the whole of the sky. Like a sudden and total eclipse of the sun.

"We got all of the children," he repeats and attempts a smile.

She chooses to believe the kindness of his lie because she

has no idea what else to do.

Machines start in with urgent sounds, the EMTs push Singh away and all the calmness drops from their mannerisms.

But Gwen's calm enough for all of them—for everyone, everywhere.

She dies right there in the ambulance, less than a mile from the hospital.

# FIVE

# THE VOICE BECOMES
# A WHISPER AT THE END

Cameron Washington wakes up to the cats playing tug-of-war with the sheets around his feet.

"How did you fuckers get in here?" he asks, but he knows how—he must have left the door open again. He rolls over and kicks at them gently.

Now that he's awake, they're up by his face, kneading his arms and incessantly peeping, which is what Elm calls it when they meow.

He touches her cold side of the bed and says, "Six more months," then wishes he hadn't said it or even thought it. Wishes he could stop himself from thinking entirely.

The cat's peeps increase, seeing one of their two favorite hands emerge from beneath the covers.

"Can you two shut the fuck up for a minute?" he asks, sits up and they scatter only to converge in the kitchen, peeping anew.

"I get it!" he yells. "Food! How original!"

He gets out of bed, can't find his slippers, but finds an empty beer bottle next to the bed. He knows immediately what it is when his toes topple it over, but it still startles him when it hits the hardwood and rolls out into the hall. He soccer kicks it down the hall, aiming in the general direction of the recyclable container in the kitchen. It's not the only empty bottle lying around.

Shit. He'll have to clean this up before tonight's Skype date with Elm. She'll want to see the little monsters.

He pulls their bag of food from under the counter, the cabinet door suspiciously ajar, like one of them has figured out where he keeps it and is willing itself to grow thumbs.

He pours equal amounts of food into each dish, separates the boys, then watches them fight over and eat from one dish, leaving the other untouched.

"You're idiots," he says.

He flips the on switch on the coffee maker and goes into the bathroom to take a long, beer-stinky piss. He doesn't wash his hands, but splashes water on his face. He sort of walks, sort of falls out of the bathroom and into the living room onto the couch. The remote's nowhere but he probably needs to get dressed anyway. If he gets into work early, he can leave early. Right? That's a thing people do, leave early?

He notices the coffee maker sounds weird, has a half-recollection of drinking coffee far too late last night.

"I don't have time drink it anyway, so the joke's on you, drunk Cam," he says. He drinks a mouthful of water from the kitchen sink faucet instead.

He looks down at himself.

At least change your shirt.

He finds a clean work-branded one in a laundry basket full of partially folded clothes. Well, it's clean. That's a small miracle. Another day sitting in there and he'll have to throw them in the dryer again, or just rewash everything.

"Why do they make the distinction between 'miracle' and 'small miracle'?" he asks the cats who, now that they're fed, stretch out on the kitchen floor. "Are there ever any large miracles? Or is life just a shit-show, punctuated by tiny bright spots?"

The cats look at him until he stops talking and then return to cleaning themselves and glaring at each other.

"I should write this stuff down," he says and then smacks his forehead comically like he's just remembered something. "But you dummies can't read, can you? And you're my only audience. So."

With Elm in Europe for a year, hc talks out loud. Is it more or less crazy that he addresses the cats when he talks to himself? What's he supposed to do? Sit in silence or run the fucking TV all the time? Are those options less crazy?

He finds his keys, wallet, phone and grabs his vape-pen from the little charging station by the front door. That reminds him. He ducks back into the kitchen and Xs another day off the calendar. Three weeks.

"Hold your applause, please," he says but is proud of himself. The vape-pen is douchey, no doubt about it, but it isn't a cigarette either. He'll feel good about himself whenever he can.

On his way out, he pauses briefly at the front door.

"Be good, monsters," he says.

They full on ignore him this time.

It isn't quite six when he starts Elm's little hatchback. He hasn't told her that he's been using her car for almost two months. His tags expired, and he hasn't made it over there yet to renew them. He hasn't even looked into it. He'll have to soon—hers only have another month or so on them. It isn't procrastination, exactly. He just can't be bothered with mundane, everyday stuff. Or he's lazy, sure. That's what people call it. But how many lazy dudes get to work two hours early?

The Starbucks line is insane, so he hits the Circle K instead and probably saves ten bucks besides. The guy behind the counter nods at him with recognition, or maybe boredom. Cameron responds, just as ambivalent.

He finds yesterday's coffee in the cup holder, dumps the contents onto the ground and tosses the empty into the passenger's foot-well. It won't occur to Elm that he's trashing her car. He's the neat-freak and she's the slob. Then she left the country and he had to be both.

Another way his body expresses missing her. Add it to the list.

He turns wide into the parking lot, makes a fast half-circle and centers himself perfectly into a parking space. He's as far from the store as he can get, right next to the road. There're a few other cars over near the breakfast place. He can smell bacon suddenly and wishes he didn't have a nose. He isn't hung-over, just hungry. He's pretty sure he has granola bars or something in his desk.

Almost through the parking lot and he sees a kid—*a child*—just standing on the sidewalk watching him cross the parking lot.

The kid stands in front of Eyeglass World. The kid stares at him, follows him with their eyes. Cameron gives him (her? It's hard to tell) a small wave and his best *Don't you know it's rude to fucking stare at strangers?* face.

There are sometimes children around, his store even has a section still, and there's a Target a few stores down and a

Dollar Tree on the other side. But he hardly ever sees a child alone, anywhere. Elm says there's supposedly huge bands of roving preteens tearing through Europe, but that's one of the dumb myths she's there to dispel. He'll have to tell her about this creep when they talk tonight.

He deactivates the alarm and relocks the door when he thinks maybe he should call someone. It's so unusual to see children alone in public now. It's been, what, almost twelve years? He'd be surprised if the kid was half that.

He wishes it was like the tags on his car, but he can't ignore this.

He finds the store phone in the charger, grabs it and goes back up front. He sees the kid still standing there, staring into the parking lot.

Is it an emergency, like a 9-1-1 emergency, or should he call the operator? He opts for the latter and hits 0.

The child looks to the right suddenly and Cameron follows their gaze. A woman bursts from the diner with leftover containers in one hand, beckoning for the kid with the other. She calls the child something, but Cameron can't hear it through the glass, curious because he isn't sure what sex the thing is.

The kid takes the woman's hand and they walk to one of the closer cars.

He hangs up on the operator menu.

He watches them go and wants to believe that the woman is the child's mother—its real biological mother—but knows it's impossible. The kid's far too young, six at most. He was always good at guessing ages, child or adult, but that talent is rapidly atrophying. There are fewer kids all the time and the remaining ones are now usually hidden away.

If the kid's five or six and it's been eleven years since

every woman that gives birth—be it natural or cesarean, early or late or right on time, religious or secular, black or white or anything else—dies? Well. Sorry, kiddo.

He hears of women hanging on for an hour or two, but they're never even conscious. The death toll is in the tens of millions now, he saw on a news-ticker in a bar the other day. All the bombast and conspiracies of the early years have fallen away. All the doubters are silent. None of the prayers have been answered.

There's a child, he assumes, an eleven-year-old somewhere who's the last child born who still has her real mom. Maybe they're walking hand in hand like those two.

What's the point of thinking about it? Where's the hope? They can't track the pattern of how it spread or where it started.

It was suddenly everywhere at once.

He remembers these women from right here in his hometown, a year or two after the first cases. There were thirteen of them. That's easy to remember. They'd all had children previously and were from the same church or neighborhood or something. They believed the deaths were all first-time mothers and they were going to band together to prove to the world that there's still hope.

They all died.

None of them lasted five minutes post-birth. None of them ever held or saw the children they gave their lives for. A twenty second Google search would've told them that their hypothesis was wrong, but they had belief instead.

That's something they talked about on their first date. Elm isn't from here, but she was at Notre Dame at the time, a couple hours north.

"I dropped out the next week," she said.

"Really?" he said. "I thought you had your degree?"

She nodded and sipped her beer.

"Mm-hmm. I finished up online. Catholic school?" she said and made a gagging face.

"Right," he said, half-remembering, "they backed those women, or something right? Supported them?"

"At least," Elm spat. "There's some pretty compelling evidence that they put them up to it in the first place and there's definitely proof that they helped them financially and with discrete medical assistance."

"Crazy," he said.

Elm shrugged.

"They've changed so much," Cameron said.

This had been four years ago when they'd first met, and the news-cycle had been full of the Catholic church accepting woman priests and giving a belated thumbs up to contraceptives and a begrudging OK to abortion.

"Eh, they're a business as much as they are a religion," she said. "Can't make money if you're deemed a cult like the Mormons and outlawed. But credit is due, I guess."

He was less cynical about religion than her.

Cameron sets the phone on the counter.

He returns to these conversations when he thinks about her, and it bugs the shit out of him. What about times she laughed or kissed him? Nope. Stupid, pointless conversations about the world around them that they can't change.

He didn't want her to go. Not because it's far and long, but because it's pointless. Why study it? Every brilliant mind on Earth has been thinking about nothing else for nearly a dozen years. There's no solution.

She said, "It has to be Europe. The U.S. is always behind. Especially in attitudes. That's where people are on the forefront, pushing boundaries."

"Like The Thirteen?" he said before he could stop himself. "They were thinking outside the box."

She tensed up, but quickly relaxed.

"Yes, actually," she said, "but with a healthy dose of scientific discipline."

It's all they talk about when they find the time to talk. The five-hour time difference makes it hard. Then it's all he thinks about and that helps no one.

Even the pleasant things, those small miracles, he can't enjoy them because what good are they, really? What do they accomplish?

He thinks about that last kid with her mother still alive and how lucky they must feel, how blessed. How much love that mother has for her child and how she'll live to see her grow up. But their joy is in direct proportion to the rest of humanity's misery. That kid's going to grow up and not be able to share that simple experience of holding her own child's hand as they walk.

Where's the hope in being the last of something?

The phone on the counter rings and his stomach sinks. It isn't even seven yet. The store won't be open for another two hours. He ignores it. It stops, rings again and stops after ten rings. He retreats into the stockroom to avoid the noise.

Then his cell phone buzzes in his pocket and his heart sinks with his stomach. It can be no one else.

He looks at the lock-screen and sees DON'T ANSWER, which is what he replaced Missy's name with after she started contacting him again.

But he wants to feel like shit today, so he answers it.

"Yeah," he says and hears her crying and talking like he hasn't answered the phone. Like he's listening in on a call that's been in progress for minutes.

Missy always talks like this. She speaks as soon as something occurs to her, enters a room mid-sentence so he catches the last words of whatever the hell she was saying and then has to start over, annoyed at him for not having super-hearing or telepathic abilities.

He sighs.

Missy isn't talking like he's been avoiding her calls for months and deleting her voicemails for years without listening to them. She's talking like they're still together, like she's relating a story about something that happened to her at work or asking him to pick up a few things at the grocery. With tears, of course.

"I think I blocked it out, you know?" she says between stifled, showy sobs.

"No, you didn't," Cameron says, irritated, knowing not to engage but unable to stop.

"What?" she asks, thrown off by him responding or even answering the phone in the first place.

"It's bullshit, Missy," he says, breaking another rule and using her nickname and humanizing her. "You never blocked it out. You could never stop thinking about it. That's why I left."

"Yeah, that's why you left," she says, voice souring, turning on him. "You left me for that whore—"

"Melissa," he says, "do not her call her that. I hadn't even met her. I don't know how else to say it so you'll understand. I didn't meet her for years."

"Whatever," she says. "Are you at work? I tried the work number."

"I'm not there," he says, "and don't call me there. That's my job, c'mon."

He hears a rustling, and the line gets quieter, but her voice is venomous.

"You talked me into it," she hisses. "There should be a law or something."

He smiles.

"There are plenty," he says, "but not the way you're thinking. If I tried to talk you out of getting an abortion, I'd get arrested. If I got you pregnant without your consent, I'd go to jail. Should I go on? It'll take a while to make it to Indiana, but I hear on the coasts they're passing laws requiring men to get snipped when they hit eighteen if they can't show—"

"Stop," she says, and he does.

He holds the phone, but she doesn't say anything. He can hear her ragged breathing. He forces himself to not feel bad for her. He knows this is hard on her, but it's hard on everyone. It's hard on him.

"Melissa?" he says. "Missy, you can't call me anymore, OK? This isn't good for you."

He hears her take in a breath.

"What if all of this is our fault?" she asks him for the hundredth time, but says it like it's a secret she's been carrying alone for years.

He sighs. She's in pretty deep. The only good part about her being so low is that it'll take a long time, months probably, before she's this low again.

"Jesus," he says mostly to himself.

She's louder again, suddenly, emboldened somehow.

"We did this," she shouts.

"Melissa, it was thirteen fucking years ago."

"We did this," she repeats even louder. "We killed our child! You did! You made me do it! You made me kill our child! And now all the mothers die! I was a mother and I didn't want it and I took it away from the world! You—"

He hangs up on her.

He wanted to feel bad about himself because of the depression of the last few months, but hit a plateau during her tirade. He feels bad about himself until the feeling turns somewhere else and he starts feeling bad for her.

But she's crazy and he'd rather feel nothing about her at all.


He accomplishes nothing that morning by getting in early. Wasted potential—put it on his fucking tombstone.

He blocks Missy's number again. She doesn't try the store phone again, at least. Alex shows up and says "Hcy, Boss," like always, and he realizes he needs to open the damn store.

He tosses Alex the keys—you open. I need to sit here for a damn minute.

"I'll bring her back in one piece," she says, making car noises as she strolls to the front, unlocks the door and hits the OPEN sign button.

"Move that clearance cart of DVDs onto the sidewalk," he yells from his open office door. "But leave the Blu-ray one inside by the summer reading table."

"Beep-beep," she responds.

His stomach reminds him he's starving, and he finds two granola bars in his desk. He eats both, writes GRANOLA on an orange Post-it note and sticks it in his wallet with a thousand other forgotten Post-its of various hues.

He needs to check numbers from yesterday, put them in, call Cheryl and keep himself from bashing his brains in on the side of his desk while she drones on about whatever the fuck it is she talks about every day. Sales? Units? Christ.

She's always in the car when they talk, regardless of the time or who calls who. He imagines her crisscrossing Indiana, Ohio and Kentucky endlessly. She vomits the same bullshit about improving numbers and nixing overtime to all her managers, but only half-heartedly, as she's perpetually distracted by the road. She comes to the store every week or two and she's on the phone then, too, her arms loaded with a drink, purse, laptop and weird promotional materials. She always gives Cameron a few advanced reader copies like she's been saving them for him, but he suspects she's simply cleaning out her passenger seat.

He has a stack of the fucking things in a bin under his desk.

Snyder blips past the office.

"Hey," Cameron says, craning his neck to see him. The big man turns on a dime and adjusts his walk into a mechanical robot lumber.

"Mr. Washington, sir," he says in a robotic monotone. His arms are bent ninety degrees and his hands stick straight out with fingers extended and thumbs pointing up. He moves his arms back and forth slowly, hugging them close to his body. He looks straight ahead when he robot speaks to Cameron, over his head. "I am not here yet."

Cameron looks around the room suspiciously. Same shit, every day.

"Then how come I can see you?"

"Adrienne had to drop me off early," he says dropping the android act, leaning into the doorframe.

"Clock in," Cameron says. "You can get a jump on the scanning before the unwashed masses arrive."

"Zombies," Snyder says.

"What?"

"The customers. Zombies," he says. "Kirk came up with it, I think."

Cameron leans back in his shitty office chair.

"Huh," he says. "Seems a little too obvious. Whatever. You can leave early if you start working now."

He salutes. Cameron hears the time clock beep from next to the back door.

With two of them here, he can duck out for a minute. Find some excuse.

He speed-dials Cheryl on speaker. She answers at once, wind tearing through her car and rasping over her car phone microphone.

"Cameron," she says.

"Hey," he says. "Can we do our call this afternoon? I got a bunch of shit to take care of this morning."

Keep it vague, come up with specifics later. She probably won't even ask.

"Yeah, sure," she says. "Better for me anyway. I have to pick up the kids."

"What?" he says.

"My children?" she says. "Gotta pick them up, dentist, all that fun stuff."

"Right," he says, and they hang up.

Cheryl has kids? Did he know that? It sort of shatters his weird road-warrior vision of her. Existing only in the car and gas stations, eating fast-food, no home, just zipping around, bouncing from store to store.

Kids. Huh.

He gets up and goes out. He nods and says good morning to a couple regulars that have already wandered in to check the new arrival vinyl bins or the back-issue comic boxes.

Alex is behind the buy counter scanning a stack of graphic

novels.

"Anything good?" he asks, peeking.

She glances around for whoever brought them in.

"Meh," she says.

"I'm gonna pop out for a minute or two," he says, coming up with a lie on the spot. "We need toilet paper and a few other things."

"Yup," she says, not breaking her stride. So the boss needs to walk around to keep from murdering everyone and himself. That's the way it is.

He checks his pockets for the store credit card and, more importantly, his vape-pen.

He exits right out of the store, even though Target's in the other direction. He wants to circle behind the shopping center and come up between Target and—what's over there? A mattress store? —and go in that way because it takes longer.

He rounds the corner. He stares at the ground as he walks to avoid eye contact if anybody's back here. He hates getting drawn into small talk.

He hears something as he passes a dumpster, and reflexively his eyes dart towards the sound. He sees tiny shoes out of the corner of his eye, moving around behind the dumpster. Children's shoes.

"Hey," he says and stops. He takes a step back and there's nothing there. He walks behind the dumpster and still nothing. No child. He looks beneath and around the dumpster. It's shut and locked. There's nobody back here. A back door nearby slams and a kitchen worker Cameron sort of recognizes comes out with a bag of trash. He gives Cameron a surprised *Are you dumpster diving, Homie?* look. Cameron holds up his vape-pen in his palm with a shush. The dude smiles and nods and Cameron gets out of there. He looks at the dude's feet as he leaves, but they aren't the shoes he glimpsed. Those were kid's shoes—chunky, bright and tied all wrong.

He shakes his head and vapes more. Idiot, you're just imagining it. That kid this morning freaked you out more than you realize. You miss Elm so much and all this shit is tied together. You can't think about one without worrying about the other. A call from The Psycho probably didn't help.

"It's in your head," he says aloud, as if his cats were here.

He doesn't leave early from work. He even stays a little late to avoid rush hour. That's what he tells himself, anyway. But he has to go home sometime.

He stops by the barbeque place a few blocks from his house. Most of the items are crossed off, but a few things are left. He gets an order of sausage jalapeño poppers and half a smoked chicken with potato salad.

He realizes when he gets back into Elm's car that he forgot his coffee this morning, only taking a few sips before he got to work and abandoned the rest of it in the cup holder all day. He never missed it, not once, all day.

Seeing it sit there with a little drop of evaporated coffee on the lid depresses him beyond measure to comprehend.

He feels so completely shitty about himself in that moment that it's almost impossible to go on, impossible to not just abandon the car there, leave the door ajar, the sack of barbeque take-out containers on the roof and just walk towards the horizon until he disappears or drowns in the nearby river or falls to pieces or dies of starvation.

After a moment he gets into the car and drives home, not finding the will to live, necessarily, but not the motivation to die either.

The barbeque smells incredible and he eats it at the

kitchen counter, too excited to make it to the couch and waste precious seconds finding something to watch in place of company. He plans to eat half of it and take the rest for work tomorrow but after a few bites that clearly isn't going to happen. He usually skips lunch anyway, not for time's sake, but out of the simmering low-level depression. The same thing making him forgetful, lazy, and sloppy.

He finishes eating, checks the time, sweeps the trash into a garbage bag, takes it straight outside and leaves the door cracked. He knows the cats aren't even curious about the outside world.

He pushes, kicks and throws the recyclables into the other bin. He looks up from bending over to find a beer bottle that got away from him, and sees a child standing near the end of his driveway.

He blinks and half-jumps out of his skin.

In a flash, the child reveals himself to be one of the Cuban teenagers from two doors down. He nods at Cameron, picks up a Frisbee from the street, whips it in the direction of his house and trots away.

Cameron stares after him like a creep and becomes self-conscience even though nobody else is out here. He goes back inside and locks the door.

He picks up other shit around the house, mostly by hiding it behind or under something else. He checks on the cats to confirm their status as living. He finds them in the bedroom on the bed at opposite corners, as far from each other as they can be and still be on the same piece of furniture. They glare at each other and flip their tails around, each angry that the other one exists.

"Monsters," he says. "Behave."

He opens the laptop on the coffee table, plugs it in and

situates it for a good, cleanish view of the house. He picks a burnt CD at random from a stack near the stereo and puts some music on at low volume so he will seem more like a human when Elm calls. He opts for a sparkling water over a beer. She thinks he drinks too much since she's been gone. This is entirely correct.

He sits on the couch in front of the laptop and waits for her call.

He wakes with a start two hours later, sitting on the couch, sparkling water tipping from his hand into his lap with the cap thankfully still on. The CD player lights blip and dance across the screen. Whatever he listened to is long over.

He checks the Skype and nothing. No missed calls.

He checks the time. It's after two in Amsterdam. Too late to call now.

He finds his phone and has a couple texts from her in that weird international app they use.

She went out with some other researchers. She was sorry it was last minute and could they talk tomorrow? Then a goodnight one a little later.

He responds, yeah tomorrow's fine and he fell asleep after dinner and he sends her a heart emoji and a smiley face one or something similar a human being would send another human being in the real world even though it doesn't feel like it, even though it feels like he's in some malicious experiment and Elm isn't real anymore and the texts are generated by some algorithm and the phone calls are reconstructed out of old recordings of things once said.

He feels like the only person in the whole world when he hasn't talked to her in a while. When he has a couple days off in a row and he doesn't leave the house, when he realizes he hasn't talked to anyone, just yammered at the cats, it's like the world is his little house and he wants to watch TV at moments like that, like the news or something, like tune into a channel with something happening right now, something that's outside of him and his little bubble, but he doesn't have TV anymore, hasn't had it for years, not in the way he used to. He has Netflix and Hulu and one or two other streaming services, but that's all removed from the current timeframe. It isn't happening right now—you don't turn it on and one thing's ending or there's canned laughter and you've missed the joke and you'll just have to wonder or be let down by it years later in reruns. You can watch everything now, but nothing really sticks, and nothing is now. It's all old, decades old sometimes. Look, right there, under the Just Added banner: *Action!* starring Jay Mohr, a show he remembers from college that lasted half a season or so and it'll sit there for a few years and people will watch it and go, "Huh, wonder when they're making more of that?" Never. Those six episodes are twenty years old, but none of that means anything. The radio. Maybe he can listen to the radio. He switches to the tuner, but when did he have an antenna for this thing, when's the last time he listened to terrestrial radio? In his car he has CDs, in a rental, it's satellite, at the store it's whatever that one station he's allowed to use or a CD here and there when he's sure nobody's paying attention or dropping by any time soon. He tries tuning the radio, tries remembering call numbers, rifles through old jingles in the cobwebby corners of his mind, blips over static, more static, and weird artifact-like noises coming through, songs that sound like they're playing under glass. He gets freaked out and turns it off. Thinks about it a minute more, then unplugs it, afraid the strange ghost radio can leak out and make his world more unreal.

The internet, Google News, anything. But how real is any

of that? If his girlfriend's a couple lines of code responding to him here, how hard is it to fake an active, hostile world outside of his experience?

He sits on the couch with his eyes closed. Where do you go from here? What's the next logical step? How real is he? How likely, how fully realized, is his back story, his dull-ass life? All of this just to convince him that the world's real, is still out there, so he can convince himself that he's real, too.

A car horn blaps somewhere nearby, and he hears another one screech by even closer and the spell is broken and he's the same. Just depressed and missing Elm and not really having anything else in his life besides dumb work.

He tucks his legs up onto the couch, flails around for a throw blanket and goes to sleep right there, leaving the laptop open in case she calls.

She doesn't.

The next day's so like the previous, it barely deserves a mention.

Cameron gives it almost no thought and the day rolls by like fog as he barely notices.

At least he sees no children standing alone with far-off looks in their eyes.

He clears the table that evening, tacos instead of barbeque, and tidies up again, marveling briefly at how messy the house can become in twenty-four hours when it's only him and the cats and he's gone nearly ten hours a day and asleep for another seven.

He puts on a different random CD, opens the laptop, checks the battery and sits on the couch.

Elm calls in less than five minutes. There she is—half a

world away, but he sees her, and it is her. No apocalyptic thoughts. He feels himself smiling.

They spend a couple minutes stepping on each others words, saying What? a lot and awkwardly waiting for the other to say something while the video lags and makes their expressions weird impressionistic versions of human emotions. But they find the rhythm of it, falling comfortably into the pattern.

"I, uh, had some weirdness yesterday," he says, not wanting to bring up children, which always derails their talks, but running out of shit to say. The way she's glancing down at the clock on her laptop, she'll try to hang up soon and he just wants to look at her for as long as he can.

"I saw a child," he says. "Or children, but separately. At different times."

She perks up noticeably, probably more amazed that he's bringing up children than whatever mundane story he's about to share.

"I got to the store," he continues, "a little early—"

"How early?" she interrupts. "You work too much."

"Just a little early, Dad," he says, and she flips him off but with a smile.

He tells her about the creepy kid in the morning watching him in the parking lot, the feet he knows he saw in the back and, reluctantly, how he thought a Cuban teen down the block was another lost mystery child.

"I'm proud of you," she says.

"For what?" he spits, more out of shock than disgust, but there's a fair amount of that too. Why would anyone anywhere be proud of him for anything?

"For not smoking, dummy," she says. "It has to be hard without me there."

"If you could text me some gentle nagging about it throughout the day that would be a big help," he says

She laughs.

"And for calling about a lost child. I mean, you were going to anyway," she says.

"It's the thought that counts," Cameron says.

She nods.

"It is," she says. "Missing children, instances of people spotting them, is way down. The numbers don't add up. It's certainly weird to see them alone now, after everything. Some states are ratifying some measures to make it a crime if you don't do the right thing, kind of the reverse of that kidnapping thing."

Cameron's vaguely aware that kidnapping a child is a capitol federal crime. It doesn't seem right to him. A kid's only parent put to death for taking them?

"Anyway," Elm says, and he realizes he's missed whatever she's been telling him. "I don't want to say that it was all in your head…"

"But I've gone insane?" he ventures.

"No," she says. "but the dumpster one? Just the shoes? I dunno, it's kind of coming up a lot, or things similar anyway."

"So mass hysteria," he says and puts his palm to the screen when she begins to protest. "I know I'm not crazy and I know I didn't see a kid back there."

He shrugs.

"I'm just tired, working too much and as fucked up by this thing as anyone," he says. "And I miss you. Like crazy, for sure."

"I miss you, too," she says.

He worries he's pushed too far into the maudlin.

But she blinks a few times, wipes at her eyes once and

says, "You wanna fool around?"

"God, yes," he says and adjusts the screen, taking off his shirt. She's doing the same. "Real quick: How do I hide the little screen of me? If I see myself doing that again…"

The next morning, after a couple employees arrive, Cameron takes his usual bogus errands walk around the shopping center. His employees think it's about vaping, but he does that in his office when he's alone. It's about getting out of the store for a damn minute.

He goes the opposite way this morning, around the Target side, cuts between the Dollar Tree and that Subway he always forgets is there.

He notices that the dumpster where he'd imagined seeing a child's shoe scurrying away is not as flush with the back wall of the shopping center as it appears when you approach it from the other direction. It's angled slightly to create a gap. There's a notch in the wall right behind it, like a half-door size. It's shallow, only two feet deep at most, and the same building-block gray of the rest of the structure. There are drag or push marks on the ground where someone shoved the dumpster. Six inches, maybe, so someone small enough can squeeze back there. He's thinking maybe he did see someone when he hears a scrape behind him. The sound of shoes coming up short.

A child stands there, a seven- or eight-year-old. A little girl with short hair, dirty clothes and bright chunky children's sneakers.

"Hey," he says. He sees her eyes dart around looking for an escape. "Wait. Are you OK? Are you lost or something?"

Elm always laughs at the way he talks to children, in his normal voice with his normal words. "I dunno," he'd say.

"They're just smaller people."

The kid doesn't run. Maybe she finds his way of speaking to her different enough from whoever it is she's run away from.

"Do you have any food?" she asks, gruff sounding or trying to be, anyway.

"No," he says, checking his pockets, even though he knows he doesn't have any. Who has food in their pockets? Maybe he's just stalling for time.

"Do you need me to get you food?" he asks.

She nods OK with one quick jerk of her head.

"Do you want to go to that diner?" he asks, hooks a thumb back in the direction of the place and takes a tentative step forward.

She's having none of that and leaps back into a crouching position like a runner preparing for the start pistol.

He puts his hands up, palms out, in surrender and takes a step back retreating into his original position.

"OK," he says. "Alright. I won't make you do anything or go anywhere."

She relents her stance a little.

"I'll go get you something and bring it back here," he offers.

That quick sharp nod again.

He turns towards a gap in between businesses. She stops him.

"Put it on the curb over there," she says and points. "You won't see me."

It's his turn to nod. He rounds the corner, hears her move somewhere back there as her shoes scrape and scurry.

He veers off to the Subway he remembers exists. They'll be faster and designed for portability more than the diner.

The kid's starving and that's the only time to eat Subway.

There are no customers and one employee who shouts something from the back when he hears Cameron set off the doorbell, but the dude emerges promptly, drying his hands.

"Sup, man," the guy says, exuding chillness like only a twenty-something fast food worker can. "You gonna get a sandwich?"

"Yeah?" Cameron says, confusion clearly in his voice.

The dude nods and slips on a pair of transparent gloves.

"Cool," he says "didn't want to waste a pair if not. Lots of people just get cookies for breakfast."

"Gross," Cameron says.

"No judgments here, man," the dude says, because of course he does.

Cameron realizes he has no idea what kids eat. He gets a foot-long turkey and bacon on white with all the veggies. She can pick those off if there's something she doesn't like.

"Mayo or anything?" the dude asks.

"No," he says, "well, do you have packets? I'm going to eat it later."

"Sure," he says. "Mustard, too?"

He slides it all into a bag with the Doritos Cameron picks out and rings it up with two bottles of water.

"You want some cookies?" the dude asks. "Since you're eating it later."

Cameron agrees to two chocolate chip, puts it on his debit card and leaves.

He glances around nervously as he walks back to the dumpster but it's before ten in the morning. Another hour before it's lousy with customers.

He places the weird cylindrical bag used only by paperboys and low-end sandwich chains on the curb and sets the water bottles on the ground next to it. He stands there a second, feeling foolish.

"I can bring more food tonight," he says. "But I'm not just going to buy shit and put it on the ground, hoping you're still around. OK? I'll be back around seven. I'm in the bookstore, kid. If you need anything. I'm Cameron."

He walks away. He's tempted to pretend to walk away but hang back.

She's probably too smart for that.

Most of his days go by quickly, a benefit of not paying attention to what's around you. Work days, specifically after lunch hours, seem to fly by. It's only at home with nothing to busy himself with when time crawls by.

Except today, of course.

Today, the hours don't just crawl—they inch. The seconds tick one at a time, each frozen there as an epoch with a beginning, middle and end. He feels high. It's why he never smokes weed. He micro-sleeps on weed, blinks in and out of consciousness, a dreamless jerkiness that stretches the minutes excruciatingly.

He tried to explain this to Elm once, which didn't work because he was high while trying to explain it.

Instead he said, "My brain's not connected to my brain."

She still gives him shit about that even after he explained more thoroughly the following day.

He checks his phone again. This time, his brain isn't connected to time.

Lunch happens, but he doesn't eat anything. He sits at his desk and stares into the middle distance for most of an hour, then it's back to the floor where he's just as useless.

"Did you have Subway for lunch?" Alex asks him in the

early afternoon.

"What?" he says, and tries to act casual. "How'd you know that?"

She wrinkles her nose.

"You stink like bread," she says. "Gag."

It's easily the most interesting thing that happens all afternoon.

To everyone's surprise, including himself, Cameron leaves on time from work, ducking out right at six.

He sticks his head behind the stores, but doesn't see the kid anywhere. Well, she's still got an hour to show. The Subway is long gone. He spies what could be the remains of discarded tomatoes near the curb and makes a mental note: No tomatoes. Easy to remember—Elm has the same aversion.

"They feel like chewing my own tongue," she's said.

He stops home, checks on the cats and heads back out for errands. He crosses a few to-do items off a month's old list. He remembers to haul the trash/recyclables to the curb rather than waking in a panic upon hearing the trucks in the morning.

He stops by the bank drive-up and takes care of some things at the ATM. He considers getting some money out for the kid, but nixes it. When he finally convinces her to go home or to the cops, food they'll understand, but not cash.

He picks up a few cleaning supplies and then it's a quarter till, so he hits up the McDonald's drive-thru. He orders a Big Mac for himself and gets her two Small Meals.

Cameron feels an intense wave of depression knock him down. When did they drop the Happy Meal name?

He drives back to the shopping center and parks in the loading zone off to the side. All kids like McDonald's, right?

When he gets out of the car, he remembers that he's supposed to make sure she's there before he gets the food, but he sees a flash of her back there.

"It's just me," he says. "Cheeseburgers."

She comes out of the shadows, sees the bag in his hand and laughs a little.

"What?" he asks.

"I thought you said, 'it's me, Cheeseburgers' like that was your nickname or something," she giggles.

She takes a Happy Meal—marketing be damned—from him and sits on the curb. Her giggle and the way she sits pulling food out of the bag—she's just a normal, lost, scared kid without a mother. They all are. Cameron hasn't spent any time with any of the Orphans, but Elm has and says it's weird how they're just children. Everything else is projected onto them. They know nothing of horror yet. Well, looking at her dirty clothes and messy hair, some of them might.

But, right now, she's just a normal kid sitting on the ground eating a tiny, flat cheeseburger.

He sits down a ways from her but sees her tense as her eyes measure the distance between them.

He takes his Big Mac out, eats it and, unsure of when he's last washed his hands, wishes it came in a wrapper instead of a box.

He opts to not imagine how dirty the kid's hands are.

"There's another one in there for you," he says, and points the bag. "If you're still hungry. Or you can save it for later."

She chews thoughtfully.

"Ain't going to try and talk me into coming with you?" she says while shoveling fries into her mouth. "Get in your car? Maybe you're not a pervert."

He looks shocked briefly, then takes another bite.

"It depresses me that you even know that word," he says. "If you want help, I can walk with you into any of these stores and we can call the police.”

“No cops,” she says adamantly.

He laughs at her and she looks sideways at him.

“Sorry,” he says, biting off more chuckles. “But how old are you? You sound like a bank robber on the lam.”

“Lamb?” she asks.

“L-A-M. It means on the run from the law,” he says.

She nods and files it away for later use.

“Seriously, what are you, four?” he asks, intentionally low-balling her age.

“I’m almost seven,” she says, instantly falling for it.

She’s one of the Orphans, as if there was any doubt. He thought maybe she was small for her age. She sounds older than she looks. He’s heard about a few kids born later with birth mothers still alive but it’s always in far-off, remote places and other countries. Always vague. Urban legends.

That’s what’s so hard. Tragedy touches everyone. Every family’s affected. Without digging too deeply, he thinks of a dozen women he’s known who died and that’s not considering the children, husbands or partners, parents and siblings left behind. It goes further. How many women does he know? How many potential mothers will never get the chance, or if they do, will die for their child?

He looks at the kid and flashes on a story from a couple months ago. A father on trial for raping his daughter. The man’s defense was that the Orphans can reproduce without complications or death. He was beginning the repopulation of the earth and that isn’t a crime or a sin—where did Adam and Eve’s grandchildren come from if it was?

His daughter was ten years old.

Sadness presses down on Cameron. He finds it impossible to swallow. Feeling bad for someone besides himself feels better and worse all at once. Why has this little girl run away from home? What horrible shit happened to her? What terrors wait for her in the future?

She catches him staring at her.

She balls up the wrappers and drops them in the empty sack. She stands up and rubs her hands on her pants, the fronts of which have already become slick and shiny with grime. How long has she been out here? Two days, three?

"Hope," she says.

He blinks at her.

"My name," she says, "my name's Hope."

"Fucking terrible," he says, not able to stop himself. "That is one sick joke."

She sighs, nods and turns away into the darkness. He sees the gleam of tears on her eyes even in the shadows. She's simultaneously older and younger in the moment. The weight of everything shrinks and expands her simultaneously.

A kid who never gets to be a kid at all.

"My aunt named me," she says. "Says she found something from my mom that said that's what she wanted my name to be. But I don't know. Never met my dad. He was killed by the cops the day I was born. Don't like cops."

"I understand that," Cameron says. "Do you know anything else about your parents?"

She shakes her head no, but doesn't appear to be listening.

"I'm sorry, Hope," he says, after a minute in silence, a breeze rustling the empty McDonald's bag. "I'm sorry you never got to meet your parents. I'm sorry your aunt named you that and that I immediately crapped on it when you told me. I don't think she meant anything by it, kid. Back then, we thought things would get better."

"She still does," Hope says. "She checks the paper every

morning, falls asleep watching the news every night."

Cameron lets out a long breath.

"She's not the only one," he says. "My girlfriend's in another country studying, trying to learn everything she can about it, with no end goal. If there's no solution, what good is obsessing over the problem?"

She stands up.

"I'm gonna go," she says. "Thanks for the food."

"Are you going home?" he asks.

She shrugs.

"Sometime," she says. "I've got places I can go."

"Your little nook behind the dumpster?" Cameron asks. "Doesn't look like much to sleep in. I can give you a ride home, kid. Or we can call your aunt and I'll sit here with you until she arrives."

She wrinkles her nose.

"No thanks. See you later, Cameron," she says.

She heads off, away from the shopping center and into the grass and trees behind. What's beyond that? An apartment complex, maybe? It's hard to remember—everything blurs when he drives right past the same shit every day.

He calls after her. She's already out of sight among the overgrown grass. She doesn't respond, but he hears her stop moving in the grass.

"You want breakfast tomorrow?" he asks.

No response.

"I'll bring breakfast," he says.

Silence for a minute, then a rustling away. Not a confirmation, but he thinks she'll be there.

Cameron wakes early and kind of sleepwalks through his morning routine. He thinks real breakfast food this morning and not that Subway garbage. Maybe breakfast burritos?

He drives a different way to work, but when he gets within sight of the Mexican place he changes his mind. He drives past it, pulls up on the shoulder and puts his hazards on.

He takes his phone from his pocket and dials.

He watches. He has to. He owes her that, to sit in his car and watch as the cops scoop her up.

It's his day off, so he parks in a weird spot and hopes no one sees his car.

The dispatcher transferred him to a detective and he'd told her the whole thing, copping to the McDonald's and the sandwich earlier in day, and told her that Hope ran off with the food before he had chance to call it in.

"Why didn't you call last night?" the detective asked.

"I didn't know where she went," he said. Which is mostly true. "I didn't want to waste your time. She's back there now, so you can grab her."

A few more questions and she took down his info as dispatch had.

"You working today?" she asked.

"I'm off, but I can meet you over there," he said.

"All right. We'll grab her," she said, "and I'll meet you at your store, I dunno, quarter after 8?"

"Sure," he said, and they hung up.

Now he sits in his car on the edge of the parking lot and watches them walk her out from behind the buildings. She comes willingly, no tears that Cameron sees, but her jaw's set hard and he's sure she's not talking. She looks filthier and smaller in the morning light.

He picks out the detective he talked to. There are only two police not in uniform and the other is a middle-aged guy with a hefty paunch. The detective's about his age with her hair pulled back into a tight ponytail. It's always weird to meet people his own age with serious jobs. He's worked in restaurants and retail his whole life, from teenager until now in his late thirties. It feels childish.

She's bent over, talking to Hope in the backseat of one of the cruisers. She straightens, shuts the door and says something to officers in the front. They take off slowly. Hope's too short for him to see her through the window. The detective talks to her partner for a minute, then he screeches away, and she stands there in the parking lot, checking her phone.

He exits his car and walks over to her.

She becomes aware of someone approaching and repositions slightly without looking in his direction.

"Detective Bollinger?" he says when he steps onto the curb. He sticks his hand out. "Cameron Washington."

She shakes it while appraising him casually.

"You watch from your car?" she asks and looks back into the parking lot.

"Yeah," he admits.

"Well, thanks for waiting until she was gone," she says. "One second."

They stand there awkwardly for a second as she makes a few notes into her phone. She puts it away, smiles at him and looks at him for the first time.

"She hasn't told us anything, but you gave us her name, and a woman called in the day before yesterday to report her missing, so I think we'll wrap this up pretty cleanly," she says.

Cameron lets out a long sigh.

"That's good" he says. "I hope she'll be OK."

Bollinger shrugs. *Are any of them going to be OK?*

Cameron hooks a thumb over his shoulder.

"You wanna talk in the store?" he asks. "I've got a little office in the back and it's not open for another forty minutes or so."

"You got coffee back there?" she asks.

"No," he says and feels suddenly inadequate. That feeling of being a child talking to a real adult magnifies. Why doesn't he have a coffee maker back there? How much money would that save? How many half-drunk and forgotten Starbucks does he leave in his car every week?

She points to the diner, which is slow between the pre-work breakfast crowd and the early lunch one.

"Let's go there," she says and walks briskly in that direction.

He follows her, trotting to keep up. She breezes right past the hostess stand and sits in a booth with her back to the wall, well away from any other patrons. She wears her badge on a chain around her neck and seems at ease going where she pleases. She removes her sunglasses once she sits down and is friendly with the waitress when she comes over for drink orders.

"Have you had breakfast?" she asks him, and when he shakes his head no tells him to eat. He orders two eggs and toast, his brilliant breakfast burrito idea long forgotten. She orders a croissant and yogurt.

"I already ate one breakfast today," she explains. "Well, yesterday, but I'm working a swing-double, so I haven't been to sleep yet. When your day begins and ends with breakfast…I dunno. There should be a word for that."

"Overlong?" Cam tries.

They sip coffee and breakfast arrives with lightning efficiency. He figures she always receives service like this.

Badge visible or not.

They eat mostly in silence. Cameron forces his food down, forces himself not to pick at it and move it around on the plate. He doesn't need any more of feeling inadequate. He does OK and even eats his toast crust.

She finishes eating first, but doesn't rush him or launch into questions while he still has mouthfuls of food. She sits back and scans the room calmly or watches him, not smiling exactly, but not sour-faced either. She has kind eyes and soft features, actually, and Cameron supposes that she pulls her hair back tightly and goes sans makeup to harden her features. She taps a thin wedding band on the Formica tabletop.

"Tell me the story again," she says as he sips the last of his coffee. She signals the waitress for more.

So he tells her and tells it straight, all of it. Her phone's in front of her where her plate had been, but she doesn't take notes or record him. She asks no questions as he talks. She watches him intently and listens closely. Her hands are folded on the table in front of her, when not touching the hair near her temples absently. If it's a tell of some sort, Cameron doesn't know what it tells.

He finishes and adds creamer to his cup. The waitress won't let it get close to empty. He changes his mind and pushes the mug out of easy reach. How many has he had? Three? Four? He's going to get the shakes if he doesn't stop.

"And then here we are," she says and spreads her hands to encompass the table, or maybe the whole diner. He feels a little mocked or at least parroted—he talks expressively with his hands. She seems too controlled for that.

"You didn't tell me all of this on the phone because," she says and pauses briefly, but he doesn't have the impression he's supposed to fill it in. It's more like she is organizing her thoughts. "Because time was a factor, you wanted us to scoop up the kid before she bolted again."

He shrugs.

"I think you might be leading the witness," he says.

She smiles, and her posture relaxes a notch.

"You watch too much TV," she says.

"I really don't," he says.

"Well, then you read too many books," she says.

He concedes the point.

"Look, I don't give a shit why you told me what you told me on the phone, and why you came clean now," she says. "We got the kid and that's the thing."

Her phone lights up, she glances at it and swipes something away.

"Her aunt's there already," she says. "She'll be home and probably grounded within the hour."

Cameron sits back in his chair, aware that he'd been leaning preposterously forward on the edge of his seat.

"She's just scared," he says. "She acts angry because she's so scared, because everything is starting to sink in. She's beginning to comprehend how fucking terrifying everything is."

"Then she's smart," Bollinger says.

"Yeah, of course," he says, but feels like she's not quite getting it. "She doesn't need to be punished is what I mean."

She puts a hand up, palm out.

"I get it, Cameron," she says. "But our part's over."

He sips his coffee, realizes what he's doing and nearly drops it. How the fuck did the mug get back in front of him? He opts for his water instead.

"Will you take that fucking thing away from me?" he asks, eyeing the coffee.

She smirks and pulls it nearly to the edge of her side of the table. She stands up and he begins to stand as well, but she puts a hand on his shoulder and eases him back down.

"I'm not gonna use your name or anything in the report I have to pass on to the DPEA," she says. "Things will work faster this way if I just leave you out of it. Can I make a suggestion?"

"Sure," he says.

"Sit here for a minute," she says, "make yourself an easy goal, like drink a whole glass of water before you can leave the restaurant. It'll give you a smidgen of control. Then probably don't go home. You seem like a guy that can sulk. Do you have any immediate pressing concerns that can't wait a couple hours? Good. Go to the movies. Hell, see two. Your mind needs escape, so let it."

"OK," he says.

She looks at him for a minute, then slips her card onto the table in front of him. She puts her sunglasses back on, gives him a single curt nod and leaves.

He hears her argue with the cashier up front—they don't want to charge her for breakfast, but she insists. He hears the door jingle a moment later and she's gone.

He slowly sips his water and stares out the window as his feelings dial down. He checks his phone. An "I miss you" text from Elm. No emails that aren't spam. He checks the movie times of the theater in the mall across the street and picks one out that starts in twenty minutes. He finishes his water, uses the diner's restroom, thanks them and leaves. The staff stares strangely at him, as if he's some wanton criminal, but since the cop didn't think so, maybe fuck off.

He stops at the Dollar Tree and grabs a box of theater candy because why not if he's going to blow the late morning and early afternoon watching a movie he has only a vague interest in.

He stops at the store in case it's on fire, but everybody's occupied with customers. It's nice out so he considers leaving his car and walking over to the mall, but doesn't. He'd be pissed later when he just wants to get home.

He parks in the garage and secrets his candy before heading in. He dodges mall walkers and teenagers, even though he's pretty sure it's a school day. It's the latest Marvel movie, but at least a month old so it's just him and two other weirdoes. The movie's familiar, pretty and that's about it. He's probably a dozen sequels behind at this point, but it doesn't seem to matter, although a few cameos blow right over his head. The plot's overly familiar, hits all the normal beats, the villains are forgettable, but he enjoys it. It gives him nothing to think about, which is what he needs. The eye candy ends and Cameron splits, leaving the weirdoes who stay for some post-credit nonsense.

Passing the food court, he realizes the Mike and Ike's did nothing to fill his stomach. He grabs a plate of hot deliciousness from the Döner Kabob place. Some type of seared meat in sauce over rice and vegetables. He points at the picture and the guy prepares it for him—no language barrier when neither man speaks.

He finishes it with a Diet Coke and decides, fuck it. See another movie.

After the enjoyable hangout-vibe of charming super-dudes trading quips, he could use Liam Neeson glowering and shooting some fuckers.

He pops back into the theater. The girl at the counter doesn't recognize him or doesn't give a shit. She off-handedly waves in the direction of his theater and doesn't bother him about his outside drink.

He sprawls out in the theater like he lives there—no company this time.

He likes this one too, turns his mind off to the obvious plot and lets the progression surprise him.

When he leaves the theater an hour and a half later, he makes a commitment to see more movies at this poorly attended throw-back theater. Jesus, the matinees are still five bucks.

He drives straight home, eager to practice his Liam voice on the monsters, blinking at the sun and wondering where the hell his sunglasses went.

He sees her feet sticking out from the porch, hidden from the street by the bushes, but clear from the driveway.

If the mail carrier had come by today, they would've saved him the trouble of finding her body, but that's not how it happened.

He thinks at first—impossibly he knows—that they're Hope's feet, even though they're clearly a grown woman's. Besides the fact that they're there at all, there's something else wrong with the way the feet lie there. They stick out wrong like they're two separate feet and not a pair belonging to the same person. He imagines some horribly impractical contortion nightmare scenario as to what the rest of the body will look like. He gets out of the car anyway.

It's Missy and she looks normal, considering, as if she's napping on his porch. Her eyes are shut, and something trickles from her mouth that's not drool. Even her feet take on a normal appearance now that he can see the rest of her. The angles are no longer strange, like an optical illusion that's been explained and spoiled forever.

• • •

He has Detective Bollinger's card, so he calls her immediately after calling 9-1-1. She arrives thirty minutes after the regular cops and they defer to her.

She takes him inside and sits him on his couch.

"I took your advice," he says. "Went to the movies."

She nods.

"Ex-girlfriend?" she asks.

"Yeah, from way back," he says. "She called me a couple days ago, all upset. We had an abortion years ago and after, well after all the mothers started dying…"

"She blamed you? Herself? Seen it a ton, sadly," she says.

"I tried to tell her how stupid it was. I wasn't nice to her the last time we spoke," Cameron says.

"She try to call you since?" Bollinger asks.

"I dunno," he says. "I blocked her number again."

She sticks her hand out. He unlocks his phone and hands it to her.

"Yeah," she says after a minute. "There's a dozen voice messages in the blocked folder. I'm gonna need this for a bit. You don't want to listen anyway."

"No, I do not," he says.

She slips it into a paper envelope and into her pocket. She says, "I'll get you a receipt."

He sits there and stares into his hands that lie limply in his lap.

"She probably texted you, too, but I don't know how to recover those," she says. "Maybe our I.T. guy does."

Cameron bobs his head that doesn't feel like his head. He feels far away.

"She didn't text," he hears someone saying with his voice. He feels his mouth muscles move and it sounds like him, but that's impossible. How can he speak if he can't move? How can he talk if he can't think?  "She was weird about texting, thought it was rude somehow."

The room is silent for a moment.

"She was sick," the voice that's his voice and not his voice continues. "A long time but wouldn't get help. She didn't want to get better. After a while, I just wanted…I just wanted her to go away." The voice becomes a whisper at the end.

Bollinger doesn't move or say anything for a few minutes and Cameron starts to feel unreal again. Not the only person in the world this time, but a ghost. She puts a hand on his shoulder and the feeling evaporates. The ghost dissipates, on to its final reward.

She says nice things to him. Comforting, practiced things she learned over time on the job. They make sense and he believes them. They probably help. If his brain was connected to his brain he might be receptive to all the wonderful, true things she says. They do sink in, a little. And she doesn't seem to mind that he kind of just sits there, nods and moves his mouth every so often.

She asks if he has ticket stubs or receipts for the movies and food he bought. She asks this in an apologetic way that says this is a formality—I'm not asking but somebody later may ask. Cameron doesn't mind and understands she has to and nothing more. He finds the receipts in his pockets, crumpled up under his keys, and hands them to her. She puts those in another paper envelope. He thinks about all the times he's not kept receipts or thrown them out immediately upon being handed one. Did some part of him know, somehow, that he would need all these today?

He shrugs inwardly. He'd paid for everything on his credit card anyway.

"I didn't see any blood," he says.

Bollinger nods.

"She took something," she says. "There's something around her mouth. And there is a little blood, actually, on her palms."

"Her palms?" Cameron asks, the strangeness snaps him out of it a little.

"Yeah, she could have coughed some up," she says.

"Jesus," he says.

"Her hands are really dirty though…how long have you had that security door?" she asks.

"The metal screen door thing? The landlord put it in," he pauses and searches his memory, "Two months ago, maybe? There were some break-ins in the neighborhood, one of his other houses got hit, so he installed these in all the rest. Kind of ugly, but it's his house, I guess."

"So the door wasn't installed the last time Melissa was here?" she asks.

"I didn't even know she knew where I lived," he says.

She finishes making a few notes in her phone and puts it away.

"She'd probably been by before, just to see, you know in her mind, that was it, just to see where you lived, just to know," she says. "I don't think it's a coincidence that she did this on your day off either. She probably thought you'd be home or would be returning soon. She hadn't planned for the security door and had maybe taken whatever it was that she took before she got here, then couldn't get inside. Bloodied her hands up trying to pry that thing loose."

Cameron sits up straighter, shakes off the last of the fog.

"She saw my car here and not Elm's," he says. "Jesus. She thought I was home by myself."

"Is that your roommate?" Bollinger asks. She gets her

phone back out.

Cameron shakes his head.

"My girlfriend. She's been out of the country for six months. Studying the Mothers and Orphans in Europe. The tags on my plates expired, so I've been using her car," he puts his head in his hands. "But Missy wouldn't know any of that."

"How long is your girlfriend going to be out of the country?" she asks.

"A year," he says and then corrects himself, "well, a year total, so another six months."

Bollinger makes more notes into her phone, excuses herself for a moment and steps outside. His little house seems strange to him. Not the sinister malice he feels when he misses Elm, but dull—a deadness to the house around him like it's abandoned. Not haunted, not even that, just utterly forgotten.

Bollinger returns. He hears commotion outside in the moment when the door's open to the world. The world where shit moves on, where things continue, and people have places to go.

"They're going to take the body, now," she says. "Some techs are going to stay and finish up out front. Is there another door you can use?"

"Sure," he says. "Don't want me trampling your chalk outline?"

She smiles her first genuine smile since breakfast this morning.

"I told you, you watch too much TV," she says.

"C'mon," he says, "I know I've seen crime scene photos and newspaper pictures with those."

Her smile broadens.

"Probably," she says, "but only if the victim is still alive. They do it so they can move the body and get the person help but have a record of how they were positioned."

"Huh," Cameron says with genuine interest, until he remembers why they're talking about this in the first place, and his face falls.

She realizes it too and her smile vanishes.

"Does she have any family?" Bollinger asks awkwardly.

"No," he says. "A father, maybe, but I don't think they've had contact for, geez, twenty-five years?"

"Well," she says, and braces him for bad news. "You might have to come down and identify the body."

She stops him before he can protest.

"I know, I know," she says. "You already have. I might be able to get the M.E. to pass off on that, but he might be a stickler, and you'll have to do it downtown. It'd be tomorrow at the earliest."

He sighs and nods.

"I'm gonna take off and get started on the paperwork," she says. "They'll be out there for couple hours probably but you can leave if you need to."

"I won't," he says.

She sticks her hand out, he takes it and stands up to see her out.

"You've had a hell of a day, Cameron," she says.

"To say the least," he says because he has nothing of value to add.

"Hang onto my card," she says. "If you need anything."

He nods, and she leaves.

He goes back inside and falls asleep on the couch, although the world's full of noise and motion and he's positive he'll never sleep again.

He sleeps and wakes and sleeps again. He cycles through

the night and the next day. He has a sip of water or a plain tortilla as needed. He watches no TV, listens to no music, reads nothing. He doesn't check his phone or email or leave the house. He sleeps like he's hibernating, like he's discovering rest for the first time. Sleeping like he'll never get the chance to again.

He considers calling in sick the next day, but wakes up at the normal time and feels refreshed and cooped-up. He runs through his routine with vigor, gets to work on time and remembers to bring his coffee inside.

He opts to not take his usual mid-morning stroll, knows he will cave in the coming days, but promises he will no longer wander behind the buildings. Leave Dumpsterville to the Orphans and the birds and the Mexican kitchen help.

He calls Elm from his office for an unscheduled chat and doesn't tell her anything about the last few days. He will, but he wants a normal conversation where she does most of the talking, he listens, pictures her face and misses her.

They talk for ten minutes, but it's all Cameron needs, and it carries him the rest of the morning.

They make a date to talk longer tomorrow and he'll have to tell her everything then.

He has a granola bar at his desk for lunch, not entirely sure where they've come from. Maybe he remembered to buy them or maybe they materialized from thin air like other things he's sometimes needed.

He's out on the floor for a couple hours before Snyder tells him he has a phone call. He takes it at the buy counter but it's Bollinger, so he puts her on hold and makes the long walk back to his office.

He can't do it. He can't see her body again. He can't. How can he get out of it? Can they make him, legally? Is it crazy or suspicious to refuse?

"I was hoping you wouldn't call me," he says.

She laughs.

"Yeah, I have that effect on most people," she says. "But you don't need to come down here. Turns out she had reconnected with her father a few years ago. He's already come and gone."

Relief washes over him.

"That's good," he says.

"Which?" she asks. "That you don't need to come down here, or that she had a relationship with her father?"

"Both, I guess," he says. "I was really hoping I wouldn't have to see her like that again. I mean, that sucks for her dad, but…"

"It's OK to be selfish, Cameron," she says. "Actually, that's why I called."

She takes in a long breath.

"Do you want to get coffee again? Or a drink? I know you drink. I saw thousands of beer bottle in your recycling bin," she says.

Not knowing what else to say, he says, "Were you investigating me?"

She laughs.

"Poking around a bit, I guess. I'm kind of a professional snoop," she says.

"I have a girlfriend," he says. "I told you that right?"

"You also told me she's gone for another six months," she says. "Look, I'm not trying to fuck your shit up. I would like to have a drink or two with you. Maybe more, and maybe more than once. Then in six months, I'd like to have a built-in reason to detach."

He wants to ask her what would happen if she gets too

attached to him, but his ego is human enough to know that won't happen and fragile enough to not be able to handle her laughing in his face. She's hitting him up for casual sex and, whatever her hang-ups or motivations, she must at least find him attractive. That makes him feel better about himself then he has in months.

He tries not to, but he thinks of Elm, thousands of miles away, and their screen relationship. How they talked most days until it became once or twice a week. He remembers a month ago when he slipped and told her about feeling like the only living person left, like he was an apocalypse survivor. He started to tell it straight, to try and confide these feelings to her and bridge the distance—the borders, the immeasurable tons of earth, the fathoms of ocean—between them. But the very curvature of the earth separates them. They exist at different times.

The gravity of trying to tell Elm these things that he's felt since she left him—he could see it on her face that she didn't get it. She couldn't understand, and he becomes embarrassed telling her as he says it, and he sort of peters out and finishes by twisting it into a joke. Like, isn't that weird? Isn't that funny?

"It's not weird," she says and shocks him with her grasp of what he's trying to articulate. "Look around, Cameron. You are a survivor of the apocalypse."

He shakes thoughts of Elm away. She isn't here. She chose to not be here with him. He wants to be supportive. He knows what she's doing is important, if futile, but it still feels like rejection. He's not enough for her—she must solve the mysteries of the world before she can settle down with him and grow old.

Bollinger—well, he should start thinking of her as

Melanie if they're going to do this—is still chatting him up.

"Are you going to marry her when she comes back?" she asks.

"Yeah," he says. "I plan to."

"You know divorce is down? Like, way down, now that people aren't clashing over raising kids? Isn't that fucked up?" she asks. "I mean marriage rates are down too, overall, but percentage-wise, it used to be as high as one in every two marriages ended in divorce. It's not even one in ten now. Isn't that nuts? We told the children of divorced kids for decades, for generations, that it wasn't their fault, but look at those numbers. Jesus."

"I should've been a therapist," Cameron says. "They must be raking it in."

"I dunno. I wonder," she says. "Look at church attendance. You religious?"

"Sure," he says. "Well, I don't really do anything with it."

"Exactly," she says. "Church attendance skyrocketed in the months following the first deaths. Now, it's bottomed out. Entire denominations no longer even exist. People see the empty churches and they assume that whatever used to be there was declared a cult for not supporting abortion or birth control or whatever, but a lot of times people just stopped showing up."

The way she talks about current events reminds him of Elm, so he tries to think of a way to change the subject

"Can we talk about something else?" Cameron asks.

He hears her smile over the phone.

"Yup. You want to have drinks with me?" she asks. The coyness in her voice ringing false, but not in a grating way.

"I do," he says. "I don't really have friends anymore, you know? Everybody's moved away or paired off. We can be friends, right?"

"Friends," she says. "Sure."

They meet for drinks the next night and she wears her hair down and Cameron can't believe how much it lightens her appearance and softens her features. Although she isn't rescuing a runaway or investigating a suicide, so maybe that helps. No badge tonight either.

He worried she'd be a hard-drinking detective but, as she loves to tell him, he watches too much TV. She nurses one drink the whole time.

They snack on tortilla chips at the bar, then decide they're hungry enough for a proper dinner, they move to a table. When the place gets too crowded and noisy, they leave.

After dinner he asks her if she wants to go see a movie or something, but she smiles and takes his arm and says, "Nope."

They go back to her place.

She knows what she wants, tells him simply and he gives it to her. He tells her. They switch back and forth and it's matter-of-fact, unfussy and passionless. But it's full of warmth, comfort and friendship.

She doesn't ask him to stay the night or make him leave, so he sleeps next to her because it's suddenly very late.

In the morning she makes coffee. He turns down breakfast and leaves to go home and feed the cats and change before work. The cats look at him in a judgey way, but they are cats after all.

He goes to work and talks to Elm and everything continues normally like this. He sees Melanie a couple times a month and they have drinks or share a meal or have sex, but not every time. He even talks her into a movie once. She's uncomfortable in there, sits in the back row, and is more concerned with whoever enters or shifts in their seat than in what's on the screen, so he doesn't ask again. He likes seeing movies by himself now anyway and sees at least one every day he has off, sometimes seeing the same film more than once. It's like he's a kid again, when you couldn't just stream or download every movie ever made.

He tells Elm about Melanie, sort of. That he's made friends with the detective whom he connected about Hope and they have coffee or drinks sometimes, and she doesn't press him and probably doesn't want to know. If she asks him about it when she gets back, he'll tell her. But only if she asks.

He thinks he sees Hope through the plate glass of the front window or taking the trash out when there's no one else to do it. Someone, a child pretty obviously, has vandalized the front of the store a few times, but it's small time stuff and he doesn't report it and it stops after a couple of weeks.

The six months pass by like this.

The year is up and Elm is back and she's so different that it's bizarre and so much the same that it hurts.

Cameron supposes it's like this for her as well, even if he's always the same to himself. Maybe not—he never left, so he never had to return.

He hopes he never sees Melanie again, not because he doesn't like her or they left it on bad terms, but because it's over and some things need to end and not be revisited. Besides, she's a cop, and people who see her are having the worst day of their life. Finding a dead woman, a woman that looked like someone he used to know—if only vaguely at that point—had certainly been the worst day of his life. He has no desire to try and top it.

Elm never asks him about her, and he never asks her if she had her own Melanie when she was abroad.

Elm slips back into her life, into his life, into their life, and it's the same as it was before she left. Except for the parts that are different.

And it's a good life. Except for the parts that aren't.

There are less of those, Cameron knows, and he tries to remember to be thankful for that.

# SIX

# THE UGLY LITTLE THING

**D**oris turns off the two-lane highway, down the unmarked gravel road and zips past all the DO NOT ENTER and NO TRESPASSING signs in English, Spanish and one or two other languages she isn't sure of. Not that she really sees the signs anymore. They fade into the background with everything else about this drive—the highway overpasses, the clumps of trees, any other vehicles.

*"You're like a mother without any children."*

Gina's words echo in her ears, turned all the way up in her consciousness in the same way the scenery is turned all the way down. It bounces back and forth between her ears and echoes around inside her brain.

A mother without any children.

She turns the phrase over and over, dissects it and tries to make sense of it. A mother without any children doesn't exist. It's meaningless—is that the point? Is Gina trying to tell her that she's useless? Less than useless, maybe? Purposeless, of no value, a pathetic thing that has little reason to be.

Poof. Those words spoken and like magic, she becomes nothing.

But the mother thing…

Doris always wanted to adopt, and Gina reluctantly agreed. As the process stretched from months to years, they still weren't approved, even as friends of theirs adopted a child, sometimes even a second. She suspected Gina of sabotaging the process somehow, but it was such a horrible thing to think of her own wife that she never asked. Instead, she let the paperwork lapse and the whole idea faded away.

Mostly.

She comes to the first of two chain link fences topped with coils of gleaming razor wire, still on autopilot. She slows her car and cracks the window enough to flap her parking pass into the red beam of the flashing scanners.

The gate in front of her shudders and rolls aside with a monotonous ratcheting. The gravel becomes dirt on this side of the gate, and huge plumes of dust kick up in her rearview mirror as the gate cycles through the jerky process of closing. There are cameras, and probably drones, watching her, but they're too far or too well hidden for her to see, particularly in her distracted state.

Whatever Gina's words meant, they were meant to hurt her. It worked. She got the fight she was looking for. Doris even threw a coffee mug at her, shattering it far to her right against the kitchen wall.

No, that's not right. Her coffee mug was already empty. She threw her nearly full cereal bowl. Will that be easier or harder to clean up when she gets home in eight hours and it's inevitably still there in pieces on the floor, streaks down the wall?

She feels guilty for throwing something now but will never apologize for it. Likely, Gina will never bring it up. Doris will come home and clean it up while Gina watches TV in the other room. They'll go to bed and in the morning, it will be better or worse, but it won't be discussed. Maybe she should leave the shattered bowl on the floor until Gina mentions it. That'd be different.

What had Doris screamed at her after she stood there blinking, moving her gaze slowly from the wall to her face? God. Had it been something about the failed adoption all these past years?

She reaches the next fence and needs to get out, open all the doors, the trunk and do a tight circle with her hands in the air holding her ID badge. She sees a guard tower now, but the highly reflective tint of the windows betrays nothing about its interior.

She hears two loud intercom squawks, shuts her trunk and passenger doors in the reverse order from which she opened them and returns to her seat. She refastens her seatbelt due to some deeply imbedded muscle memory.

Once her driver's side door shuts, the second gate begins to creak its painfully slow opening.

The dirt road continues, but she already sees the solid concrete wall that will be her last checkpoint, from the outside anyway. It looms large even this far back. It's twenty feet high and topped with spikes jutting out at a forty-five-degree angle. The razor wire of the two outer fences are tame by comparison. This is a wall, not a fence, and if you need a reminder of the difference, visit a prison.

The road splits and she follows the left path. In a quarter mile, she parks near half a dozen other vehicles as dusty from the journey as her own.

She gets out from the car, grabs her bag, double checks that she has her keys and locks it.

She makes the last stretch of the jaunt across the stark openness of the parking lot. The feeling of being totally exposed as doubtless dozens of men with firearms and weapons-equipped drones watch her every step, finally pulls her out of her stupid little fight with Gina and she readies herself for the day.

Was it really a little fight, or is it truly just one long sustained war that's punctuated by brief ho-hum moments of serenity between skirmishes?

Ah.

There it is, trying to creep back in and steal her attention. She pushes it all the way down inside and closes a door on it.

She reaches the entrance and turns to the Plexiglas guard booth to the right and holds her ID up next to her face. She does her best impression of herself from that photo and receives a curt nod from the man behind the booth. There's an intercom system, of course, but they almost never use it. Instead, the guards mostly nod or point at things.

He glances towards the keypad and she punches in her unique six-digit code. She expects retinal scanners or blood samplers any day now.

There's a loud clanking sound like an enormous bolt being thrown back, and Doris places her bag into the large metal drawer. It vanishes into the wall to wait for her to retrieve it on the other side, sans cell phone, keys and any sharp implements forgotten in there. Once, she'd left nail clippers in her bag, somehow, even though she can't imagine why nail clippers would ever be in with her work stuff.

The guard hand-scribbles her receipt tickets for the unallowed items and buzzes her in. She pushes the door open with one finger, still amazed at the lightness and maneuverability of such an important door.

Inside the prison at last.

There are two guards in the hall. The closest one to her is Dennis—a perfect prison guard name. Much more believable than Burt or Jerry or the few other names of guards she remembers. Those are too much like movie names for guards, as if they got the jobs after being plucked right out of a pile of headshots. These are just people, this is their job. They have wives, ex-wives, girlfriends and, some of the older or lucky ones might even have children.

*"You're like a mother without any children."*

She swallows and tries to think of some way to keep that damn thought from popping into her head. She has work to do.

Dennis smiles and nods at her.

"How ya doin' this morning, Doris?" he asks while retrieving her bag for her from the metal table bolted to the floor. He's one of the few guards who's friendly to her and they small talk when his shifts overlap with her day here.

She smiles back and pushes her fight with Gina from her mind again. It's good to have a friend.

"I'm OK," she says. She knows better than to complain about a spouse to a man. Ugh. She's been down that road before. You say one negative about your wife in a non-joking manner and you can see the wheels in their heads turning and the erections forming in their pants. She hopes Dennis wouldn't be that way, but they all are on some level. Why bother to test him and find out?

No expectations mean no disappointments.

She knows she is no prize, isn't much to look at, and she certainly cultivates the unattractive parts of her appearance when she comes here. More for the staff than for the prisoners. Inmates will whack off to anything, but she won't be able to do her job if the guards are hovering around her constantly worried about her safety or virtue or whatever.

They chat as he escorts her through the halls, talk about some disaster he had with a propane grill last week and his sons being terrible at sports. She talks about a scatterbrained coworker and a crazy man at the grocery store.

"Crazy?" he asks, shocked. "Isn't that word a no-no in your profession?"

"Eh," she shrugs. "Maybe to some of my colleagues, but honestly? Some people are just shit nuts."

He laughs, a strange but not unwelcome sound in this serious place.

Most of the guards walk her to the end of their respective territories and then pass her off onto the next unlucky sap, relaying her through the Byzantine corridors of the prison until she finally plops down into the office she shares with the various outsiders they bring in for specialized services. Not Dennis. He walks her the entirety of the route through the prison and deposits her to her destination solo. He nods at each successive guard in turn as they shuffle backwards to fill the vacancy of the previous one's spot. She imagines it unwinds itself in reverse after he leaves her to work, but she'll never know.

She asked him once, a few months into her job here, why he walks her all the way when nobody else does.

"Well," he said, "I can't speak as to why they choose not to, but the biggest thing about prison, for them and us, is that it's boring. Any change of pace that doesn't result in someone in the infirmary or the morgue is OK with me."

She understands this impulse to change things. It's why

she hardly keeps regular office hours at the clinic or her own offices, but she finds it strange coming from a prison guard. They're creatures of habit. Their more adventurous brethren take to the streets in uniform if they disdain routine so much, and Dennis has worked here nearly twenty years.

The more you learn about people, the less you know.

They finish their long sojourn through the dull, gray concrete of the prison to her office. He tips his hat to her before he leaves.

He immediately turns back on his heel towards her and hands her a cord with a flat plastic box on the end of it. The box is that beige, yellowish-gray color of early Apple computers—that dirty, rugged hue that perfectly fits into these institutionalized surroundings. Inset on either side of the broader faces of the rectangle is a button that maybe once was red or orange but is now that old plastic shade of the rest of the thing.

"You know the drill," he says. "Wear it or don't but keep it close and don't hesitate to press it. We don't mind false alarms around here. We prefer them, in fact."

She nods and takes it, not as reluctantly as she once had. The strange over-cautiousness of the place has wormed its way inside of her and taken up permanent residence.

He executes another perfect turn on his heel and is back off down the hall. His ease of fluid motions makes Doris wonder if he'd been a military man before this. She's pretty sure it's never come up, and she makes a mental note to figure out a way to ask him the next time they chat.

She leaves the door to the office open and goes behind the desk to get her things in order. She glances at the clock on the wall, and she has exactly five minutes before her first session. Prisoners are a punctual bunch.

She skims her schedule and corresponding notes for each inmate. Nobody new this week. Should be straightforward.

She works her eyes over the list. Nine, fifty-minute sessions, each inmate arriving at five after then departing at five till. Five inmates, then a break for lunch, which will be brought to her in this room, then four more inmates and finally out the way she entered. Only exiting will be the faster of two routes, another thing separating her from the prisoners.

Of the nine, six see her because of a court ordered, mandatory reason, one is pretending he needs help in some misguided attempt to be transferred to a lighter security facility or a step-back on some of his charges, even though she's repeatedly told him that's not what she does and has no contact with parole boards or any other body, and two are genuinely trying to work through some issues and maybe improve themselves or at least feel better.

Of the six forced to sit across from her and, God forbid, speak, two of those cooperate in any real way and the rest answer in single syllables or grunts or merely stare at her until the clock runs out.

She has no group therapy sessions any longer. She phased out the last one a few months back. She found nothing useful about them for the inmates. The sessions turned into microcosms of the lives and power struggles they live with every day. They were fascinating to her, of course, and could probably generate thousands of pages of research, but that's not why she's here. She takes only the barest of notes and these she leaves in full view of the inmates.

This is a volunteer position and she tries to help these men and gain nothing from them in return.

Kitson, Arturo is first. It's always preferable to schedule him first thing. His session is mandatory; he gains nothing by coming in here and he puts forth no effort. They small talk for most of an hour while she avoids sharing anything personal with him, and he makes up various lies about himself or his past that change from week to week. He does this without a malicious attempt to deceive her. He's more of a bullshitter than anything else. He's a conman and petty thief on the outside, and is serving life after a woman was accidentally killed during some botched job. She learned this from his file since he can't be trusted to tell you the color of the sky.

When his fifty is up, he straightens up from the casual posture of their sessions—stretched out in his chair with legs extended and feet crossed at the ankles, hands laced behind his head, staring over her head as he spins his web of harmless shit. He bows at her as if it was a performance and strolls out nonchalantly as if leaving a bar in the afternoon and not headed back to a cell.

Flint, Joe is second and another good one to have before lunch, as the big man never says more than ten words to her and only one at a time. In the slow crawl of the afternoon, those sessions are agonizing.

They stare at each for fifty minutes and then he's led away. It isn't a menacing or hostile stare, exactly, but it isn't thoughtful either. It's a flat stare, devoid of anything she tries to project onto it. She remains keenly aware that this man killed two people with his bare hands in a gas station parking lot in broad daylight in front of a dozen witnesses.

"Why don't you want to talk about anything, Joe?" she asked him during their second or third session.

"Pointless," is all the man said in his slow baritone.

She nodded. He's on death row and declined the appeals process. He will be put to death before the year's out. She isn't here to make anybody do anything or talk about anything, she's just available if they so choose to.

Not even a single word from the big man today. Which isn't a record but probably ties for one. He nods once when his time is up and lumbers away.

Espinosa, Marcos is one of the good ones. Whatever that means in a maximum-security facility filled to capacity with the worst humankind has to offer. He's a real hard-luck case who tries to improve himself, keep his nose clean, and is desperate to get out of here through legal means.

He's what Gina calls a "shit magnet." A human whom, even the most cynical of observers must admit, simply has bad luck. Shitty people and situations spiral around him and make his life shitty through no fault of his own.

He claims it started at birth when his nine months pregnant and ready to burst mother got turned around trying to sneak over the border and he was born on the Mexican side, less than a quarter mile from the United States. He was orphaned soon after and grew up in various Mexico City street gangs, usually as a mascot, as he was one of the smaller and weaker kids. In his teens, he became less of joke and more of a piece of meat to passed around between older, lecherous types. Barely twenty, his blood, fingerprints and a suspiciously consistent signature suddenly turned up as evidence peppered all through a major joint effort between the Federal Mexican Police and the DEA. He's indicted, charged and convicted as the mysterious "Giant Squid" of the Mexican drug trade, who had tentacles in all aspects of the drug operations, even though Mexican traffickers do not produce or even handle drugs—they merely provide border access to the American buyers via internationally sanctioned checkpoints.

He was extradited to the U.S. to serve multiple life

sentences, despite the phony evidence and that some of the acts he was accused of occurred when he was less than six years old.

Eventually, he gained enough support to be retried and acquitted. He met a woman in the U.S. with dual citizenship and they were immediately married and became pregnant. He was captured by ICE while his wife was in labor and deported before his daughter was born, even though his previous charges had been overturned. Cops hate being proven wrong.

This was a little over thirteen years ago. His daughter, as far as Doris can tell from her research, is one of the last children whose mother survived giving birth to them. Reports began coming in as early as ten hours after the birth of Marcos' daughter that recent mothers were dying after childbirth in record numbers.

Whole hospitals worth, then whole cities, then whole countries and then every single one everywhere on the planet. No matter how remote, no matter any variable anyone could theorize or evaluate.

Marcos claims he knew none of this. Doris believes him. He was dropped off in Mexico and instantly turned around and began the long sneak back across the border to see his newly born daughter.

When he finally arrived and found his family a series of farcical events bordering on the slapstick came to pass and he was fleeing with his daughter. He spent a mere twenty-four hours with her before he was apprehended.

The kidnapping of children, even your own, as a capital offense punishable by death was swiftly passed and back-dated to include any offenders since the earliest day of the tragedy. And, since Marcos' wife died in a car wreck on the way to court to defend him and prove that their daughter was not one of the Orphan children, he was convicted, sentenced to death and is serving his time out here.

Doris rubs her temples. It hurts her head re-familiarizing herself with it for the hundredth time—how must he feel living the nightmare?

Marcos enters. A slight man, he trips over his own feet walking into the room and catches himself just short of sprawling out onto the concrete floor or dashing his own brains out on the corner of her desk.

He smiles sheepishly at her and takes his seat.

He's recovering from a recent black eye and maybe a newly chipped tooth.

He reads her concerned look and tries his best to shrug and smile it off.

"That Octopussy nickname is really catching on," he explains. Light glints strangely off his mouth as he talks. Definitely a freshly chipped tooth.

When the other prisoners found out that he was once, although briefly and mistakenly, The Squid of the Mexican drug trade, they referred to him as Octopussy, one gang going as far as to force a prison tattoo artist to ink a large pink octopus on his forearm. The guards broke it up after a single tentacle was drawn. The unfinished tattoo looks very much like a large, pink penis pointed at his left hand.

He collapses, rests his head in his hands and whimpers.

"I'll never see my sweet daughter again," he moans.

This is the usual crux of their talks.

"You will," Doris says and hopes she isn't lying to the man. She details her recent efforts to try and arrange some sort of visitation while his lawyers, also found by Doris, work diligently to get him a new trial.

Normally, she's as positive as she pretends, with all the

moves in the correct direction, but this is Marcos "Octopussy" Espinosa, the human shit magnet. She's ready for the rug to yank out from beneath them at any moment.

She goes through a few more things with him. He slowly perks up as she tries to help him find ways to avoid conflict with the other inmates, even though she knows he's doing everything he can. As they reach the halfway point, a bright smile crosses her face. She shouldn't hold back much longer.

"Marcos," she says. "I have something to show you."

She reaches into her bag and realizes at that moment that she hasn't checked to see if it was confiscated. A sickness spreads in her stomach when she doesn't feel the slickness of it. Of course they took it. It's Marcos' luck that she'd try to surprise him with a simple kindness and they took it and she'll have to tell him because she hasn't prepared a lie. It will break his heart a little bit more.

But wait.

There it is. She feels the smooth, tackiness under her fingers, the way a photo's finish is both sleek like a snake and slimy like you imagine a snake to be.

She pulls out the photograph and hesitates before handing it to him.

"I can't let you keep it," she says. "They won't let you have it, and it would be pretty obvious who smuggled it in for you."

He nods, still not knowing what she has, or not daring to dream that big.

She turns the picture of his daughter, taken three days ago, face-up and hands it to him.

He blinks down at it in wonder, up at her and then right back down again.

He makes little sounds with his mouth like he's trying to

form words, but can't remember how to speak. He's burping up single, isolated syllables as if "ut" or "ag" are something she'll understand. Which she does.

"It's her," Doris says. "Taken last week. She's thirteen years old, Marcos."

He strokes the photograph softly as his eyes brim with tears. The brighter red rim of the bruised eye make it appear wetter than its black and blue twin.

"I know," he says and repeats it a few more times.

He asks her questions about his daughter for the remainder of their time. She doesn't mind, like he doesn't mind that she hardly has any answers for him. He doesn't seem to notice at all—he stares at the photo and fires off a series of questions, one after the other, not taking enough time to absorb any information. He repeats himself several different times.

It passes too quickly and when there's two minutes left, she asks him for the picture back. He hands it to her automatically but holds on a little extra as she plucks it from his grip. He follows it with his eyes as she replaces it between some papers and shoves them back into her bag.

"I promise to bring it next time, Marcos," she says. "Maybe another one, if I can swing it."

He thanks her, and she imagines him mentally filing it away in his brain where no one here can sully or take it from him.

He does his best to harden his features in the last minute before the guard arrives and takes him away, but he'll always look out of place here and she hopes he can hang on long enough to get out.

Washington, DeVante the Third is next and it zips by in a blur. Doris barely recognizes his presence or why he's here.

She zooms through his session on autopilot and doesn't feel too guilty about it. He treats therapy as a joke, and if he hadn't killed a liquor store owner during a robbery and a fellow inmate in a lesser jail, he wouldn't be here anyway. He leaves, and she instantly forgets everything that transpired in the last hour.

One of the guards comes in with a tray of food.

She isn't that out of it, is she?

"Don't I have one more before lunch?" she asks.

"Not today," the guard says, whose name is something like Jim or Tim. "Wood's not gonna make it today. Long lunch for you, I guess."

She nods.

She learned early that to get along with the staff, she needs to outwardly appropriate their Us versus Them attitude towards the inmates, so she doesn't ask if he's all right. She'll find out sooner or later. Wood is one of the uncooperative ones. No big loss if she doesn't see him for a bit. There's often one missing for disciplinary, medical, or various other reasons.

She thanks Jim or Tim and he sets the tray on the desk. She stops him at the door.

"Do any of you guys have a newspaper or something?" she asks with her best smile. "Gets a little boring in here."

He nods.

"I think I saw Craig with it," he says. "I'll send him your way."

She thanks him, and he leaves. She sits down to discover what delights the kitchen staff cooked up today.

Ham, baked macaroni and cheese, collard greens and a cookie, even though she always tells them no dessert. She will take the can of Diet Coke they included. Pop is a perk only for the staff.

The ham is wet but not moist, probably boiled or some other atrocious method of preparation. It reminds her of her grandmother's cooking. She was such a fantastic cook with baked items or sides, but meat… The main course of nearly every meal was always out of her grasp. Overcooking and drying out meats was her usual transgression. She was mostly OK with ham or pork roasts, as they're forgiving to those who try to destroy them. But poultry, turkey in particular, was always a disaster. With turkey there was gravy, so you could dunk the dry meat into it in some half-successful attempt to reconstitute it like resuscitating an abandoned astronaut or a forgotten army grunt.

The greens are serviceable, though she suspects the little chunks of dark meat is more of the listless ham when bacon is preferable. But when isn't it?

The mac and cheese, however, is good. Really good. It looks the least appetizing of all the elements of the meal—a medium brown or a kind of orange and yellowish block. But it holds together like good casserole and yields when prodded with the plastic spork. The noodles are perfectly proportioned and precisely cooked, not chewy or gummy, and there are little, finely diced onions mixed in. The cheese is silky and pleasantly tangy while the parts that made contact with the pan are delightfully caramelized and crispy without being burnt. She's lucky enough to have a corner piece. The crumbled topping is also spot-on. She assumed it was breadcrumbs before biting into it, but its texture is flakier than that with a great buttery taste. One of the larger chunks gives it away with those recognizable dimpled ridges. Ritz crackers. She makes a mental note to apply them to her own recipe in the future.

After a tasting bite from everything on her tray, sans cookie, she finishes her ham, greens, macaroni and cheese and half her Diet Coke in that order. She's eyeing the cookie, considering a poke or squeeze test to determine if it's even worth it, when another guard strolls in and slides a well-read newspaper onto her desk. He half-heartedly reminds her that prisoners are not allowed outside materials, especially anything that can enrage them, like newspapers, so if she'll give it to whoever collects her tray or secret it in her bag before her next appointment that'd be swell. She nods agreement and he walks out.

She prefers a national or bigger city paper to the local one, but it's this morning's at least so why complain. She flips around haphazardly at first, skimming the back and front pages of various sections. She reads magazines backwards, but newspapers are a little trickier with that method of perusal. Mostly, she makes a lot of noise and a fair amount of mess.

The paper is the usual mix of horror, mundanity and pointless fluff. Doris wanted to be journalist once, but is that even what this rag is? She flips to another section. They only publish this twice a week now? This used to come out every morning and there was a second local paper in the afternoon. There's 400,000 people in this city, it can't sustain a daily paper?

She worked on her high school paper, rose quickly through the ranks to an editor position, partly because she works hard when she loves something, and partly because those jobs needed to be filled no matter what.

Even then, over thirty years ago, the newspaper business was dying a long, slow death from the wound inflicted by TV. Internet garbage was a few years away and it was longer until the majority had the connection to appreciate it. A few years after that was the outright attack on the medium with the pivot to small-chunk video because that's easier to control, restrict access to, and push out independent sources.

It's not like she really cares or that any of this bothers her.

She burnt herself out in high school over the pointlessness of trying to give people the information they need versus the information they think they want—the push/pull of that dichotomy stretches you beyond your ability to snap back into shape until you're nothing but a soft lump or a collection of broken edges. That happened by the time she was eighteen.

But she fell into a journalism scholarship, so she took it. When it ran out in two years, she switched to English. If nobody cares about written word that directly affects their lives, they sure don't care for words about lives only lived on paper. She quickly switched majors again, stumbled into the humanities and careened slapdash into social work and therapy.

She maintained a few inroads with her journalism friends, launched the campus' first website for and by the students, took classes that interested her, and worked on the campus literary magazine. But she never once worked on the newspaper. When something's dead to her, it's dead, buried and never spoken of.

She flashes on Gina in that moment and pushes it aside. She hopes they aren't there yet.

She finishes the paper, does her best to refold it into some semblance of a rectangle and slips in under her tray.

Only then does she eat the cookie.

It's a white chocolate macadamia nut cookie. It's salty, sweet, soft and chewy. She's glad she waited and glad she ate it. She has just enough Diet Coke to wash it down and, miraculously, she doesn't choke on the last sip of pop.

The same guard who delivered lunch retrieves her tray and smiles in thanks that she included the paper.

She has fifteen minutes or so before work resumes and nowhere to hide now. No food to try and lose herself in, no newspaper to distract herself with. Just thoughts of Gina and their increasing fights and disintegrating marriage.

The amount of pain and suffering a human mind can stuff into itself in fifteen minutes is staggering. How many times will she hear her say those parting words, that cereal bowl-shattering phrase, over and over in her head with nothing else for it to bounce off of?

Her first appointment after lunch is Avagyan, Robert. He was apprehended a couple years ago during the bust of a regional kidnapping ring.

Two of Bob's fellow acquaintances waiting on death row in other prisons have already been murdered by fellow inmates, so the soft, nervous man is kept in isolation. A lot of men are here for kidnapping, but it's their own children or not-quite legal girlfriends, whereas Bob and his associates took other people's children. They lured them with fantasies about their mothers being alive and waiting to meet them.

Nearly every man in this prison has children if not an Orphan child.

Usually, Doris finds these sessions fascinating. Bob was a mere underling in the gang with no knowledge of its workings or affiliations to trade for a lighter sentence. The ringleader—a man that still terrifies Bob—was shot and killed by the DPEA. He can spend hours talking about this disturbed individual and the crimes they perpetrated together. The isolation means Doris is the only person Bob ever talks to.

But today she can't focus.

The teacher that died rescuing those local children from

Bob's gang is Gina's hero as she's a fellow educator. So, Doris is thinking about their fight again.

The appointment blips by like a single sonar artifact on a submarine's screen. She figures no one's getting anything out of her ghostly form today so she pulls herself together enough to signal a guard from the hallway, tells him she isn't feeling well and needs to leave early. If he can apologize to her last two clients for the day, that'd be wonderful. Maybe she can spend extra time with them next week.

She must look as bad as her claim—he doesn't laugh at her for the last part.

As she leaves in the reverse order she came through earlier, she sees a few faces of mild concern for the early departure, but mostly they look as if they expected it. As if she's washing-out and they're right in their judgment.

This is her projecting, she knows. This is a way for her to feel better about faking an illness, a pre-investment in feeling smug and superior next week when she shows up.

Dennis is out strolling the parking area.

"Ducking out early?" he asks, waggling his eyebrows. It's a comical gesture and not a come-on.

"Not feeling the best," she says, and then decides to confide in him. "Well, I may have fibbed a bit. I just can't seem to focus. Lot of extraneous crap from my life getting in the way today, and if I can't listen I'm not really doing anybody any good. We'll try again next week."

He winks at her.

"Your secret's safe with me," he says. "The wife says, 'sometimes you need a day off because you've got a cold, and sometimes your brain does.' Or something like that."

He excuses himself, says some of us have no choice but to stick around and work, but he says it with smile to show that he's ribbing her. She laughs and gets in her car.

On the outside of the gray prison walls, the process of leaving grinds to a halt once more, but she's in her own car with her own things and she checks her email and her phone and blasts some classic rock at too loud of a volume to think around and it passes without much fuss and she's soon off the property and cruising down the two-lane highway and back towards town.

The DO NOT PICK-UP HITCHHIKERS and FEDERAL PRISON signs soon give way to mile-markers and gas station and hospital signs. *Be on the lookout. We gathered all the worst people in the world and put them in one place. It's locked-up tight, but you never know* segues smoothly into *Here's a Shell gas station with an included combination Taco Bell and KFC, if you're that kind of maniac.*

The world eases back from insanity to normalcy.

It's all strip malls and fast-food joints.

No, she thinks, what are they called? You have to go up and order, but they bring it out to you? It isn't quite a restaurant and is more expensive and slightly nicer than a McDonald's?

Oh, well.

If that's the only term she can't recollect today, she'll consider it a win.

She zips through the outskirts of town past the truck stops, and switches highways. Now, in the fancier neighborhoods the dwellings all look the same and appear to be more garage than house, with well-kept and tiny, treeless yards. She likes to imagine that no people live in these neighborhoods, that it's a subdivision of automobiles that can finally afford all that garage space they've been longing for out here in the suburbs. Even that guy down on all fours in the grass with a pair of scissors perfecting his lawn—he was hired by the robot-cars to maintain the plush exterior. She smiles. This ridiculous notion that if the cars become sentient their main concern is the same as those of their obnoxious owners.

It pushes the impending doom of arriving home and having to clean up that cereal mess away just a bit further.

An older couple ride by on their weird lounging bike things and wave at her, ruining the robot fantasy. She considers flipping them off but manages a friendly wave instead.

The fancy houses of today slip into the fancy houses of ten years ago and then slide into twenty as the streets whip by. The fancy grocery stores and higher-end big box stores quickly become a Walmart. This never fails to make her happy since she knows it drives the residents around here nuts. *Gasp! They are better, surely, than Walmart people!* She smiles at the self-loathing they feel every time that, in the middle of the night desperately needing some crucial necessity, they find themselves staggering around and blinking in the harsh 24-hour glow of Sam Walton's living monument.

This gives way to lesser chains—Dollar Trees and Circle K's and then suddenly and abruptly, nothing. Just abandoned and shuttered businesses, churches and homes. This is where the drugs are dealt and people are murdered, or so the newspapers and politicians would have you believe. But nobody lives or works here, in this half-a-block of crumbling infrastructure, in this urban demilitarized zone. Or so the politicians and news sites say.

Doris doesn't buy it.

If no one lives here, why are they murdered here? Maybe it's a good place to dump a body, sure, but do you get killed in places you never go? She can't deny that bad shit happens here. This is where Bob Avagyan and his kidnapping ring were hiding out.

Just as quickly, the no man's land is gone, and the check cashing places and ethnically-specific grocery stores and Laundromats spring up and then segue even faster into the tallish buildings of downtown.

The city is like a target—concentric rings of income levels and industries, suburbs, DMZ, downtown. Entering from any direction and shooting into the city like an arrow, you'll pass through these rings unless snagged and caught up in one by either destination or poor marksmanship.

There are little pockets of variables. Little neighborhoods that are better or worse or newer or stranger than their surrounding overall area. Doris and Gina live in one of these northeast of downtown, called North Broadway or NoBro.

Nestled in the disintegrating prefab mid-century nightmare of the neighboring streets, NoBro is about four-square blocks of some of the earliest houses still standing in the city. Late Victorian homes, yes, but unlike similar streets or neighborhoods dotting the area around downtown, these are all single-family homes that haven't been sliced up into units for college kids. Many of the homes have been passed down through families for generations.

But of course, there aren't families anymore, not the way there used to be, and one or two of the homes are unoccupied now. Others might go up for sale (can you believe it?) or even, God forbid, be rented out.

Her neighbors are all mortified and Gina with them. They live in her grandfather's house after all. Doris, however, is taking a perverse satisfaction in it. NoBro thinks they're better than the outside world. It's nice to have the outside world encroach on it a tad.

She sighs.

She shouldn't shit on it. She loves it here in their big old house in their quiet, well-established neighborhood with her neighbors that enjoy being here too. There's something comforting about how un-hip the area is. It isn't transitional, and it isn't a stepping stone to anywhere else. In a medium-sized Midwest city full of people settling on a hometown that they hate, it fills her with pride to live in a place where people want to be there.

She turns into her neighborhood and, being the middle of the day in a working neighborhood, it's devoid of activity.

She turns right again and sees Gina's car on the curb, which is strange. Is she also so overly bothered by their fight that she came home early as well, maybe to clean up that damn shattered cereal bowl and wipe the slate clean through that simple act? She feels an over-abundance of emotion towards her in that moment, like maybe they are still more similar than different. Like maybe that's where the friction in their relationship comes from—their mirror-image rough patches grinding against each other in an attempt for the same things.

Then she sees a strange woman exit the front door of her house and all these thoughts vanish.

She comes to a slow halt in her car. She doesn't break exactly but kind of drifts to a stop. Her foot slowly lifts from the gas pedal at first to prepare to slow down and turn into her driveway, then she lifts it all the way, floats to the shoulder of the road and pulls over next to her neighbor's house. This saves her from being discovered by the strange woman who pays her no mind as she walks across the street and hops into a small hatchback in need of a wash.

The woman puts the ugly little thing into reverse, backs

into the neighbor's driveway across the street and zooms away down the opposite end of her road.

Preoccupied with backing her car up and reapplying lipstick, she didn't see Doris at all.

Doris thinks maybe she recognized the woman from somewhere but can't place it. She can think of only one reason a strange woman would be at her house in the middle of the day when Doris is supposed to be out of the city for around ten hours. Gina isn't supposed to be here either.

The woman's car recedes quickly in Doris' windshield and she knows she has something important to do, one way or the other.

Her brain screams at her body to do something— anything. To take an action. She sees the turn signal blink left at the end of her street. Her body remembers to drive, tears away from the curb and narrowly misses Gina's car.

She zips down her street, hangs a fast left and doesn't bother to check for cars, signal, or slow down. She feels like she might tumble into her own passenger seat from the force of the turn but wills herself to stay in place.

She sees the woman's car breaking up ahead and somehow finds the fortitude to slow down to a normal speed instead of simply continuing to accelerate and smash the woman's puny car with her SUV and crush it under its wheels like a demolition derby grand finale.

The woman goes straight through the intersection and Doris follows, thankful that a couple more cars join them. She doesn't know anything about tailing someone but maybe fall back a way and let other cars get between you.

When the woman turns right on Spring just after downtown, she knows where they're going and where she knows her from.

She's heading to campus. She's one of Gina's students.

She avoids going to school functions when she can but there are some times when Gina needs her wife to help with a charm offensive or something. That's where she recognizes this homewrecker from.

Let's be honest—her home's been wrecked for years. But is that the point? Does Gina get to deceive her this way, to say horrible things to her to win an argument or a fight and also behave like this?

No. She doesn't get to sleep with another woman. Well, girl, practically.

She follows the girl the rest of the way to campus to be sure and to show herself that she isn't crazy, that she's thinking it through.

She drives past the parking structure when she sees the girl pull into it, and waits in a handicap spot. She glances back and forth between the dashboard clock and the pedestrian exit.

Three minutes later, the girl exits the structure and saunters off into the tangle of walkways towards the various buildings.

She sits in that parking space, grips her steering wheel and doesn't know what to do. She leaves when campus security rolls by with its flashing yellow lights and gives her a blip on its horn to tell her to move on.

She has no idea what she'll do, but she turns her vehicle towards home.

She parks on the curb again at the end of her street and gets her phone out. She has no new texts. She sends Gina one.

coming home. left early if you wanna come home early too

She follows this with the smirking devil emoji—their code for sex.

Gina responds almost instantaneously with

ooh that sounds nice. been stuck in meetings all afternoon. i'll try

Then, as further insult, a smiley face.

The front door to their house opens moments later and Gina sprints to her car, jumps in and lead-foots it down the street.

This time, Doris is even more tempted to play demolition derby.

But she waits until Gina's car turns the corner, drives the rest of the block to their house, pulls into the driveway and turns the car off.

She looks at the texts again and imagines Gina saying it to her face. Imagines how she lies to her face, how many times she already has, how many bullshit texts she's sent, how many meetings or classes she's invented, how many late nights sprang up at the last minute, how many conferences she's been to.

How much of their life has been one big mound of bullshit?

Doris knows she should respond. She knows it's suspicious if she doesn't send back an "aw" or sad face and she doesn't want Gina prepared. She wants Gina to have no idea that she's on to her, no clue that she's about to tear her world down and burn everything they have in a fire as hot as she can make it.

She realizes she's holding her breath, lets it out slowly and remembers to breathe back in again after her lungs are empty. She sits there gripping the steering wheel and re-teaching herself to breathe until she can no longer feel her pulse hammering in her ears. She relaxes her grip on the wheel, pulls each finger away from it as if they were entirely separate things, like she doesn't have something called a hand that operates as whole, she just has fingers.

Eventually, she even gets out of the car and goes into the house. She locks her car with a press of the fob and remembers to shut the front door behind her like everything's normal. What else can she do? Sit in her car and grip the steering wheel aware of her breathing until the world ends?

No. Gina's acting normal. Doris will act normal. If Gina can act fast and loose and casual about their—

She laughs. She stands at the bottom of the stairwell and laughs. She remembers the term she was trying to think of earlier. Fast-casual—that's what you call that type of restaurant that is a step up from Burger King.

She chuckles her way up the stairs.

In her office, she sits down at her desk and digs around in the bottom drawer until she comes out with a blank notebook.

She loves notebooks, pens and really any kind of school or office supply. Her favorite part of school was the week or two before when she'd pick out all her notebooks, folders and pencils. She looked forward to helping her own children with this but that never happened. She got her tubes tied a month after all the first deaths hit the news. Now, closing in on fifty, it'd be too late anyway.

She takes comfort, in a small way admittedly, that she's an adult and can buy whatever she wants whenever she wants. Hence, a drawer full of Mole Skeins and Field Notes. Spiral bound repurposed metal covered ones with recycled paper. Wood backed ones with handmade paper and chunks of unevenness to illustrate how real and authentic they are. Perfect bound blank notebooks with completely smooth paper that ink might not even adhere to, or will at the very least smudge if you don't let them dry enough.

Ruled, un-ruled, quad ruled, grid ruled. Spiral, glued, stitched, loose. Newsprint, velum, Bristol. No, it's not a verse from a bad Billy Joel song—it's the bottom drawer of her desk where she deposits all her favorite new notebooks until the universe gives her a purpose for them.

She finds a stenotype notebook about the dimensions of a half sheet of printer paper. It's spiraled at the top, the pages are a bright canary yellow and ruled with green lines horizontally from top to bottom with no margins and a dark, red line that bisects the pages vertically.

It's the perfect canvas to draw her plans.

"Whoa, are you writing longhand? I never see that anymore."

Doris stops mid-word and looks up, blinking the real world back into existence. She's in the wine bar around the corner, after feeling trapped inside her own home.

It's that neighbor. The one that had the failed yoga studio and spa that Doris and Gina had tried a few times. She's got that husband with the weird name that works at the library or a bookstore?

"Yeah," Doris says. "Just trying to get some thoughts down before they vanish."

Adrienne. That's her name.

She plops down in the seat across from Doris.

"What are you writing about?" she asks.

"Uh, I don't know yet," Doris says, off balance.

"Really?" she says. "That's so interesting. My brain doesn't work in words very good. I just figured you had it all planned out in your head or something."

"Maybe for somebody, but not for me," Doris says, buying time, trying to figure out a polite way to get rid of her.

"I just kind of scribble until I figure it out."

"Huh," she says and reaches over and rifles the corner of the notebook. Doris sits on her hands to keep from smacking Adrienne's away from her stuff. "You have to have some idea by now, you've almost filled this whole thing."

"Oh, well, I don't know," Doris stammers.

Doris scoots back in her chair. If she can't get Adrienne to leave, Doris will be the one to bolt.

Adrienne sags.

"I'm sorry," she says and pulls her hands back across the table. "I'm being nosey. Snyder always says I'm too nosey."

"It's OK," Doris says, even if it isn't.

Adrienne nods to the glass and the mostly empty bottle of wine next to Doris' bag.

"It's just, you seem so intense or upset about something," she says. "I thought maybe you could use a friend."

Doris bites her tongue to keep from saying *We're just neighbors.*

"You and Genevieve really helped me out when I had my spa," she continues. "It was so sweet, and it kept my dream alive for a little bit longer than it would have been."

"Oh, Adrienne. It was a great space. We really loved it."

They sit in silence for a moment.

Finally, Doris flips the notebook back to the first page and shows her the header she scrawled there a few hours ago:

WHAT TO DO ABOUT GINA

Adrienne gasps and covers her mouth.

"No! You two are having problems?" she says softly.

"Yes. She's cheating on me," Doris says, and tells her the whole thing. This woman she barely knows.

Afterwards, Adrienne nods and looks away. Doris knows what's coming next.

"I'm not doubting you," Adrienne says, "but there has to be at least a couple reasons that woman would be at your house. How can you be sure that's what this is?"

Doris smiles. It's devoid of humor—it's all teeth.

"It's exactly the same," Doris says. "Years ago, this is how we met and got together. I was the other woman."

Gina's on her hands and knees scrubbing the floor when Doris stumbles home from the wine bar. There's a slight wet discoloration where Gina's already cleaned the wall and Doris wonders if it'll always be there or if it'll fade or if she'll still be able to see it in her mind's eye even after if it's long gone. If she'll ever be able to not see it.

"Feeling guilty?" she asks, because she can't help it.

Gina's back is to her so she can't see her face, but she does see her stiffen and stop.

She rings the sponge out into a bucket.

"It didn't seem like you were going to do anything about it," she says, and resumes scouring.

Doris almost asks if they're still talking about the splattered cereal and the broken bowl, but clamors upstairs and goes to bed instead.

On Friday she calls and moves her prison day up to Tuesday from Wednesday. She has all these excuses ready but doesn't end up needing them. They don't care—it's all the same shit to them.

She asks for Dennis and, after a few he comes on the line. She explains what she needs, says it's for a clinical study and he says, "Yeah, I think so. I'll see what I can do."

He can probably have it ready for her on Tuesday.

She thanks him and hangs up. Still a few days to go,

including what promises to be an awkward weekend with this woman that's supposed to be her wife. Three days of living and pretending everything's normal. Of politely deflecting Gina's advances or attempts to makeup when she wants is to puke all over her. Of watching the news sitting next to a stranger resembling her wife.

Time and the weekend pass at the rate they always do even if she feels it differently. Faster and slower all at once.

Threatening to crawl out of her skin, she meets Adrienne at the wine bar Sunday evening. They drink and talk about everything that isn't pertinent.

She does not tell Gina where she went.

Monday chugs along through the miasma of a hangover. She has extra appointments to make up for rescheduling everyone from Tuesday but it's smooth enough.

Tuesday arrives and she leaves as if going to work but puts in her prison day instead. Gina's oblivious to her deception, clearly wrapped up in her own.

After her shift, Dennis meets her in the parking lot with a cardboard box.

"You know how to work any of this stuff?" he asks, placing the box gently into the back of her car.

She shrugs.

"I'll Google it," she says.

"Fair enough. You don't have to tell me what it's really for," he says. "Just promise me it ain't illegal. Or at least lie to me that it ain't."

She looks in the box, pokes at its contents.

She smiles.

"It's not," she says. "I just need to observe some people who agreed to be observed but before they think it's happening."

He scratches his head.

"OK," he says. "I don't pretend to understand that."

"So," she says, trying to keep from lapsing into a full-on condescending teaching moment. "Students studying in psychology or sociology need to acquire so many hours as test subjects to pass their classes. So, they have to go out into the world and sign up for tests. Easy stuff like watching pornography while somebody monitors their heart rate."

He makes a squeamish face.

"Don't be such a prude, Dennis," she says and cuffs him lightly on the arm. "So, for an experiment this year I'm going to test how people feel based on whom they perceive to be around them. OK, it's going to work like this: the student will come in for the test, sign some releases and then sit down in the waiting area and fill out some more paperwork about their overall mental health, how they view themselves, others and the world at large. The waiting area will be full of other people appearing to do the same, but they'll really be actors."

"Actors?" he asks.

"Yes. The waiting room is the test," she says. "After they fill out the other questionnaires and turn them back in at the front desk, we'll make an excuse that we have to reschedule the test and they'll come back and to do it again, but this time the actors will be different, and will be playing either seedier characters, or affluent, preppy ones, depending on who we had them with the first time."

He nods, getting it.

"And you're going to film them with video and sound to pick any behavior changes from group to group," he says.

She beams at him and gives him the thumbs up.

"That's pretty clever," he says.

She almost tells him the truth right then, but somehow

finds the fortitude to convey a thank you and depart.

In her car, she feels as if she's vibrating at an unsustainable frequency. Like she might erupt. She breathes and squeezes the steering wheel until it passes.

You're almost there. Explode after you've burned everything to ash.


She has other things to prepare without tipping her hand. She fills a few boxes in the basement with her things, but she doesn't have a lot. They have quite a few things together, but as she walks around the house and evaluates it all, she doesn't want any of it. She just wants clear.

She has a large bookshelf of books in her office which Gina rarely enters but does walk past several times a day. She packs all the books away into three heavy boxes she can barely lift, lays some newspaper down around and under the bookshelf, finds an old can of primer and old paint swatches in the basement and places them prominently to finish the scene.

The guest bedroom is probably where they fuck.

Gina's twisted sense of morals would rationalize it—she would never sleep with this whore in their marriage bed. As if that's what Doris would have a problem with. But she knows her and that's how she thinks.

The girl, she doesn't know.

She could think about it. She could find the perfect notebook for sussing-out the mistress' motivations. This book, doubtless, is down in that drawer somewhere waiting to transition from a vessel into its purpose fulfilled.

Doris won't do it. Fuck the bimbo. She doesn't deserve a notebook.

• • •

"I'm relieved we never adopted," Doris says near the end of their second bottle. "Fuck. That sounds so terrible."

Adrienne pats her on the hand.

"No, it doesn't," she reassures her.

"Well, it feels terrible," Doris says. "I know it would be messier and more difficult and I'd never really be free of her because we would have this other person that tied us together, but…I don't know."

"You always wanted kids?" Adrienne asks.

Doris sighs and nods and gulps more wine.

"Of course," she says. "At least one little girl."

"I guess that's the difference between our ages," Adrienne says. "I was only nine or ten when the Orphan stuff started. I think I grew up in a different world than you. I don't know anyone that wants children."

"Shit. I forget how young you are. People must think you're drinking with your grandmother."

"No, no," Adrienne says. "Well, mother, maybe…"

Doris flips her off.

"There used to be these things called Pro-Life and Pro-Choice," Doris says in her best lecture voice.

"C'mon, I'm not that young," Adrienne says. "I know what those mean."

Doris chuckles.

"Seriously though. You know what the words mean," Doris says, "but you don't know what it was like when everybody was one or the other with no middle ground."

Adrienne divvies up the rest of the bottle.

"And even that wasn't true, at the time. Rich religious people still got abortions when a baby would be inconvenient for them. Liberal feminists with no maternal instincts became mothers. Cognitive dissidence."

"Cog what?" Adrienne asks.

"It's a term for when your beliefs crash into your reality. Like, you think you'll act one way, and even tell others how to behave, but you can't be sure until you're in the situation. You never know what you'll do until it's done."

Adrienne nods sort of vacantly. Doris recognizes she's not as dumb as she pretends.

"I always wanted kids," Doris says. "But a month into the Orphan crisis, I got my tubes tied. I'm not going to die for it."

"But you'd let somebody else die for it? Raise theirs?"

This is the kind of lawyer mumbo-jumbo Gina used to spring on her when they were trying to adopt. She lets it slide.

"I don't think we'll ever know," Doris says.

"I was just teasing you with that crack about your age."

She waves her off.

"It's fine," she says. "I just keep thinking about how we used to argue about abortion. There's still so much we disagree on. So many things where you must pick a side. What horrors does the world have waiting for us, to take those other choices away?"

She almost doesn't go through with it.

She almost leaves a note—or nothing at all—and drives away.

But this isn't a movie and there aren't end credits or a snappy score to hide the fact that she must stop her car somewhere. She must end up somewhere or explain where she comes from.

She can't drive away from thinking about it.

Gina still assumes she's out of town on Wednesdays, so that's when she'll catch them, she hopes. Ha. She actually hopes it's a weekly tryst, so she won't have to live in this charade any longer.

The cameras are wired with sound and motion sensors. She can upload it wirelessly to Gina's email account and send copies off to her bosses at the school and never have to see it. She can ruin Gina's life without ruining her own brain.

That next week jumps by faster than the previous one. She calls movers to meet her Thursday morning to put her shit in storage. Gina will receive her email with video of her fucking her student and call Doris' cell phone, but it'll be traded in for a new one with a new number. She'll call her work, but she's taken a leave of absence starting that day. She'll race home and find all traces of her gone.

From that point on, she'll never see her again. She'll only communicate through lawyers.

Not that Doris thinks she'll make much of an attempt. She tried to brain her with a cereal bowl for an innocuous comment during a standard fight. Gina will have to wonder what would she do if she got a hold of her in this state of rage?

She always takes the easy way out. Why else sleep with a student rather than work on their marriage?

The week ticks by in these perfect snapshots. Single frozen images like a filmstrip slowed all the way down. Like pulling the celluloid through her fingers so she can see the progression of time but without motion. No transitions. No movement. Nothing she can feel.

She waits out the week calm and serene, a pause before the storm, exuding an eerie stillness. She breathes it out like it's inside of her, like her body makes it.

She leans harder into appearing normal. Those around her only seem slightly distant, a little out of touch but pleasant enough. She knows these things because she's outside looking in—above it and looking down in mild amusement.

Thursday speeds into Friday which zooms through the weekend with both days squashing into a blob indistinguishable from each other or any before or after. Like it's one long day and she takes a little nap in the middle. Monday pops up and pops away just as fast. Even the uniqueness of Tuesday and her time at the prison doesn't slow the rate at which the hours whiz by.

Suddenly here it is, Wednesday.

She pretends to leave for the prison but only goes a block from her house to a coffee shop since the wine bar doesn't open until the afternoon. Mug/Shots is the trendiest place in the neighborhood. It's owned by some big restaurant group and she had signed the petition to keep it from opening, but it beats trudging miles away to an independent or all the way to the Starbucks with the impossible parking lot or the Dunkin Donuts inside the library downtown.

Adrienne wanted to join her, but Doris had nixed it.

"You've been a great friend," Doris had said, "but I need to do this part alone."

"Just remember that you aren't alone," Adrienne replied.

If they stick to their schedule as Doris believes it to be, it'll be more of an after lunch or early afternoon delight situation. So, she has hours to kill. She orders a coffee, a breakfast scramble and a pastry because, fuck it, why not.

She sits at a table by the window, eats her breakfast slowly and refills her coffee several times. She's pretty sure she knows a few of the faces that pop in for something now and then. They look at her sidelong as much as she does to them. Maybe the boycott isn't as universal as she believed.

After breakfast and an excessive amount of coffee, she takes a nice solid shit in the customer restroom, something she avoids doing in public restrooms unless it's a dire emergency but instead feels a grim satisfaction here. She switches to sparkling water to slow her nerves down and settle her stomach. It isn't anywhere close to lunch time, so she buys a USA Today and reads the whole thing from cover to cover in her strange, back-to-front way. She's not sure if any of it sticks but that's hardly the point. She only needs to pass the time.

It's almost one when the motion sensors kick the cameras on and they start recording. All morning the sound sensor picked up various ambient noises but when the motions didn't pick up any movement in the vicinity, the buffering cycled back, and the cams returned to standby.

They're rolling now.

She discovers that when it continues recording, any pretense of wanting to crack the application open and take a quick peek vanishes. It was never the plan, but some deep part of her brain thought she might.

Now she has zero desire to see what's happening. She wishes she didn't even know. Wishes she could go back two weeks and remain ignorant and happy. Or if not happy, apathetic.

The caffeine burnt itself out of her system a while ago, but her jittery, jangled nerves reemerge, and she can't keep her knees from jumping and her leg muscles spasm in a tug of war between flight and fight. She stands to compensate. It doesn't help. It's like a panic attack—a sudden, jarring need to get the fuck out of here.

She exits abruptly, leaving the disheveled paper and glasses on the table. She sweeps her computer, phone and small purse into a larger bag with one swipe of the arm. She tosses the bag in the back of her SUV. Before shutting it, she digs through the bag and finds her phone and keys. She shuts the hatchback, standing there with her hands on the back windshield as if she uses it for support. As if it's holding her upright or sticking her to the ground. As if she doesn't maintain this slight touch, she'll either be crushed by her own weight or float into the sky.

After a few minutes, she pulls herself together enough to step back from the vehicle without bursting into shards or puffing into vapor and, instead of opening the driver's side door and getting in, she walks away from the car.

She walks towards downtown.

She can't bear to be inside anything right now. Not even the small mobile utopia of her own vehicle where everything is hers and the way she likes it.

She walks as aimlessly as she can, hitting a corner and turning, zipping across the street when no cars are approaching. Not stopping and waiting for crosswalk lights to give her the go-ahead, she weaves in whichever direction is unobstructed.

Keep moving. If she stops, she might never move again.

She has no idea how much time passes. It feels like she's been walking all day, all week. Everybody else is in slow motion. Or maybe she's a ghost and the world passes by without her feeling the motion of the earth skim by beneath her.

She finds herself outside her own house at her front door. That shitty little hatchback is parked on the curb across the street. Was she headed in this direction all along? Did her body drag her mind here? She looks at the time on her phone. She left the coffee shop maybe fifteen minutes ago.

She stares at the screen on her phone, not out of disbelief about how little time has passed but because her mind is trying to make a further connection about her phone. About how her phone isn't just a phone. It's a tiny computer for your pocket. It's a calculator and a meteorologist. It's a banker and a clock and a compass and a fitness tracker and a camera and—

And a camera.

She brings the camera up with a quick swipe of her thumb and just as easily switches it into video mode. She's in the house and tiptoeing up the stairs and hearing their hushed voices and grunts and giggles and she's in the doorway now and they don't see her, they can't see her because they're tangled up with each other in the spare bed on top of the covers like animals and Doris can only think about how weird that it's such a beautiful day out today while this is also happening right here in front of her and how can that be possible and she continues to videotape them without really seeing them even though it's all she can see, even though she's seeing nothing but them on the little rectangle in front of her face and they still don't know she's there and she could do anything to them, really, she knows that, they don't control her with their actions they've given all the power over to her, they're small and insignificant and tied up in each other and their lives and the world and she is so far removed from it, so far above them and everything else that she holds their lives in her hands and she only has to decide and she will have locked their fates into place and they'll struggle or accept but they'll never change, never deviate from the path she sets them upon today at this moment.

She pushes these two ceramic cats from the dresser next to her to the floor. One's black, one is white. They were a couple hundred dollars apiece and she never really liked them, but she talked Gina into buying them for reasons she cannot possibly fathom in this moment. She sees their heads cock, their bodies stiffen in the instant before the cats shatter on the hardwood of the floor, as if they sense it coming or maybe they hear the faintest of scratches as the unglazed bottoms of the ceramic paws slide across the wood before exploding on the floor.

They look at her, all wide eyes and gaping mouths and wild hair, and she continues filming them and then, because there's nothing they can do to her, she gives them a little wave and leaves.

She hears Gina shout something like *"Wait!"* and there's something like sobs and loud noises and curses as they probably step on broken cat shards, but it's all far behind her and she's well down the street now, taking the most direct route to her car this time, and she gets in and it starts and she checks her phone and she remembered to turn off the camera and save the video and she emails herself a copy and then emails one to everyone who works with Gina, to all their friends, to all of their relatives. Then she drops the phone out of the window and crunches over it on her way out of the parking lot.

She knows it's folly.

She knows she can't drive and never stop. She knows there's nowhere to go and nothing to do if she leaves this place and her responsibilities. She knows she can't drive towards a sunset and keep pace as the earth turns beneath her.

She knows all of this but is going to try anyway.

# SEVEN

## SOMETHING SO TINY
## MAKES SUCH A HUGE NOISE

**H**eidi unfolds and refolds the empty sugar packet. Finally, she flicks it across the table to will herself to stop fidgeting with shit.

Just sit here. Just sit.

She looks down and sees a straw wrapper in her hand.

Gemini sets a fresh cup of coffee in front of her, sits down with their own cup and smiles at her in that desperate, whipped-dog kind of way they have. She's going to scream or claw their eyes out or jump out of her own fucking skin.

"Can you sit over there, across from me, like a normal person?" she asks.

They look hurt. Of course they do. They never argue, talk back, or complain but they always look hurt.

They push their cup across the table, slide out of the booth and take the chair opposite her. They never take the booth side. They opt for the chair when not feeling brazen enough to practically sit on top of her.

"It's just," she says, even though they don't ask, "I want to be able to look at you when we have a conversation."

"It's fine," Gemini says, and reaches for her hand.

She pulls back, instinctively, and then tries to make it appear as if she reaches for her coffee cup. Gemini does their best to act like they don't notice, like they believe her. Like everything is OK.

"Everything's not OK," she says aloud, ostentatiously to Gemini but really in conversation with herself.

"What do you mean?" Gemini asks with real fear in their eyes.

Heidi stares at them, lets the mask fall away and shines intense contempt towards them. Gemini gasps audibly. She's not going to let their scared, little puppy bullshit work on her this time.

"Everything is wrong," she says, louder. She spaces out each word as if Gemini is foreign or hard of hearing.

As if on cue, a visibly pregnant woman enters the coffee shop.

She's tall and slender—model-height really. Her long blonde hair's piled in a messy bun, and large mirrored sunglasses rest on her smooth face, tilted up. Her clothes and jewelry are few but exquisite.

Everything about her says class. States it as if it's a fact.

And then out in the open, like it has any business being there—like it just fucking belongs there—a nice, round belly beneath her silk blouse.

The whole place focuses on her, not silent exactly, but hushed as if in awe of this brave, stupid woman.

"See?" Heidi says. "Like I said, everything is wrong."

Gemini looks confused.

"What?" they ask, completely serious.

They're the only person in the place who doesn't see the pregnant woman. They can only ever see Heidi.

God. She might scream after all.

Finally, it dawns on them.

"Her?" they laugh and shake their head. Ridiculous. Heidi's surprised they don't slap their knees or fan themselves.

"She's nobody. She proves nothing. Just some rich bitch," Gemini says with more venom then Heidi ever thought possible. "They're everywhere. I used to mow her lawn when I was a kid."

Heidi gets low in her seat, pushes her coffee cup to the side and bends forward.

"She's fucking pregnant," she hisses. "Are you simple?"

"Are you?" they say before they can stop themselves. Then, with more authority than they've shown speaking on any subject, "It's fake."

Heidi's never thought much of them but never thought they were insane.

"What the fuck are you talking about?" she asks.

"Yeah," Gemini says, "I read about it on Newsweek or Time or something. Rich ladies are wearing fake pregnant bellies as high fashion now, mostly on the coasts, but it looks like it's making its way to the Midwest."

"Bullshit," she says but there's no force behind her words.

Gemini nods.

"Some of them inflate, to take you through the, the, uh stages," they say. "What's it called?"

"Trimesters," she says without pause.

"Right," they say. "Trimesters. Or they make successive sizes that you swap out. Some are meant to feel real, so you can push yourself up against strangers on the subway or whatever. Pretty gross, huh?"

"But you can't know for sure," she says. "Do you really know her? What's her name?"

Gemini sips their coffee. They smile slightly behind their cup like they anticipated the question.

"Jasmine," they say.

She pushes herself back from the table, walks over to the station with cream and grabs a napkin. She winds a longer way back to her table and casually passes her eyes over the woman's stuff. Right there on her cup: JASMINE.

She sits back down.

"Well?" Gemini asks.

"Well, you know her name at least, I'll give you that," she says.

They sit in silence for a while. Her eyes dart around and endlessly search while her fingers worry napkins, stir sticks or anything within reach. Gemini sits calmly and gazes at her mostly. Their smile broadens when her eyes pause on them.

Jasmine leaves.

Heidi and Gemini continue to sit. Most of the place clears out, just them, another couple in the corner and the ever-present guy with his laptop at the counter.

"I have to know if it's real, or not," she says.

"It isn't—" Gemini tries.

"But you don't really know," she interrupts. "You're probably right, but you can't really know."

"You should've said something while she was still in here," they say. "I could've yanked it off her or something."

Gemini laughs. She stares at them until they finish.

"You said you know where she lives," Heidi says.

They start to laugh again until the expression on her face interrupts them.

"Are you fucking serious?" Gemini asks quietly.

"Completely," she says. "I wanna know if it's fake. And if it is, I'm gonna back over it with my car."

"What, why?" they ask. "Why do you give a shit?"

She shrugs.

"Fuck her and her disposable income for such heinous shit," she says.

"But, what if it's real?" Gemini asks.

"I thought you were so sure it's fake," she says.

"I am," they say, "but what if? What if she's really, yuck, pregnant?"

"Then," Heidi says, "we cut it out of her and steal the fucking thing."

Their hands cover her. They want it. They're making her want it for once. Usually, she resists and resists until finally giving in, but now she wants it. Gemini has Heidi's clothes off. When had that happened? They still have their underwear on, but she sees their erection bulging. Gemini kisses her stomach, thighs, brushes their lips over her pussy.

"Please," she begs.

Gemini slides two fingers inside her and licks her clit, sucks on it. She comes in less than a minute.

"Don't you dare put a condom on," she says. "I want you to cum in me."

Gemini enters her without hesitation, holds her down and fucks her. They pin her hands above her head. She comes again as they suck on her tits. Gemini comes moments later, Heidi's legs wrapped around them. A warm wetness spreads inside her. They keep thrusting.

Heidi loosens her hands, flips them over and rides. She straddles them, rakes at their chest and smacks Gemini 's tits around. They get harder and harder inside her. Gemini tries to say something like "Wait," but she won't slow down. She can't slow down.

When Gemini comes the second time, they grab her ass with both hands and almost bucks them both off the bed. She collapses on top of them and doesn't roll off until they've completely softened inside her.

They sleep.

She wakes in the dark and finds them already awake, staring at the ceiling.

"I was going to break up with you in the coffee shop today," she says before she realizes she's saying it.

Gemini sighs, barely audibly.

"I know," they say. "I pick up on more than you think."

She says nothing.

"Do I need to run to the pharmacy? Do you need Plan A?" they ask.

"No," she says. "When I was fifteen, my parents gave me a hysterectomy or something."

They go rigid beside her.

"What? Jesus," Gemini says. "That's not legal, yet. Is it?"

She nuzzles closer to them, tries to relax their body with her touch.

"Sometimes," she says. "If they can show you're at risk, they can get it done to you."

"Jesus Christ," they say.

"Yeah," she says. "I took them to court and lost. They had all these email transcripts and text message threads. They had installed something on my phone that saved all my Snapchats. They read them in court, while I sat there. Nothing I could do. You know the best part? It was all bullshit, stupid teenage talk.

I was still a virgin. But I had broken my hymen when I was eight or so, never told them because I was too embarrassed, and here they are staring at me while all this stupid, filthy shit I had written was read out loud. The cops took me straight from the courtroom to the medical facility. The procedure took less time than it took the court to decide I was at risk to get pregnant. My mom was waiting in the lobby to take me home when they wheeled me out. I pretended to be out of it and went to the bathroom. I was going to figure out how to kill myself in there, but somebody had cracked a window, probably smoking in there. I slipped out the window and down the street. I blew a trucker to get me out of town. Let other ones fuck me. I've never seen either of my parents since."

Gemini opens their mouth, probably to say "Jesus Christ" again, thinks better of it and holds her tighter instead.

"I tried to get the procedure reversed, a couple years later when I was an adult, but they had fucked up the procedure, or maybe I did scrambling out the window," she says. "It's permanent."

They lie in silence.

"Maybe after we steal Jasmine's baby, we should find your parents. Burn their house down or something," Gemini suggests.

She laughs.

"Shit," Heidi says, "where have you been hiding?"

They make up a rough plan.

Heidi wonders when all this will wear off or sink in or become a joke or become too real. As they plan, she sees the panicky, old Gemini under the surface. The unsure one that exists to try and please her every whim when all they manage to do is to piss her off. But mostly, they're different. Better.

This escalation, this continuing the plan, it's Gemini's fault. They're supposed to be the one to stop her, to talk her down, to mellow everything out.

But they aren't.

They're forging ahead, arm in arm with her, even guiding the way sometimes.

Now they sit in her car on the street, two houses down from Jasmine's.

Gemini's in the driver's seat, dressed all in black, and skims a medical textbook by streetlamp. Heidi sits in her own passenger seat and buzzes with nervous energy. She's not jumpy though, as she goes over their crude hand-drawn map of the partial interior. Gemini's only seen the downstairs.

She's dressed all in black too.

"OK," Gemini says, "the lights have been off in the downstairs for forty minutes and half an hour upstairs."

She blinks at them.

They're really going to do this.

"Should we wait longer?" Gemini asks when she doesn't respond.

"No," she says. "We don't know when the husband's coming back. Let's do it tonight."

Gemini saw the husband leave with a suitcase this afternoon. He's in insurance or something. A Lyft picked him up at the curb. It was a small roller bag. He'd only be gone one night, maybe two.

It must be tonight.

"Let's move the car farther away," she says. "Is there a way to get into the backyard from another street?"

They think about it and glance around nodding.

"Yeah, I'm pretty sure," they say. "I used to do most of this street. The fences are low back there. There's an alley for everybody's trash and recycling."

Gemini pulls out, uses just the parking lights and creeps around the block.

"Don't go too slow," she says. "People will notice."

Here's the jumpiness. She clamps a hand down on her left leg to keep it from spasming.

Her foot taps to compensate.

They park under a tree next to the alley entrance. No house faces them head-on. She's feels invisible, like part of the landscape.

They exit the car. There's a moment of panic when the overhead light flashes on, but they shut the doors quickly and mostly quietly.

"They get a lot of trash divers back in here in International Waters. They don't like it, but I think they'll ignore us if they think that's what we're doing," they say.

"International Waters?" she asks.

"Sorry," they say, and chuckle nervously. "That's what we called all these alleyways and paths when I was a kid."

"What do they care?" she asks. "About the garbage? It's shit they're throwing away."

Gemini puts their hands up in mock defense.

"Hey, I agree with you. Fuck them," they say.

While keeping her right hand lightly tracing the backside of the fences, just like Gemini does a few paces in front of her, Heidi follows them down the alley. It's grass and not concrete—so unlike her idea of what an alley should be.

Gemini counts quietly under their breath.

They stop, and she bumps into them softly.

"It should be this one," they whisper.

They grip the top of the fence and pull themselves up to see over. They do this twice. Heidi bites her tongue to keep herself from asking about how she thought this part of the fence was supposed to be short.

"Yeah," they say, "this one."

They find the back gate locked, but the wood is soft with rot. They pull at it, twist back and forth with their hands. It falls away from the post silently, the wood like taffy. They toss it into the grass.

Headlights flood the alley with light.

It only lasts a second. Just a passing car. They allow themselves to breathe again. The gate opens jerkily as it catches on the overgrown grass.

"Guess they never found a replacement for me," Gemini says.

She chuckles silently. Not because it's a funny joke but because this is crazy. They're crazy. She's crazy. Everything's crazy—might as well laugh about it.

They creep across the backyard.

She stops them at the sliding glass door and points to an ATD sticker on the window.

They shake their head.

"Fakes," they whisper into her ear. "The husband printed them off the internet or something. He gave them to all the neighbors."

She decides to believe them, but how can they know this?

They check the windows on the back of the house. A smaller one above the kitchen sink is unlocked.

Gemini looks at her apologetically.

"It's going to have to be you," they whisper.

"What?" she says stupidly.

"Unless you wanna try the front, or break one of the others," they whisper. "I can't fit through this one. You can, easily. I can boost you up."

She nods slowly.

"I don't see any dishes in the sink," they say, "but be careful anyway."

Gemini slides the window up. It opens it like a tiny mouth. The kitchen beyond yawns massive and pitch-black. They crouch down and lace their fingers together like a scoop. She steps into it with her right foot and they easily boost her up to the window. She grabs the sill with both hands and bends her elbows inside.

Without dropping her foot, Gemini pivots around behind her, releases her foot and grips her by the thighs. They steadily push her up through the window.

She's inside.

That weird smell of an unfamiliar house.

The sink's empty but a full drying rack and useless small appliances clutter the immediate counter space. She makes little noise dropping into the metal sink. Adjusting her feet directly beneath her, she climbs out onto the floor like a spider emerging from a hole. Mindful of her legs, she forgets her elbows and the faucet blasts on for a second before she shuts it off.

She stands in the absolute dark of the kitchen in the deafening quiet and feels the fine mist that sprayed her settling on her skin.

She slows her breathing down but can do nothing about her heartbeat.

She orients herself from her memory of Gemini's map and makes corrections as she sees them. She slips past the island, through the dining room, around the table, bumps into a couch but it's soft and silent, and finally arrives at the back-patio door.

Gemini's on the outside, hunching down to make

themselves small, invisible and statue still. To make themselves part of the darkness.

They make eye contact, and Gemini points down.

To the ground? No—to the bottom of the sliding-glass door and the bar jammed into the gutter to keep the door from opening even if unlocked.

She reaches for it and then stops, staring down.

She hears soft tapping on the glass above her.

She looks up and sees them tapping on the glass with one finger, that old panic firmly re-established in their eyes. In their whole face. Gemini puts their hands up, palms flat and shrugs their shoulders with exaggeration. A clear *What the fuck?* mannerism.

She stands back up to her full height, leaving the bar in place. She traces a heart shape with her index finger on the glass over their face, turns and walks alone into the dark house.

She makes a circuit downstairs and memorizes the layout. She considers unlocking the front door to save some time if she needs to exit quickly but nixes it. She doesn't want Gemini finding a way in.

One car parked in the garage barely makes a dent in the cavernous space which she finds strange but doesn't know why.

She shakes her head. She's focusing on all the wrong things and avoiding the upstairs. Silly, stupid. Scared.

The stairs aren't carpeted so she slips her shoes off and carries them up. No family photos dot the staircase wall. No pictures of anything are on any of the walls. She replaces her shoes in the upstairs hallway.

All the doors, to various degrees, stand ajar except a narrow one at the end that's probably a linen closet. Be extra quiet, she thinks. The last light to go off in the house would be the farthest one down the hall on the left. She checks all the other rooms first—nobody.

Heidi slinks into the master bedroom. She sees a shape on the bed. She sits briefly at the vanity and examines the clutter in the dark. No fake belly hangs from the back of the chair. She slips into the walk-in closet. No fake belly rests in a special box among the clothes. She checks the master bath. No fake belly lies discarded next to the sink.

She prowls the whole area a second time and checks every surface again. She checks all the drawers and all the hangers. Matching nightstands flank the bed, but the drawers appear too small for practical use, so she skips them.

Heidi tries to make sense of the pile on the bed. Would she sleep in it if it was fake? Did they make them so that something kicked you as you were trying to get to sleep? Did they press on your bladder just right, so you had to get up and pee every hour? Did they give unbearable heartburn or gestational diabetes?

An idea ricochets through her brain.

She turns from the bed and reenters the master bath. She shuts the door quietly and stuffs a towel from the rack into the crack at the bottom of the door. She stands up and flips the light on and holds her breath in case it's wired with a fan. It isn't. Her eyes adjust to the light.

In the medicine cabinet she finds one prescription in the husband's name among the bandages and aspirin. That same nagging feeling from the garage plucks at her, but she pushes it away.

Then she sees what she's looking for, right there on the counter next to the toothpaste: Prenatal vitamins.

Case closed.

She hears Gemini's dissenting voice in her head, but she's more confident now. Could all of it be an act? Sleeping in that fucking monstrosity, taking pills and buying maternity clothes? Just to, what, trick her body into releasing hormones or something?

Jesus.

No one knows what kills the mothers, but it could be hormones. She's sure she heard that once on TV.

She wants to grab the bottle, force Jasmine to take the whole thing and wash it down with toilet cleaner from under the sink. No. Impossibly, it isn't an act. This woman is really pregnant and treats it like it's the most natural thing in the world.

Heidi turns the light out, replaces the towel on the back of the door and opens the door, replicating its forty-five-degree angle.

Jasmine is stirring in the bed.

Heidi hears her say "Fuck" and the covers whip back. Her shape rises from the bed, a black shape against more blackness. Heidi wants to freeze, she wants to stay in the bathroom doorway, to stay still and invisible.

But of course that's where Jasmine's going, that's why you mutter "fuck" to yourself in the middle of the night and stagger out of bed.

Heidi retreats quickly and tries to remember where the shower is. To her left? Yes—she feels the partially open curtain, brushes past, steps in as quietly as possible, and flattens herself against the shower wall. Thankfully, there's no tub to amplify her steps or trip her up entirely.

Jasmine hits the door with her body coming in.

"Dammit," she says.

Guess Heidi hadn't opened it to the correct angle.

She listens to the woman piss, long and hard. She risks a peek out of the shower. Jasmine's either naked or in something so sheer it's practically transparent. Heidi sees the outline of a large, round belly.

With a huff she pushes herself off the toilet and towards the door, either forgetting or not bothering to flush. Heidi takes a cautious step out of the shower and follows her.

They both see the shadow in the door at the same moment.

"Nathaniel?" Jasmine says with uncertainty.

The shape grows larger, spreads out from the doorway and pours into the bedroom. Heidi knows it's Gemini, logically, but is terrified anyway. It looks insane. It looks like the darkness in the air solidifies into a person-shape and stretches out again to overtake the whole room.

It's not a monster made of shadow, it's Gemini moving right at Jasmine.

They hit her, and she falls to the ground on her side, catching herself on her hands and elbows.

Heidi wants to scream at them to be careful of the baby but can't find her voice. Jasmine pulls herself up from her knees, clawing and crawling up the bed. When they hit her again in the back of the head or neck, she slumps over with her legs dangling off the bed.

"Jesus, turn her off her stomach at least," Heidi says.

Gemini paws around for the light switch, hesitates, decides against it and crosses back over to the bed.

Heidi turns the bathroom light on and pulls the door mostly shut, giving them just enough to see by. She shrinks back into the shadows in case Jasmine wakes up. If she can wake up.

"She's not fucking dead, is she?" she asks.

They make a little disgusted sound with their mouth.

"C'mon. I barely hit her," they say.

Gemini checks her pulse anyway.

"She's fine," they say.

"What about the baby?" Heidi asks, emerging from the shadows a little. She freezes when she hears something like Velcro tearing and something heavy lands on the floor near her. She toes it gently. It feels like a large, hairless cat.

"See for yourself," they say. She hears the smile on their face, the *I told you so* in their tone.

She reaches down and feels it. It's warm to the touch and firm but yielding. It starts beeping sharply from somewhere and Heidi jumps back.

"No," Jasmine says from somewhere far off. "No. Give it back. Hurry! It's electronically monitored! I can't take it off, they'll find out! I can't lose the baby!"

Gemini straightens to their full height. Jasmine shrinks back slightly on the bed but continues asking for her baby.

"It's not a baby, you fucking freak," Heidi says, and Jasmine jumps, realizing there are two strangers in the room.

She nods furiously on the bed and sits up straighter.

"It will be," she says. "you have to let me put it back on. The agency monitors it very closely."

A cell phone next to the bed begins beeping in tandem with the sounds from the blob on the floor.

"Fuck!" Jasmine screams. "That's them! They're checking on me! Please, please give me the baby back."

"Fine," Heidi says, picks it up and tosses it onto the bed. "Fucking weirdo."

As Jasmine frantically reattaches the apparatus, Heidi grabs the cell phone. It stops ringing before she reaches it.

"Look at this," she says and tosses Gemini the phone. They catch it one-handed, displaying the beginning and ending of their athletic prowess.

They do a classic double-take. Heidi laughs and imagines them slipping on a room full of banana peels. Jasmine continues to fiddle with the fake belly, forgetting them completely.

"A fucking adoption agency?" Gemini asks. "That's who she's so terrified of? Fuck, I thought it was the CIA or something."

They laugh.

"I have to call them back," she says, suddenly standing close to them at the foot of the bed. With the belly attached, it ceases its chirping. Neither of them noticed her move off the bed. "If I don't, they'll just call again. I have to talk them out of pushing my due date back."

They share a look between the two of them. They have no idea what to do.

The phone in Gemini's hand goes off again.

It's the adoption agency.

"Fine," Heidi says, keeping her head down and hair in her face but speaking firmly. "Put it on speaker. Do not mention us, or I put every knife in your kitchen through that fucking thing. While you're still wearing it."

She nods furiously.

"Fine," she says, "whatever, just give me the damn phone."

Heidi snatches it from Gemini and, instead of handing it to Jasmine, sets it gingerly on the bed behind her in a small act of defiance to maintain control.

"Hello? Hello?" Jasmine says, easily putting some panic into her voice.

"Mrs. Fontenont? It's Virgil, from the adoption agency," a voice says clearly.

"Oh, hi, Virgil," she says with a slight, exasperated laugh. "I know why you're calling."

Heidi hears the smile on her face and is sure it transmits over the phone. Jesus—she should be an actress.

"Let's start with your verification number first, please," Virgil says.

Jasmine rattles off a dozen practiced numbers.

"Thank you, Jasmine," Virgil says after a second's pause. His tone relaxes considerably. "So, what's up? I got a notice that you detached from The Bump."

"Sort of," she says quickly. "The Velcro, or whatever it is that attaches it in the back?"

"It's not Velcro," he says, easily slipping back into formality, "It's a proprietary fastening system that…well, it doesn't matter. I know what you mean. Continue, Jasmine, please."

"Right," she says, "well, the fastening thingy, the comforter or sheets got caught in there and pulled it open, and it fell off when I shifted on the bed, I guess."

They wait in silence. Jasmine mouths "fuck you" and "cocksucker" at the phone with exaggerated force. Virgil taps a few things into a keyboard audibly from wherever he is in the world.

"So, this was after you used the restroom?" he asks.

Jasmine flips off the phone.

"Right," she says, exhaling audibly. "Sorry, I'm still disoriented from, well, everything."

"It's fine," he says, "take your time, please."

Jasmine and Heidi both wince at that "please." Something's awful about how he says please every time he addresses her.

She repeats her invented version of the events, starting

earlier with waking up to pee.

"So that's pretty much it," she concludes. "I heard my phone of course, but was worried about getting…The Bump situated. I was just about to call you guys back when you saved me the trouble."

Heidi heard her pause noticeably before saying "The Bump." They must discourage referring to it as a baby.

More silence and more keyboard tapping but no more silent swears from Jasmine. She sits very still on the bed with her eyes closed tight and forces herself to breathe as evenly as she can. She crosses fingers on both hands.

"OK," Virgil says cheerfully. "Everything looks good. No big deal. I figured it was something like that, but you know all the policies and everything I gotta call and check. If you can remember, after you get up from the toilet, or any sitting position really, run your hands along the seam back there by your spine. It smooths everything out and gives the contacts better holds. How are you otherwise?"

They chat amiably for another minute and then Virgil says he'll let her get back to sleep.

Jasmine hits the end call button and falls onto her back on the bed.

"Fuck you, Virgil," she says. "You anal-retentive prick."

She lies with her palms pressing into her eyes for a minute and then sits back up with a groan. She sees them and her face droops further.

"Christ, I forgot about you assholes," she says. "Fuck you two as well. Get it over with it."

"Get it over with?" they ask in near unison.

"Yeah," she says, yawning. "I need to get back to sleep, so steal whatever you want, I don't care. Take it all."

Heidi and Gemini glance at each other.

"You know I'm not going to report it," she continues. "I won't even tell my husband that one of them was Jared who used to cut our grass, but is now all grown-up and a woman, maybe? And breaking into people's homes with his coffee house skank."

This horrible sinking feeling sickens Heidi's stomach. It threatens to pull her through the floor, through the bottom story, through the ground and into the earth. She's never known Gemini as anyone else and she knows it pains them to be reminded of their past.

But besides all that—Jasmine knows who they are.

"I'm not—" Gemini tries but Jasmine waves them off.

"Shut up, I don't care. All I care about is the baby," she says. "I won't report this because the agency has access to my phone, all my records. Do you get it? If there's a police report, they'll push my due date back. Fuck, they might reevaluate my whole pregnancy."

Heidi slaps her across the face.

"You're not pregnant, you dumb psycho," she hisses. "You get that, right?"

Gemini places a hand on her arm, gently.

"Let's just go," they whisper. "she's not going to say anything. Look at her."

Heidi shakes the hand off.

"Fuck her," she spits. "She gets to pay people to feel like she's pregnant? She should have to feel like the rest of us. She's not fucking special."

Jasmine reevaluates them and fear seeps into her eyes.

"What the hell do you guys want?" she asks.

Heidi crowds her as Jasmine inches back on the bed towards the headboard.

"I want to tear that thing off of you and toss it off an

overpass," she says.

Jasmine hugs herself and covers as much of The Bump as she can. She's pressed all the way against the headboard now.

"I want you to lose something important to you," Heidi continues. "I want to see your face when it happens."

Jasmine glances back and forth between their faces, silent for once. Her eyes plead and her brow sweats. She settles on Gemini but doesn't speak. She tries to sway them with her eyes.

"Jared," she says, forcing calm and volume back into her voice. But she stops and her eyes dart around wildly.

Heidi and Gemini hear it too.

The garage door is opening.

"You said the husband left this afternoon with luggage," Heidi hisses at them.

"He did! I saw him," Gemini says and points at Jasmine. "She kissed him goodbye at the door and he took a Lyft."

That weird tug Heidi felt downstairs coalesces from a feeling into knowledge—there should be two cars in the garage.

Jasmine laughs and gives voice to her silent railings against Virgil earlier.

"You stupid fucks," she says. "That was my brother. He was here for the weekend."

The prescriptions in the cabinet, if the husband was staying somewhere overnight—

A door, an extremely close door, opens and shuts. Light turns on downstairs and the dimmest edges of it reach up into the bedroom.

"You dipshits need to get the fuck out of here," Jasmine whispers. "He's going to make a drink, but he'll poke his head in to check on me any minute. He will call the police, do you understand? I won't be able to talk him out of it."

"What do we do?" Gemini asks. "Heidi?"

"I'm thinking," she says and chooses not to notice her name was said aloud.

"Climb out the window," Jasmine whispers. "Or better yet, hide in one of the rooms down the hall. He should be up here and asleep in an hour or less, then you can slip out. Take my purse as you leave. We'll call it even."

"Too late," Gemini says as the hall light blasts on and they hear the first steps on the stairs.

A noise behind Heidi turns her head. The tiny nightstand drawer gapes open. Metal glints in the darkness from the gun in Jasmine's hand.

"Get under the fucking bed," she rasps at them. "Now, now, now."

The light flashes on with intense brightness. A middle-aged man stands in the doorway, his tie is loosened, and his sleeves are rolled up. He has a brown drink in his right hand.

"Uh, huh?" he says, and they are stupid last words.

Gemini dives for the gun. It goes off with a flat crack as they struggle with it and the man in the doorway falls to a heap on the ground, giving out like the bottom of a soggy grocery bag.

"No," Jasmine says and scrambles to him, conceding the impossibly small pistol to Gemini. How can something so tiny make such a huge noise? How can it take down a person so large?

Gemini stares down at the gun in their hand. It's a toy in their large grip.

Jasmine turns back towards them.

"He's dead," she says. "He's dead you fucking assholes!

They'll never give me a baby now! They won't give one to a single parent! That's why they're the best in the world! Fuck!"

Heidi gets Gemini's attention. They blink like they're stepping from a dark movie theater into the noonday sun.

"Put it down, Gemini," she says.

"Wha?" they manage.

"Either shoot her with it or put it down," Heidi says. "We have to go. Now."

"Right," they say and place the gun gently onto the bed. They cross the carpet to the door.

"You can't leave," Jasmine says but doesn't move to stop them. "Not now."

Downstairs, they hear loud banging noises from upstairs like an animal tossing furniture around. The gun starts going off wildly. Maybe Jasmine screams in the background, but Heidi can't be sure. That part could just be in her head.

They run out of the sliding glass door. Gemini must've removed the rod before sneaking upstairs.

She wants to ask them how they got inside, but they're both sprinting across the lawn now at full speed.

They reach the gate at the same moment and attempt scrambling through it simultaneously like a vaudeville act until they step aside for her.

Two cops wait in the alley.

One stands by her car writing something down while the other looks up at the second story of Jasmine's house and talks quietly into the walkie-talkie clipped to his lapel.

The one by the car sees them first.

"Hey," he says.

Heidi and Gemini take off down the alley in the opposite direction.

Heidi tears blindly through the darkness feeling trash cans

and telephone poles and junk whiz past them as she follows Gemini's hammering footsteps. She hears other footsteps close behind her and voices yelling for them to stop.

They burst from the other end of the alley and dash down the street.

She knows she should head in a different direction from Gemini, but she doesn't. They're slowing down. Heidi finds something in herself and speeds up somehow. She's even with them now that they're in open terrain and she can see where she's going.

A cop breaks the alley threshold and picks up speed too.

He yells at them again.

She almost stops running when she hears the cop stop. Gemini risks a confused look over their shoulder and she pulls completely past them.

"TASER TASER TASER!" the cop yells, and a sound like loud snapping or a metronome made of crackling fire fills the air around them.

Gemini goes ramrod-stiff and collapses to the pavement in a slow motion topple. The cop's already on them with his cuffs out.

She needs to keep moving

The cop yells again. Something hits her in the back, but something else misses over her left shoulder and she doesn't freeze or collapse. She runs.

An invisible force takes her legs out from under her and slams her into the ground. She thinks maybe her head bounces off the pavement, but it curiously doesn't feel like anything.

There's a panting cop pinning her to the concrete. She stares at the baby blue of his uniform and wonders when they're going to finally change the name of that color. What would be a good alternative?

She fails to come up with one.

She never sees Gemini again.

They're tried separately. Heidi attempts to get notes to them. She never knows if they get them or not but never receives any reply.

Some days it's easier to believe the notes do get through and, on other days, the opposite is true.

She stops sending any after her lawyer convinces her to make Gemini a scapegoat and plead down to lesser charges. She claims everything was their idea. They knew the house previously, and only Jasmine and Gemini's fingerprints were on the gun, after all.

Jasmine attempts to read a statement at her plea hearing, but the judge doesn't allow it.

Heidi thinks she maybe sees her mother in the courtroom that day but wills herself not to look towards that spot throughout the proceedings.

She's sentenced to two years. Her lawyer tells her Gemini gets twenty-five.

They'll have to serve their term in a men's maximum-security facility.

Almost through her two-year stretch, Heidi learns that Gemini dies in prison.

She hopes they're not buried with the name Jared on their tombstone.

When she's released, she takes the small paper bag of her things and walks from the prison. She has no one meeting her and no plan. She figures she'll just walk until she ends up somewhere.

A block or so from where they let her out, there are a man

and a woman waiting by a black sedan that's pulled over onto the shoulder.

The man's in his sixties and the woman isn't much younger. They don't seem familiar. It wouldn't matter if they did. Prison's made her wary of everyone.

"Heidi?" the woman says. "Heidi Chylstek?"

She stops a few yards short of them and glances between their faces. They both smile at her.

"What is this?" Heidi asks.

They share a look like they can't believe she doesn't trust them. Like this a perfectly normal way to approach a person.

"Well," the woman says, "I'm Doris Leeke and this is Lieutenant Dixon."

"Retired," he says and puts his hands up to show they're empty.

"OK," she says.

"OK," Dixon repeats.

"Would you like a ride into town?" Doris offers.

Doris suggests the front passenger seat, but Heidi opts for the back. She wants to be able to see both of them at all times.

"We're here to propose more than a ride," Doris says.

"Of course you are," Heidi says. "Is this a Jesus thing?"

Doris and Dixon both laugh.

Doris turns and faces her between the front headrests. She places her right hand on the center console near Heidi. Her fingernails are recently and professionally done, probably gel polished, in bright turquoise.

They're the most colorful, brilliant things Heidi's seen in two years.

"I knew Gemini," Doris says.

"What?" Heidi says, or at least tries to.

"I was their therapist in prison," she explains. "I am so sorry for your loss."

Heidi directs her attention out of the left window of the car. Flat, empty highway passes by lazily. She's not going to tear up in front of strangers.

"Gemini spoke of you often," Doris says. "They—"

Heidi cuts her off with a jab to Dixon's seat.

"Let me out here," she says, her gaze still fixed out the window.

"Here?" he says. "Kid, there's nothing around here."

"Wait," Doris adds lamely.

"I don't know what the fuck this is," Heidi says, "so I'm getting out of the goddamn car."

She's so angry she's not even mildly surprised that he immediately pulls over to the side of the road. The doors aren't locked.

Doris follows her out, talking to her. She begins each sentence with "Heidi" like she's speaking to a fucking child.

They don't notice Dixon get out of the car. He stands well clear of them with his mock-surrender hands up.

"Doris," he says, "you can get back in the car, if you like."

She returns to the car. Heidi paces back and forth in the dirt along the road. Other cars zoom past like nothing's happening.

"Kid," he says. "We'd like to offer you a job."

She stops and looks at him. She shrugs exaggeratedly like she's an actress in a silent film.

"What the fuck?" she says. "What the fuck are you talking about?"

He nods at the car.

"She means well," he says. "C'mon. Where are you going to walk to?"

Eventually, they climb back in. Dixon takes over and tells her about it as they drive.

She looks down towards the street from the top floor of the former hotel.

This used to be a Marriot or a Hilton back in the day, she thinks. The name's now something so generic she can't recall it. The tight, cursive gold letters of the sign vanished from her mind as soon as her eyes left them. This was three days ago. She hasn't been outside since and there's weirdly no branding inside. Oh right. HOME SERVICES is all the sign says now.

Three quick knocks tap outside her door.

Heidi opens it and a woman around her age in thick, hipster glasses stands there with her hand extended for a shake. She has a cute, crooked smile.

"Hi, I'm Elm," she says.

Heidi shakes her hand in spite of herself and the woman blows past her into the room. She gives off the impression of a fast-walking cartoon character—her barely contained energy at home amid a swirl of papers.

"How are you settling in?" she asks. "Aren't the orientation videos boring?"

"Um, it's alright," Heidi tries.

"Oh! It's not too much like prison in here, is it?" she asks.

Heidi smiles. There's no guile or malice in this woman. She probably asks people about their menstruation or bowel movements with the same cheeriness.

"It's much nicer," she says. "Premium cable. Room service."

"Yes! Room service!" she exclaims and then lowers her voice to a whisper. "You have to try the 'Cookie for Two.' Nobody will stop you from eating it all yourself. There's no law or anything."

They talk more about the menu, the TV package and the convenience store in the lobby until there's a pause and Elm claps her hands together.

"OK," she says. "Business. I'm one of the researchers you'll be working closely with. But that's all boring. You wanna go see the kids?"

"Yes," Heidi says.

A ping-pong ball goes wide and bounces towards them. Elm taps on the glass to gain the attention of the girl that hops over to retrieve it. Elm sticks her tongue out at the girl when she looks at them. The girl rolls her eyes.

Elm laughs.

Heidi reflexively touches the glass.

"They can see us?" she asks.

"Of course, it's glass," Elm says and then elbows her gently. "I'm just teasing you. We keep everything open and transparent. The kids are invested in the process."

She can't seem to pull her own hand back down.

There are two dozen early teenagers in the large game room. Playing ping-pong, videogames, sitting around in headphones, on laptops, or reading.

"They're all Orphans," she manages to say through the lump in her throat.

Elm nods.

"I mean, I know they are but, God. It's been sixteen years, but you never see it like this," she says. "They're so grown-up now."

She expects something snaky like *Yeah, that's how it works* but Elm continues to nod and smile.

After another minute, Elm says, "You've been cleared by

medical, if you want to go inside."

Heidi tries to not look as scared as she feels.

"Should I?" she asks. She hates herself for asking, but she's been asking permission for every little thing for the last couple years.

Elm shrugs.

"Hey, that's up to you," she says. She looks past Heidi down the hall and waves at a few adults who've entered from the other side.

"I know it can be overwhelming," she says. "Here's a couple teachers you probably haven't met. It might ease you into it."

Elm introduces her to two women and a man. They seem pleasant and welcoming enough, but Heidi can only focus on the woman who's around her age. She tries her best not to stare but…

After the teachers move on, Elm attempts to explain some minute office processes, but Heidi interrupts her.

"I'm sorry," Heidi says, "but that woman? Charlotte? Is she pregnant?"

Elm sets her jaw and nods.

"Yup," she says as if that says it all.

Heidi shakes her head.

"With what you guys are trying to do here?" Heidi asks. "She couldn't wait a couple years? At least? She's, what, my age?"

"Actually," Elm says, "she's almost forty."

"Holy shit, she looks incredible," Heidi says. "Never mind. Whatever she's doing is working."

Elm laughs and gives her a gentle elbow.

"C'mon, we've stalled long enough. Let's meet some of the kids," she says.

• • •

Over the next few weeks, Heidi meets all of the three dozen fifteen- and sixteen-year-olds enrolled in the first class on the premises.

There are five girls and one boy she seems to have an easy companionship with and gets to know them well. They'll make up the core of her group, although Elm and the other researchers insist that nothing should be too rigid. If a kid wants to switch groups, or feels at home in multiple ones, they're free to do so.

Over that first year, kids come and go from her group, but it stays mostly around six. She has the largest group of anyone here and is proud of it.

She tries to be as open with the kids as she can and encourages them to ask her or tell her anything they want, and not just about sex either.

She shares stories from her life that aren't too painful to recall and keeps them as PG-13 as she can but she never talks down to them or tells them something that isn't true.

Doris is the highest-ranking faculty member here and everyone has a one-on-one meeting with her weekly. Heidi still feels weird about her, so their meetings are usually short and cordial.

She becomes good work friends with Elm and Charlotte. Which, she reasons, means they're actual friends since no one leaves the grounds much.

Charlotte dies a couple hours after giving birth to a healthy baby boy.

Elm tries to cheer Heidi up by explaining all the data they captured during the pregnancy and those last few hours, but it doesn't help. How many millions of data points have been collected in the last seventeen years? What good has it done?

They find out later that same month that one of the kids is finally pregnant. Thankfully, it's not one of Heidi's girls, but it still bothers her. She finds herself lapsing into uncontrollable tears whenever she glimpses the girl, Taylor, who is still weeks from showing any physical sign.

"Maybe you should talk to Doris about it," Elm suggests. She shakes her head.

"I know you got off on the wrong foot with her, but she's really pretty great," Elm insists. "I'm not helping, and who else are you going to talk to?"

She finds the head of security instead since Dixon has always been nice to her, but she doesn't know how to approach it. After five minutes or so of chitchat, she lets him get back to work.

"Do you want to talk about it?" Doris asks during a meeting the following month. "Whatever's bothering you?"

Heidi lets out a long breath. She'll have to remember to punch Elm.

"I'm still broken up over Charlotte," she says.

"Yeah, that was tough," Doris says. "He has a good home, I can tell you that. If that helps any."

She makes a face projecting that it doesn't.

"And now, with one of the girls pregnant…" Heidi trails off.

"I understand," Doris says, but doesn't elaborate.

"It's just, I have a couple kids in my group," Heidi says, "and they're becoming active. So, I'm worried about them. Do you really think this is going to work?"

Doris glances down at her notes.

"And this is Kat and Joey, correct?" she asks.

Heidi shakes her head.

"Don't let him hear you call him that," she says. And then,

in a deeper, more serious voice, "It's Joseph."

Doris snorts.

"My mistake," she says.

"You didn't answer me," Heidi continues. "Do you really think the Orphans can survive having children with each other? Do you really believe that?"

Doris leans back in her chair. Will she chide Heidi for the use of the taboo Orphan slang?

"That's the hard part, isn't it?" she says after a moment. "It's a hypothesis. You know that. The kids know that, their fathers or guardians know that. And that's all I know, too. Belief? I don't know. But we have to keep trying things, don't we?"

Doris is right, of course. They can't stop trying. Humanity would be completely gone in, what, a hundred years? Eighty?

Despite this, and even though she knows this is happening in semi-secret places all over the world, Heidi wishes they could gamble with some other kids somewhere else.

Heidi spasms in that way that only waking from a dead sleep will shake you. There is someone else in her room.

"It's me," Elm whispers and places a hand softly on her.

She grabs it automatically and, just as quickly, lets it go.

"What's going on?" she asks. "What time is it?"

Elm turns towards the window and Heidi sees the wetness of her eyes.

No, dammit. No.

"Taylor had the baby," she says through tears. "She didn't even last ten fucking minutes."

Heidi sits up and lightly smacks her own face.

"Shit," she says.

She rubs Elm's back as she's racked with a deep sob.

"Stop," Elm says to herself and shakes her head until it passes. "She's not the first one. Well, here, yes, but there've been others. Toronto and Gallop, at least. Just last week. I'm not supposed to know about those deaths."

"Jesus," Heidi says.

Elm presses something cool and thin into her hands. She knows what it is right away. It's one of the lanyards they pass over the scanners by the doors to move around the building all day, every day.

"It's Doris' keycard. It's the only one that can get you out of the building," she says.

"What?"

"You need to take Kat and get out of here," Elm says with panic in her voice. "They're going to lock us down. They're going to isolate her and the father and not tell them there's any danger. She's going to die in six months if you don't get her out of here."

"OK. OK," Heidi says and she's up and pulling on whatever clothes are lying around. She stops. "She's going to know this badge is missing."

Elm pushes her towards the door.

"She gave it to me," Elm says. "She's the one that told me about the other deaths."

"What?" Heidi says, still half asleep.

"The cooperation uses an algorithm to pick employees that'll be easier to control," Elm explains. "But Doris has a final say in who gets hired. She hand-picked as much of the staff as she could. Understand? She can read between the lines of your life story in a way a computer never can."

Elm removes her lab coat and shoves it at her.

"Take my coat and glasses. I'll stay here and pretend to be you. You know Thad, right?"

"The science teacher? Mustache?" Heidi asks.

"Yeah, Mustache. He's in a green car parked on Washington," she explains and points straight out Heidi's window. "On the other side of the Convention Center."

"That's the plan?" Heidi asks.

Elm hands her the stuff. She shrugs.

"There's no time for a plan," she says.

Heidi wants to tell her that she was right about Doris. She wants to have a proper goodbye with her only friend left in the world.

There's no time.

Elm squeezes her hand.

"I know," Elm says and pushes her out the door.

Heidi blinks in the brightness of the hallway and adjusts the glasses down on her nose. The distortion of the lenses is too much to suffer through. The world's distorted enough.

She slips the lanyard over her neck, makes sure the picture is facing her chest and smooths the lab coat as she walks.

She sees two guards waiting for an elevator. She nods curtly as she breezes past them.

Walk with purpose. No one will stop you.

Less than a month ago, Kat was moved into her own room on Heidi's floor. She tries not to think about how difficult this would've been mere weeks ago.

Doris' keycard overrides Kat's locked door and she slips inside.

She turns the lights on instead of eliciting a scream by approaching her in darkness.

Heidi kneels by the bed and coaxes her fully awake.

"Taylor's dead," she says, and the girl's eyes fill with tears.

She takes the girl's face in her hands and forces her to

focus past the heartbreak and look into her eyes.

"We have to go," she says while shaking her own head slightly. "They won't let you leave. They will let that baby kill you. It's not worth your life."

Kat instinctively touches her stomach.

"Kat, we have to go. To save your life," she says.

Her tears are pouring freely and quietly down her face, but she nods in agreement. "OK," is all she says.

Heidi checks the hall, they exit the room and beeline for the stairwell. Only a few floors down and Kat stops.

"We have to get Joey," she says.

Heidi pulls at her arm, but the girl won't budge.

"There's not time for this," Heidi says.

"I won't leave without him," she responds.

"Fuck. Shit. Fine. Stay right here, I'll go get him," Heidi says.

She ducks into the hall without looking and runs flat-out to his room.

Joseph's already awake and easy to convince. They're back down the hall and into the stairwell in less than two minutes.

Dixon's standing on the stairs a few steps above Kat.

His weapon's un-holstered but points towards the ground.

"Kid," he says. All three of them look but Heidi knows he's addressing her. "Are you leaving from this way? North?"

She's all turned around and possess no natural sense of cardinal directions.

"Washington," she says helplessly. "Convention Center?"

He taps the Bluetooth earpiece with his free hand.

"I just saw her heading to the south entrance," he says. "Right. Probably the parking garage."

He holsters his gun. He arches his eyebrows at them.

"Well, go, dammit," he says.

They take the last few flights two and three steps at a time.

They pause at the ground floor and, before poking her head out, Heidi asks a question that's been bugging her. "How come she gets to call you Joey?"

He looks at Kat and smiles.

"She can call me whatever she wants," he says.

"Follow right behind me," Heidi says, and they burst into the empty lobby. There's a moment of sheer panic as the keycard takes a second longer than normal to unlock the door, but it does unlock, and they are outside in the world.

HOME SERVICES the sign says in gold script, and Heidi hopes there's a day when she forgets it once again.

They jaywalk across the empty street and through the lobby of a functioning hotel that's attached to the Convention Center.

They come out on Washington. A car flashes its headlights at them.

They clamor inside.

"Toss the lanyard," Thad says, and she does.

As the car pulls from the curb, Heidi turns from the front seat to tell them to get down low in the back.

Once they've cleared downtown, Thad turns towards her.

"Where to?" he asks nonchalantly.

"Does this thing go back in time?" she asks.

He chuckles.

"Darn," he says. "The DeLorean is in the shop."

She ignores him.

"Somewhere public, I guess. Maybe an all-night pharmacy where she can get the abortion quickly," Heidi says.

Thad agrees.

"After that, I don't know. I have no idea what to do.

There's nowhere to go," Heidi says, hearing the quaver in her own voice.

"It's OK," he says. "It'll be alright. It's OK to not know what to do. And it's OK to admit that you don't know."

She looks out the window as the street blurs by in the night.

She tries to stretch her mind to find something concrete to believe in. Something so easy that even children know it. Something about how this night can't last forever, and the day will return eventually.

She has trouble believing even this.

# ACKNOWLEDGEMENTS

On New Year's Day in 2018, I realized *Frankenstein* was exactly 200 years old and nobody seemed to give a shit. The Science Fiction genre was created by a teenage girl in a weekend and there was no talk about it on such a monumental anniversary. Maybe because she was a girl? I don't know. Let's reconvene in nineteen years and see if Poe is lauded on the bicentennial of creating detective fiction.

I reread *Frankenstein* that afternoon. The cells of *Night Brings Night* were already dividing in the mud of my brain, but Shelley's tale sparked something. (Groan. Sorry.) I like to start a book with nothing more than a premise and a character and then just go go go until that first draft is done. I pay the price for this ~~madness~~ method during editing, but nobody really knows how to do any of this, so find what works and hold on. I started two days later, January 3rd, and finished the first draft in 52 days on February 23rd. Much longer than a weekend, but that's the fun part anyway.

This one is for my wife, Veronica, who had to live with me during those fiftyish days and all the other days. It's also for Nick and Kenny who read it first and gave me a thumbs up and asked the right questions. And it's for Pam who found the mistakes even if I didn't fix them all. See you next time.

ABOUT THE AUTHOR

Kris Lorenzen lives in the midwestern United States
with his wife and their two cats. This is his second book.
Tonight feels like a taco night.

www.krislorenzen.com